HAPPY
BIRTHDAY

Also by Danielle Steel

44 CHARLES STREET	SPECIAL DELIVERY
LEGACY	THE RANCH
FAMILY TIES	SILENT HONOUR
BIG GIRL	MALICE
SOUTHERN LIGHTS	FIVE DAYS IN PARIS
MATTERS OF THE HEART	LIGHTNING
ONE DAY AT A TIME	WINGS
A GOOD WOMAN	THE GIFT
ROGUE	ACCIDENT
HONOUR THYSELF	VANISHED
AMAZING GRACE	MIXED BLESSINGS
BUNGALOW 2	JEWELS
SISTERS	NO GREATER LOVE
H.R.H.	HEARTBEAT
COMING OUT	MESSAGE FROM NAM
THE HOUSE	DADDY
TOXIC BACHELORS	STAR
MIRACLE	ZOYA
IMPOSSIBLE	KALEIDOSCOPE
ECHOES	FINE THINGS
SECOND CHANCE	WANDERLUST
RANSOM	SECRETS
SAFE HARBOUR	FAMILY ALBUM
JOHNNY ANGEL	FULL CIRCLE
DATING GAME	CHANGES
ANSWERED PRAYERS	THURSTON HOUSE
SUNSET IN ST. TROPEZ	CROSSINGS
THE COTTAGE	ONCE IN A LIFETIME
THE KISS	A PERFECT STRANGER
LEAP OF FAITH	REMEMBRANCE
LONE EAGLE	PALOMINO
JOURNEY	LOVE: POEMS
THE HOUSE ON HOPE STREET	THE RING
THE WEDDING	LOVING
IRRESISTIBLE FORCES	TO LOVE AGAIN
GRANNY DAN	SUMMER'S END
BITTERSWEET	SEASON OF PASSION
MIRROR IMAGE	THE PROMISE
HIS BRIGHT LIGHT:	NOW AND FOREVER
The Story of Nick Traina	GOLDEN MOMENTS*
THE KLONE AND I	GOING HOME
THE LONG ROAD HOME	
THE GHOST	

* Published outside the UK under the title PASSION'S PROMISE

For more information on Danielle Steel and her books, see her website at
www.daniellesteelbooks.co.uk

DANIELLE STEEL

HAPPY BIRTHDAY

BANTAM PRESS

LONDON · TORONTO · SYDNEY · AUCKLAND · JOHANNESBURG

TRANSWORLD PUBLISHERS
61-63 Uxbridge Road, London W5 5SA
A Random House Group Company
www.rbooks.co.uk

First published in the United States
in 2011 by Delacorte Press,
an imprint of The Random House Publishing Group,
a division of Random House, Inc., New York

First published in Great Britain
in 2011 by Bantam Press
an imprint of Transworld Publishers

A CIP catalogue record for this book
is available from the British Library.

ISBN 9780593056851 (cased)
9780593056868 (tpb)

Addresses for Random House Group Ltd companies outside the UK
can be found at: www.randomhouse.co.uk
The Random House Group Ltd Reg. No. 954009

The Random House Group Limited supports The Forest Stewardship
Council® (FSC®), the leading international forest-certification organization. All our
titles that are printed on Greenpeace-approved FSC®-certified paper carry the FSC® logo.
Our paper procurement policy can be found at
www.rbooks.co.uk/environment

Printed and bound in Great Britain by
CPI Mackays, Chatham ME5 8TD

2 4 6 8 10 9 7 5 3 1

MIX
Paper from
responsible sources
FSC® C016897

To Beatrix, Trevor, Todd, Nick,
Sam, Victoria, Vanessa,
Maxx, and Zara

May "Why not?" be an answer
that brings you joy, happiness,
and new horizons. May life
be kind and generous with you,
may the people at your side be gentle
and loving, and may you *always*
be greatly loved!!

I love you so much!
Mommy/d.s.

Life, a good life, a *great* life is
about "Why not?"
May we never forget it!

d.s.

HAPPY
BIRTHDAY

Chapter 1

November first was a day Valerie Wyatt dreaded every year, or at least for the last two decades, since she turned forty. She had successfully staved off the potential ravages of time, and no one who saw her would have guessed that she had turned sixty when she woke up that morning. She had been discreetly shedding years for a while and it was easy to believe her creativity about her age. *People* magazine had recently said she was fifty-one years old, which was bad enough. Sixty was beyond thinking and she was grateful that everyone seemed to have forgotten the right number. Valerie did everything she could to confuse them. She had had her eyes done for the first time when she turned forty and then again fifteen years later. The results were excellent. She looked rested and fresh, as though she had been on a terrific vacation. She had had the surgery done in L.A. during a summer hiatus. She had also had her neck done when she was fifty, giving her a smooth, youthful neckline with no sag any-where, and her plastic surgeon agreed that she didn't need a full face-lift. She had great bones, good skin, and the eye and neck work had given her the effect she wanted. Botox shots four times a year added to her youthful looks. Daily exercise and a trainer three times a week kept her long, lean body toned and un-marked by age. If she had wanted to, she could have claimed to be in her forties, but she didn't want to seem ridiculous, and was content to knock nine years off her age. People also knew that she had a thirty-year-old daughter, so she couldn't stretch the truth too far. Fifty-one worked.

It took time, effort, maintenance, and money to maintain her appearance. It served her vanity, but it was also important for her career. Valerie had been the number-one guru of style and gracious living during a thirty-five-year career. She had started as a writer for a decorating magazine when she got out of college, and she had turned it into an intense dedication. She was the high priestess of how to entertain and for everything that went on in the home. She had licensing arrangements for fine linens, furniture, wallpaper, fabrics, exquisite chocolates, and a line of mustards. She had written six books on weddings, decorating, and entertaining and had a show that had among the highest ratings on TV. She had planned three White House weddings when presidential daughters and nieces got married, and her book on weddings had been number one on the *New York Times* nonfiction list for fifty-seven weeks. Her arch-competitor was Martha Stewart, but Valerie was in a class unto herself, although she'd always had deep respect for her rival. They were the two most important women in their field.

Valerie lived exactly the way she preached. Her Fifth Avenue penthouse, with a sweeping view of Central Park, and an important collection of contemporary art, looked camera ready at all times and so did she. She was obsessed with beauty. People wanted to live the way she told them to, women wanted to look the way she did, and young girls wanted a wedding just the way Valerie would have done it, or as she instructed them to do on her show and in her books. Valerie Wyatt was a household name. She was a beautiful woman, had a fabulous career, and lived a golden life. The only thing missing in her life was a man, and she hadn't been involved with anyone in three years. The thought of that depressed her that morning too. No matter how good she looked, the age on her driver's license was what it was, and who would want a woman of sixty? Even men in their eighties wanted girls in their twenties now. With this birthday, Valerie felt she had become obsolete. It wasn't a pleasant thought, and she wasn't happy today.

She looked in the mirror intently as she prepared to leave her apartment that morning. She didn't have to be in the studio until noon for a taping, and she had two appointments before that. She was hoping the first one would cheer her up. And the only thing keeping her from a major panic attack was that at least no one knew her right age. But she was depressed anyway. She was relieved that the image she saw in the mirror reassured her that her life wasn't over yet. She wore her blond hair in a chic well-cut bob that framed her face, and had it colored regularly. She never had roots. It was the same color it always had been, and her figure was superb. She carefully selected a red wool coat from the closet to put over the short black dress she was wearing that showed off her spectacular long legs, and she was wearing sexy high heels from Manolo Blahnik. It was a great look and would be elegant and fashionable when she taped her show later that day.

The doorman hailed a cab for her when she left the apartment and she gave the driver an address on the Upper West Side. It was in a seedy neighborhood, and she noticed the driver looking at her admiringly in the rearview mirror. She was pensive as they sped through Central Park. The weather in New York had turned chilly two weeks before, the leaves had turned, and the last of them were falling off the trees. The red wool coat she was wearing looked and felt just right. Valerie was looking out the window of the cab as the radio droned on, and they exited from the park on the West Side. And then she felt an electric current run through her as she heard the announcer's voice.

"My, my, my, I never would have believed it, and I'll bet you won't either. She looks terrific for her age! Guess who's turning sixty today? Valerie Wyatt! Now that is a surprise! Good work, Valerie, you don't look a day over forty-five." She felt as though the announcer had just punched her in the stomach. Hard! She couldn't believe it. How the hell did he know? Their researchers must check DMV records, she thought with a sinking feeling. It was the most popular morning radio talk show in New York, and

4

everyone would know. She wanted to tell the driver to turn it off, but what difference would that make? She had already heard it, and so had half of New York. The whole world knew now that she was sixty years old. Or at least the better part of New York. It was humiliating beyond words, she fumed to herself. Was nothing private anymore? Not when you were as famous as Valerie Wyatt and had your own TV show, and had for years. She wanted to cry as she sat in the backseat wondering how many other radio shows it would be on, how many TV shows, what newspapers it would be in, or celebrity roundups announcing whose birthday it was and how old they were. Why didn't they just sky-write it over New York?

She was frowning as she paid the cabdriver and gave him a handsome tip. The day was off to a miserable start for her, and she never liked her birthday anyway. It was always a disappointing day, and despite her fame and success, she had no man to spend it with. She had no date or boyfriend, no husband, and her daughter was always too busy working to go out for dinner. And the last thing she wanted to do was make an issue of her age with friends. She was planning to spend the night at home alone, in bed.

She hurried up the dilapidated steps of the familiar brownstone, nearly tripping on a chipped step, and pushed the button on the intercom. The name on the bell was Alan Starr. Valerie came here at least twice a year and called between visits to boost her spirits or when she was bored. After she rang, a voice filtered into the chilly November air.

"Darling?" It was a happy voice, and he sounded excited to see her.

"It's me," she confirmed, and he buzzed her in. She pushed open the heavy door once it unlocked, and hurried up the stairs to the second floor. The building was old and looked tired, but was clean. He was waiting in an open doorway and threw his arms around her, grinning broadly. He was a tall, handsome man in his early forties with electric blue eyes and shoulder-length brown hair. And despite the shabby address, he was somewhat well known around town.

"Happy birthday!" he said, hugging her close to him as he smiled with a look of genuine pleasure to see her. She pulled away, scowling at him unhappily.

"Oh shut up. Some asshole on the radio just told the whole goddamn world how old I am today." She looked on the verge of tears as she marched into the familiar living room, where several large Buddhas and a white marble statue of Quan Yin sat on either side of two white couches with a black lacquer coffee table between them. There was a distinct smell of incense in the room.

"What do you care? You don't look your age! It's just a number, darling," he reassured her as she tossed her coat onto the couch.

"I care. And I *am* my age, that's the worst part. I feel a hundred years old today."

"Don't be silly," Alan said as he sat down on the couch opposite her. There were two decks of cards on the table. Alan was said to be one of the best psychics in New York. She felt silly coming to him, but she trusted some of his predictions, and most of the time he cheered her up. He was a loving, warm person with a good sense of humor, and a number of famous clients. Valerie had come to him for years and a lot of what he predicted actually came true. She started her birthday with an appointment with him every year. It took some of the sting out of the day, and if the reading was good, it gave her something to look forward to. "You're going to have a fabulous year," he said reassuringly as he shuffled the deck of cards. "All the planets are lined up for you. I did an astrological reading for you yesterday, and this is going to be your absolutely best year." He pointed to the cards. She knew the drill. They had done this many times. "Pick five and place them face down," he said, as he put the deck down in front of her, and she sighed. She picked the five cards, left them face down, and Alan turned them over one by one. There were two aces, a ten of clubs, a two of hearts, and the jack of spades.

"You're going to make a lot of money this year," he said with a serious expression. "Some new licensing agreements. And your ratings are going to be fantastic on the show." He said pretty much the same thing every year, and so far he'd been right. But in her case, that was easy to predict. Valerie's gracious living empire was sound.

"What's with the jack of spades?" They both knew she'd wanted a man in her life since her last relationship ended. She had been divorced for twenty-three years, and had devoted more time and energy to her career than to romance. But she missed being involved with someone, and was disappointed that no one had turned up in years. She was beginning to think that no one ever would again. Maybe she was too old. She certainly felt it now.

"I think one of your lawyers might retire," Alan said about the jack of spades. "Give me five more."

This time the king of hearts showed up, and the queen of diamonds. Alan smiled.

"Well, that's interesting. I see a new man," he said, smiling wider, and she shrugged, unimpressed.

"You've been saying it for three years."

"Patience, darling, patience. It's worth waiting for the right one. I like this man. He's important, powerful, very tall, and good-looking. I think you're going to meet him through your work." Valerie laughed at that.

"Not in my business. Any guy involved in decorating, lifestyle in the home, or the wedding industry is not likely to be straight. I'm going to have to meet him somewhere else."

"Maybe he's one of your producers," Alan said, concentrating on the cards. "I definitely think you're going to meet him through work." He had said that before, and no one had appeared. His other predictions were often true, but lately not about men. "I think your daughter might have a baby this year," he said, turning over the queen of diamonds and handing her the deck again. Valerie smiled and shook her head.

"I don't think that's going to happen. She works harder than I do. She doesn't even have time to date. She's not married, and

I'm not at all sure she wants a husband or a child." Nor was Valerie anxious to be a grandmother—that was definitely not on her wish list or her radar screen, and fortunately it was not on her daughter's either. Alan was off on that one.

"I think she might surprise you," Alan said, as Valerie turned over five more cards and the reading continued. It was similar to what he always predicted for her, success in business, a new man on the scene, and an assortment of small warnings about upcoming projects and deals and people she worked with. But this time the new man came up several times. Alan was adamant about it, and Valerie sighed as she listened. People always told her that she couldn't have everything, a fabulous career and romance in her life too. Life just didn't work that way. No one got everything they wanted, they said, and Valerie hadn't either. Like most people, her success hadn't come easily, and in her case she had wound up alone. The two of them chatted as she continued to turn over the cards, and Alan told her what he saw ahead for her. Most of it was good. Her health wasn't a problem, he said, and as usual her ratings would soar. He saw some kind of production deal in the Far East, possibly a line of furniture, that would be advantageous for her, and it was obvious as he read for her that he genuinely liked her. She was honest, direct, and fair. Some people said she was tough, but it was mostly a standard of excellence that she applied to herself and everyone else. Valerie drove herself and everyone around her hard. She hadn't gotten to the top of her field by accident. She had crawled up the mountain for thirty-five years, with sheer hard work and a certain kind of genius and unfailing instinct about what she did. Alan admired her for that. He loved how straightforward she was. She didn't play games, or hide. What you saw was what you got. And he didn't need the cards to know how upset she was about her age today. Valerie said several times that sixty just seemed so goddamn old, and now everyone was going to know. He could see that the very thought of it made her want to cry.

As Valerie listened to Alan's reading in his West Side apartment, Jack Adams literally crawled across his bedroom floor with tears in his eyes. He had never experienced pain like this in his life. Never. Well, maybe once or twice while playing professional football in his youth, but not since then—and surely not in recent years. He felt like someone had planted a tomahawk in his back. The shooting pains went straight up to his brain and down his legs. He couldn't stand up or walk. He made it to the bathroom and pulled himself up slowly, clutching the sink. He grabbed his cell phone off the counter and sat down on the toilet seat with a scream.

"Oh my God," he said, as he found the number in his phone. When he saw himself in the mirror, he looked like he'd been shipwrecked, and felt a thousand years old.

Jack had been to a Halloween party the night before and had met an incredible girl there at the bar. He'd been wearing a Superman costume, and she had been Catwoman, wearing skintight patent leather, hip boots, and whiskers. She had an un-forgettable body, and when she took the mask off, her face wasn't bad either. She said she was a model, but he'd never heard of her. She was twenty-two years old, with dyed jet-black hair and green eyes. He was six feet four and she had been only a few inches shorter than he was. And the sex they had later when they got back to his apartment was beyond acrobatic. They'd both had a fair amount to drink, and he couldn't remember hav-ing that much fun in a long time. She was typical of the girls he went out with, always in their early twenties, often models, sometimes actresses, and usually any pretty girl who crossed his path. Jack had never had trouble meeting women, or seducing them. Girls had been throwing themselves at him since his teens, more than he knew what to do with at times. And like candy, he could never resist them, and Catwoman had been no exception. The only thing different about her was that the last time he made love to her the night before, something in his back had snapped and he couldn't move. He had let out such a terri-fying shout of pain that she had offered to call 911, but he was mortified and refused, and tried to pretend it didn't hurt as much as it did. He had suggested she go home, and she had. And he had spent the rest of the night in agony, waiting to call his chiropractor, which he was doing now. The receptionist an-swered and promised to get the doctor immediately when she heard that Jack Adams was on the line. He sounded terrible even to her. And he said it was an emergency.

The man who answered Jack's call sounded jovial and happy to talk to him. Jack Adams had been a patient for a dozen years. "What's up, Jack? My nurse said it was urgent."

"I think it is," he said in barely more than a whisper. Even talking hurt. Breathing hurt. He had visions of himself in a wheelchair for the rest of his life. "I don't know what the hell I did last night. I think I pulled a muscle in my back or something. I may have torn a ligament. I can hardly walk." He could see himself paralyzed. The pain was beyond belief. He had almost thought it was a heart attack at first. Whatever it was, it was killing him.

"How'd you manage that, or do I want to know?" Frank Barker teased him. He knew how active Jack's sex life was. They laughed about it at times, but Jack wasn't laughing now. He was on the verge of tears, and the chiropractor could hear it.

"Probably not. Can I come in?"

"How fast can you get here?" Jack Adams was a very important patient, and Frank was happy to fit him in, particularly for an emergency like this.

"Twenty minutes," Jack said through clenched teeth. He had no idea how he would leave his apartment, but he'd get there somehow. He hung up and called the car service he used, and crawled into his gym clothes that were on the bathroom floor. He would have gone in his underwear if he had to. He wondered if he should be going to a hospital, but Frank would know what to do. He always did. And this couldn't be as bad as it seemed.

That just wasn't possible. He had passed a kidney stone once, and this was worse.

He was downstairs ten minutes later, moving slowly and bent over. The doorman saw him and helped him into the car. He asked what had happened and Jack was vague. Ten minutes later, they were at the chiropractor's office and the driver helped him inside, where they led him into a room. Frank was with him in five minutes, and examined him. Jack could hardly move, and after the examination, the chiropractor looked at his chart and smiled.

"It's your birthday, Jack! Happy birthday!"

"Oh please . . . don't even say it . . . what the hell did I do to myself last night?" He wanted it to be something minor, but it didn't feel that way. This felt like major damage. He told the doctor exactly how and when it had happened, and Frank couldn't resist teasing him a little.

"It's these young girls, Jack . . . they're a handful!"

"I think she's a gymnast or something, or a contortionist. I'm in pretty decent shape, and she damn near killed me. What did I tear?" It made him feel ancient that a night of acrobatic sex had left him in this condition, and on his birthday yet. He had turned fifty today. Such an ugly number. He suddenly wondered if he'd ever have sex again. Maybe not the way he had the night before.

"I'm going to send you for an MRI. I have a feeling you may have ruptured a disk. I hope not, you may have only herniated it. Let's take a look."

"Shit," Jack said, looking as though it were a death sentence. "Will I need surgery?" He looked panicked.

"I hope not. We'll see what the MRI tells us. I'll get you in right away." Frank was a genius at getting technicians and physicians to accommodate his important clients. "One thing's for sure, I think you'd better take it easy for a night or two." He smiled broadly as Jack sat up, wincing in pain. He had invited friends to downtown Cipriani that night, among them several young models, but he already knew he'd have to cancel. There was no way he could sit for dinner. And he had to go to the office, at least for a few minutes. He'd called on his way over to tell them he'd be late, but didn't say why. He didn't want to admit to the condition he was in, at least not until he knew more.

Jack went back to his car and went to the hospital for the MRI. Frank had set it up for him, and as he walked into the hospital, bent over like an old man, two men asked him for an autograph, which was even more humiliating. He had been one of the most important players in the NFL, had won six MVP awards as starting quarterback, was a twelve-time pro bowler, had won four Super Bowls for his team, and was in the Hall of Fame. Now he could hardly stand up or walk after one night with a twenty-two-year-old. He told the two fans he signed the autographs for that he'd been in a car accident. They had been thrilled to see him, in no matter what condition.

The MRI took an hour and a half, and they told him he'd been lucky. From what the technician could see, the disk was probably herniated not ruptured, and he didn't need surgery, just rest, and physical therapy once it calmed down. It was a hell of a way to start his birthday. He was fifty years old, and his career as a wild and crazy lover had ended with a major bang and a herniated disk. It made him feel even worse.

He had taken a painkiller by the time he got to work, still wearing his gym clothes and looking ragged. He hadn't shaved or combed his hair, but dead or alive, he had to go in for a few minutes. He had to see the producer about what to prepare for a special the next day. Jack had been one of the most important sportscasters on TV since he retired twelve years ago, at thirty-eight. He had a serious knee injury that finally put him out of the game for good, but even that had been nowhere near as painful as this. It had been an illustrious career and a respectable end. And his career as sportscaster and network hero had been satisfying too. He liked what he did and the network, fans, and ratings loved him. He had a personable on-camera presence that added new fans to his old ones, and he had always been irresistible to women, and equally unable to resist them. His marriage had ended in divorce five years before he retired. He had cheated on his wife constantly, and he gave Debbie credit that they had parted friends. He had been a lousy husband and he knew it. The opportunities and temptations constantly put in his path as an NFL superstar had been too much for him and their marriage.

Debbie had married one of the team doctors within a year of their divorce, and was happy and had had three more kids, all boys. And she and Jack had a son who was twenty-one, a senior at

Boston University, and he had absolutely no interest in football, except to admire what his father had accomplished. Basketball was his sport, since he was tall too, but he was a better student than Jack had ever been and wanted to go to law school. He had no interest whatsoever in pro sports. He didn't even watch football on TV.

Jack hobbled across the lobby when he got to the network, almost crawled into the elevator, and stood doubled over after pressing the button for his floor. He couldn't stand up straight, and didn't see the face of the woman who got into the elevator after him. All he saw were high-heeled black shoes, a red coat, and good legs. But he didn't want to think about that now. A monastery maybe for his golden years.

The woman in the red coat and black shoes pressed the button for her floor and stood near him. "Are you all right?" she asked with concern.

"Not really, but I'll live," he said, and tried to look up at her and winced. She looked vaguely familiar, but he couldn't remember who she was, and then it hit him. She was the gracious lifestyle guru of the world, and he was hunched over like Quasimodo, in gym clothes, flip-flops, uncombed hair, in need of a shave. He was in so much pain he almost didn't care. He had always thought she looked a little too perfect on TV, but there was a sympathetic look in her eyes now, which confirmed to him just how bad he looked. It was pathetic. And as he looked at her, he noticed a tiny pinprick of blood on either side of her mouth, barely noticeable, but it caught his eye. "I herniated a disk," he explained, "and I think you cut yourself shaving," he added. She looked startled and touched her face.

"It's nothing," she said vaguely about the pinpricks, as they stopped at his floor. That didn't always happen, but it had today. She had gone to get her Botox shots after seeing the psychic, and before work. She had no intention of explaining it to him, and wondered if he knew anyway. She knew who he was too, and had seen him around the network, looking handsome. He was a mess today, and seemed very sick or badly injured.

"Do you need help getting out?" She seemed sorry for him. It was obvious just how much he was hurting.

"If you could just keep the door open till I get out. If I get hit with it, I'll probably be a quadriplegic. I had a little too much Halloween last night," he said as he shuffled through the elevator door. He had been hoping to have a little too much birthday celebration too, but that was clearly no longer in the cards for him, and maybe never would be again, he thought mournfully, as he thanked her, and the doors closed behind him.

He could hardly move by the time he got to his office and collapsed on the couch and lay down with a loud moan. His favorite production assistant, Norman Waterman, came in and stared at him in amazement. Norman had worshipped him as a kid and knew all the statistics on him better than Jack did himself. He still had all his football cards, and Jack had signed every one of them for him.

"Holy shit, Jack! What happened to you? You look like you got hit by a train."

"Yeah, I did. I had an accident last night. Herniated disk. Is George here? I have to see him about the show tomorrow."

"I'll get him. Hey, happy birthday by the way!"

"How do you know?" Jack looked at him, distressed.

"Are you kidding? You're a legend, man. I've always known your birthday, and they announced it on the news this morning."

"My birthday or my age?" Jack asked, looking panicked.

"Both, of course. People know anyway. Anyone who ever followed football knows how old you are. You're NFL history."

"That's all I need. I'm going to spend the rest of my life in a wheelchair, and now they're reminding everyone of how old I am. Terrific." He told most of the girls he went out with that he was thirty-nine, and they weren't old enough to have followed his career or care. A lot of them believed him, and they were all excited to go out with Jack Adams. Announcing on the news that he was fifty was not going to help his dating career, but neither had Ms. Catwoman, who had reduced him to rubble in one night. He felt like crap. "What are you doing to celebrate tonight?" Norman asked innocently as Jack groaned.

"Suicide probably. Just get George, will you?"

"Sure, Jack . . . and happy birthday again." He said it with feeling as Jack closed his eyes, lying on the couch in agony, and didn't answer. Norman's admiration of him was touching, but all he wanted for this birthday was to be out of pain and to have his life back again. A life of sex and women.

* * *

At her desk several floors above, Valerie was going through a stack of fabric samples she wanted to use on a show about redoing your living room, and others for a segment on decorating for Christmas. Some of them were pretty good. There were stacks of samples and photographs all over her desk. Everything was in meticulous order, and she had her shows organized well in advance. She had a busy week ahead. She had checked in the mirror when she got in, to look for the spots of blood Jack had mentioned. They were tiny specks, and she washed them off, thinking that it was rude of him to mention it, particularly given the way he looked. He had always seemed very cocky to her when she saw him, and he always looked to be right off the cover of *Sports Illustrated* or *GQ*. Now in sharp contrast, he appeared as though he had been living in a cave somewhere or washed up on a beach after a shipwreck, but he'd been visibly in a lot of pain. And then she forgot about him, as she made notes for her upcoming shows. She had only two hours to work before she met her daughter for their birthday lunch at La Grenouille. Lunch at the elaborate French restaurant was an annual tradition for them, and it was the only birthday celebration Valerie would have today.

It was not good news to Valerie when her impeccably efficient secretary Marilyn had told her that her birthday had been announced on television that morning, and more than once. So not only everyone who listened to the radio now knew her age, but anyone who watched morning news too. The cat was certainly out of the bag. And it did nothing to console her when Marilyn told her that it was Jack Adams's, the retired quarterback and sportscaster's, birthday too. Valerie didn't bother to tell her she'd just seen him in the elevator doubled over in pain. Valerie didn't give a damn if it was his birthday or how old he was, it was bad enough that she had turned sixty and the whole goddamn world now knew it. How much worse could it get? The entire planet now knew that she was an old woman, and even Alan Starr's predictions for love and success in the coming year were no consolation for that, and who knew if they would happen anyway. The reality of her age was depressing beyond belief. Sixty felt like the new ninety to her.

Chapter 2

April Wyatt rolled out of bed without even remembering what day it was for the first few minutes. The alarm went off, and she was up and on her feet, and shuffled off to the bathroom. It was just after four A.M. She wanted to be at the fish market in the South Bronx by five, and at the produce market by six. She had a lot to buy for her restaurant. She was halfway through brushing her teeth when she remembered that it was her birthday. Normally, she didn't really care, but she was upset about it this year. She was turning thirty and had been dreading it. She hated "landmark birthdays." They made you measure yourself against everyone else's yardstick, and by traditional standards she didn't measure up. By thirty you were supposed to be married, have children and/or a successful job, and maybe even own a house. April had a restaurant, didn't have a husband or even a boyfriend, and was light-years away from having kids or even thinking about it. She was in debt up to her ears to her mother for the building she had put up the money for so April could open the restaurant that had been her dream and was now the joy of her life. It was doing well, but she was still paying back the debt to her mother. She never pressed her about it, but April wanted to pay it off. She figured that in another five years, maybe she would, if the restaurant kept making money the way it was. The building, with the apartment above it where she lived and had an office, was in the meat-packing district of New York. It had been a slum years before, and the building had needed a lot of renovation to bring it up to code, which April had done, spending as little on it as she could. She had put everything she could into the restaurant itself. Her apartment was a dump.

So on the yardstick of where she was supposed to be at thirty, she had a business and a career but not much else. No man, no kids, no house of her own, and a pile of debt. But she had her dream, and she loved it. She had called the restaurant April in New York. It was crowded almost every night, and they had gotten several great reviews in the three years since they'd opened. And it was her baby, one hundred percent. It was everything she had wanted it to be, and they had a flock of loyal fans. They were open seven days a week, and April was there herself day and night. She bought all the food, was the head chef, and visited guests at their tables too, although she was happiest in the kitchen. She had to show her face once in a while, particularly for faithful fans. She selected all the wines herself, and they had an interesting wine list at moderate prices. Those who loved it said it was the best restaurant in New York.

April had left college after the first year to take a year off and had never gone back, despite all her parents' aspirations for her. Her father was a medieval history professor at Columbia, and she had gone there for a year and been miserable the entire time. All she wanted was to be a chef. She had never gotten excited about her mother's passion for gracious living—all that interested her was what happened in the kitchen. Fancy weddings and table settings meant nothing to her, or how nice the living room looked. What she loved was preparing delicious food that everyone liked to eat.

She had spent six years in France and Italy going to school and apprenticing to become a chef, and she eventually worked at some of the best restaurants in Europe. She had been an apprentice of Alain Ducasse in Paris, and later an under pastry chef at the Tour d'Argent. She had worked in Florence and Rome, and by the time she came back to the States at twenty-five, she had some serious experience under her belt. She had worked for a year at one of the finest restaurants in New York, and then, thanks to her mother, had spent a year setting up the restaurant of her dreams. What she had wanted to do was serve the best of everything, both favorite delicacies *and* simple foods that people loved to eat, not drowning in elaborate sauces or a menu people wanted to face only once in a while. She offered fabulous pasta, which she made herself as she had learned to do in Rome and

Florence, steak tartare exactly the way they made it in France. She served escargots for those who loved them, foie gras both hot and cold, and boudin noir. She offered the finest salmon, unforgettable cheeseburgers on homemade buns, mac and cheese, meat loaf and corned beef hash like your grandmother used to make, gourmet pizzas, roast and Southern fried chicken, French leg of lamb, and mashed potatoes that melted in your mouth. There was caviar and blinis, spring rolls and dim sum, Maine lobsters and crab, and soft-shell crab in the summer, fabulous shrimp and oysters that she picked out herself. The menu was a combination of everything people loved to eat, and she loved to cook, with an entire section of comfort food, everything from matzoh-ball soup to polenta, pastina, pancakes, French toast and waffles, at any hour of the day, not just for Sunday brunch. She had brought the pastry chef from the Hotel Ritz in Paris to make exquisite pastries, desserts, and soufflés. She also had good, moderate-priced wines from all over the world, with an excellent sommelier to help choose them.

The restaurant had been a hit overnight, not only with her clients but with their kids as well. Her children's menu included grilled cheese sandwiches that kids and adults loved, hot dogs and hamburgers, tiny pizzas, plain pasta with nothing on it, mac and cheese, tiny bite-sized servings of fried chicken, and French fries the way she had learned to make them in France, which everyone loved. And for the kids' desserts, hot fudge sundaes, s'mores, banana splits, milk shakes, and root beer floats. When parents told their kids they were going to April's, their children were ecstatic. And if an adult wanted to order from the children's menu, that was okay too. It was the kind of restaurant that April would have loved to go to as a child, and that she enjoyed as an adult. And so did everyone who went there.

They were constantly booked for lunch, dinner, and Sunday brunch. And at this time of year, for the month of November, she served white truffles with pasta or scrambled eggs for those who loved them. She paid a fortune for the white truffles, which could only be found in one area of Italy, and were flown in from Elba every November for a brief three-week season. They had just come in from Italy two days before, and only serious food enthusiasts knew and loved the delicate roots that were found underground and were pungent and aromatic when shaved on pasta or risotto. She was going to start serving them that night. One of the things she loved about her birthday was that it was white truffle season, which she was crazy about. They were a big investment for her since white truffles cost a fortune.

April in New York was a smash hit, and it was her entire life. She had no time for, or interest in, anything else. And it was only on a day like this that she allowed herself to think about what else she didn't have in her life. In fact, she had nothing else, but she didn't want anything other than a restaurant. She hadn't had a serious romance in five years, but she didn't have time for one anyway. Before that, in Paris, she had been in an abusive relationship, with another chef who walked out on her every five minutes and had once threatened her with a butcher's knife. It had taken her two years, a shrink, and eighteen months on

Prozac to get over him, and she'd been gun-shy ever since. Since then, her relationships had been brief, infrequent, and superficial. The restaurant seemed to satisfy all her needs for now.

What shocked her, and was something of a wake-up call, was turning thirty today. Thirty seemed so grown up, or maybe just plain old. It made her suddenly wonder if she'd ever be married and have kids, and how she'd feel about it if she didn't. What if all she had was a string of restaurants instead? She wanted to open a second one, one day, but not yet. She wanted to get everything about this one right first. Even after three years, there were things she still wanted to improve on, systems she wanted to refine and change. She had just hired a second sommelier, because the one she had said he was overworked and, unlike her, didn't want to work seven days a week. April didn't mind working that hard at all. It was the nature of the business. She had no idea what she'd do with herself if she took a day off, so she never did.

As she drove to the new Fulton Fish Market in the Bronx, she thought about her birthday again. Her mother had always loved the fact that they were born on the same day, but it had always annoyed April as a child. She hated sharing "her day" with someone else, but now that she was older, she didn't mind. She already knew that this year was going to be hard for her mother. She had been dreading turning sixty for months. And if April felt a little skittish about turning thirty, she could only imagine how much worse it was for her mother, whose success rested partly on her image of youth. April felt sorry for her, and she knew that it bothered her mother too that there hadn't been a serious man in her own life, or even any man, for several years. She worried about that for April too, and nagged her about it from time to time. April didn't have time to think about it, and it was only on a day like today that it came to mind. She forgot about it again as she got out of her truck and joined in the fray at the fish market, where other chefs were selecting seafood for their restaurants. She was busy picking out what she needed until nearly six, and then drove to the produce market and spent an hour and a half there. She got back to Little West Twelfth Street shortly before eight and made herself a steaming bowl of café au lait. It was just what she needed after a cold morning buying fish. She turned on the radio in the restaurant kitchen and was startled when she heard an announcer on one of the early morning talk shows talking about her mother's age. She knew that was going to upset her even more, if she heard about it too. At least no one was saying that her daughter April Wyatt was thirty years old today. It was enough having to deal with it, without having the whole world know, April thought. She didn't envy her mother that side of her life. But her mother liked everything else that went with it, the glory, the success, the money, the acclaim, and if she wanted that, she had to take the downside too. April had no desire to be famous, she didn't aspire to be another Alain Ducasse or Joel Robuchon. She just wanted to run a restaurant where everybody loved to eat, and so far she had done well.

April had her father's natural discretion and simplicity, and her mother's passion for hard work. No one worked harder than her mother, April knew. Her father had a much gentler, less ambitious view of life. The academic life suited him well. And both her parents readily admitted that their union had been a mismatch from the first. Their marriage had lasted only eight years, and they divorced when April was seven. Her mother had already been building her career by then, and her father said he didn't have what it took to stick it out. He was in way over his head in her world. They were good friends now, and the divorce had never been bitter. They were just totally wrong for each other, and Valerie had always said to April that her father was a good man. He had married her stepmother within two years of the divorce. Maddie was a speech therapist who worked with children in the public schools, a far cry from Valerie, with her TV show, major career, endless licensing agreements, successful books, and glamorous public image. She hadn't been as big a star when he married her, although she was heading that way, but Valerie had become one over the years. Maddie and April's father had had two more children, two girls, Annie and Heather, who were respectively now nineteen and seventeen, and both good kids. Heather helped April in the restaurant sometimes in the summer and wanted to teach. Annie was a math genius, and a sophomore at MIT. They were all nice, decent, normal people, and both her parents enjoyed coming to the restaurant to eat. Her father often brought Maddie and Heather to dinner on Sunday nights, or for brunch, and Annie when she was home

28

from school. He was very proud of April, and Valerie was too. And April loved the fact that there was no animosity between them and everybody got along. It made life easier for her. She couldn't imagine living in a family with parents who hated each other after a divorce, although she had seen it happen to friends as she grew up. The only bad thing that had ever happened to her was the torturous relationship she'd had with the chef in France, which was probably why it had come as such a shock and hit her so hard. Until then, no one in her life had ever been abusive to her, or even unkind. She always said she never wanted to go out with another chef and was quick to say that most of the ones she knew were nuts.

As she drank her café au lait in the immaculate, quiet restaurant kitchen, she made some notes for additions to the menu that day. They would introduce the white truffle pasta at dinner, and they had two fish specials that day, and she added a Grand Marnier soufflé just for fun. The people who worked in the kitchen would start drifting in at nine, to start doing the prep work. The waiters came in at eleven, and the restaurant opened at noon.

April left just as the first of the sous-chefs, the under chefs, came in. She had an acupuncture appointment at nine. She went religiously twice a week, mostly to help her handle stress.

The acupuncturist she went to was on Charles Street, three blocks away. And over the years she'd gone to her, they had become friends. Unlike April, Ellen Puccinelli was married and had three kids. She had trained in England with a Chinese master, and said that she kept working just to stay sane and get some time away from them. April always enjoyed her time with her, it was part relaxation, part gossip with a girlfriend, and part shrink. Ellen usually brought her husband, Larry, and kids to dinner at the restaurant on Sunday nights. She was four years older than April, and her three rowdy boys were cute kids. She had been married for ten years. Her husband was a contractor, and life was something of a juggling act for them, living in New York.

Ellen smiled broadly as soon as April walked in, wearing jeans and a heavy sweater and the clogs she wore to work. Both women enjoyed what they did.

April took off her shoes, watch, and heavy sweater and laid her long, thin frame down on the immaculately draped table. Ellen's office was always warm and cozy. It was the perfect place for her to relax. April's long dark hair was in a braid that hung off the table. Ellen was a small woman, with short blond hair and big blue eyes. She looked like a pixie, and so did her kids. She had pictures of them on her desk.

"Isn't today your birthday?" Ellen asked her, as she reached for April's wrist to take her pulse. It always told her what was happening with her, which part of her body was being impacted by stress, long hours, or too much work.

"Yes," April acknowledged with a rueful grin, "it is. I thought about it this morning and started getting really depressed, and then I figured what the hell. I'm lucky I have the restaurant, I can't worry about what I don't have." Ellen was frowning as she took April's pulse and didn't comment. "Okay. What's wrong? My liver, my lungs, or my heart? I had a cold last weekend, but I got over it in two days," she said proudly, and Ellen smiled.

"Nah, just the usual stuff." Ellen smiled at her friend. "Some of your defenses are down, but that's normal for this time of year. We'll do some moxa." April loved the warm pungent smell of the moxa that Ellen lit on her belly and deftly removed before it burned her skin. It was both warming and healing and the part April loved best, but she didn't mind the needles either. Ellen was so good at what she did that she never hurt her, and April always felt relaxed when she left. She'd been doing acupuncture since she got back from Europe, and swore by it, and Ellen was very good. "Any new men in your life?" she asked with interest, and April laughed.

"Four of them, in fact. Three new weekend waiters, and a sommelier I stole from Daniel Boulud." She chuckled and Ellen shook her head.

"I meant real ones. There's more to life than just cooking."

"So they tell me," April said, and closed her eyes, as Ellen continued to heat the moxa on April's belly. It felt great. "I was thinking about that this morning. I used to think I'd be married and have kids by the time I was thirty. Now I can't even imagine it for the next several years. Maybe when I'm thirty-five. I used to think thirty was so old. I still feel like a kid." She looked like one as well. Like her mother, April didn't look her age, and she had her mother's looks, except for the dark hair. They had the same hazel eyes and perfect unlined skin. They were lucky. And April

31

never wore makeup, she couldn't see the point. It just melted on her face in the heat of the kitchen. She only wore it when she got dressed up and went out to a dinner party or on a date, which hadn't happened for several years.

"You've got a lot to feel good about," Ellen reminded her. "Most people don't have successful restaurants at thirty. I'd say you've done pretty well."

"Thank you," April said quietly, as Ellen removed the moxa and started with the needles. She stopped after a minute and took April's pulse again. She had an uncanny knack for sensing anything that was off balance, and she was rarely wrong.

"Are your periods screwed up again?" she asked after doing two more needles, and April smiled. Hers had been irregular for years. It was one of the ways the stress of her work manifested itself. Sometimes she didn't have a period for several months. She was on the Pill, to try and stay regular, and to cover the occasional "slip," although she didn't have many. But she didn't want to take the risk. And she hadn't had a sexual "slip" in quite a while.

"I haven't had a period in two months," April said without concern. "Whenever I work a lot, I don't get one for months. I've been pushing pretty hard. We added some new things to the menu last month."

"Maybe you should check it out," Ellen said casually as she did needles on April's upper arms.

"You think something's wrong?" April looked surprised.

"No, I don't," she reassured her, "but your pulse is funny. I keep picking something up."

"Like what?"

"When was the last time you had sex?"

"I can't remember. Why?"

"I'm probably crazy. And I know you're on the Pill. But maybe you should take a pregnancy test. Did you miss a Pill or two the last time you had sex?"

"You think I'm pregnant?" April sat up, looking shocked. "That's ridiculous. I slept with a guy I don't even like. A food critic. He was cute and smart. I plied him with our best wines to impress him, and had too much to drink myself, trying to be friendly. The next thing I knew, I woke up with him in my bed in the morning. I haven't done anything like that in years. And the bastard even gave us a bad review. He said the menu was childish and overly simplistic, and I'm not using my training or my skills. He was a real jerk."

"I don't think not liking a guy is considered birth control," Ellen said calmly, as April lay down again, looking disturbed.

"Now that I think of it, I only missed one Pill. I was so hung over the next day, I forgot, and I had a sore throat. I hope he got it. I had strep." She remembered it now, although she had given herself a pass for the indiscretion and had done her best to forget. She almost had, but it came back to her now, with Ellen's questions.

"Were you on antibiotics?"

"Yeah. Penicillin."

"That can knock the Pill out of commission. I think you should check it out."

"I'm not pregnant," April said firmly.

"I'm sure you're not. But it never hurts to check."

"Don't freak me out. Today is my birthday," April reminded her, and they both laughed.

"I'm sure it's nothing," Ellen reassured her, but it was too late for that. April was already stressed about it.

"So am I," April said firmly, trying to convince them both.

They talked about other things then, but Ellen reminded her of it again when she left. April didn't want to think about it, and she was sure she wasn't pregnant. She had no symptoms, other than the period she often missed anyway. She was still annoyed at herself for sleeping with him. Mike Steinman. It had been a stupid thing to do. She was old enough to know better, but he had been good-looking and intelligent. It had happened over Labor Day weekend, at the beginning of September, two months before. She hadn't allowed herself to think of him since.

She walked past a drugstore on the way back to work, and she felt stupid for doing it, but she walked in and bought a pregnancy kit. She hadn't worried about something like that in years. She had had a scare once in Paris, but fortunately she hadn't been pregnant. She was sure she wasn't this time either, but she bought the kit anyway, just so she could tell Ellen that she had made a mistake and to reassure herself. That was a headache she didn't need.

April stopped in the kitchen on her way in. Everything was in order, and the prep was well under way for lunch. They weren't opening for another two hours, and she had to go upstairs to dress for lunch with her mother. The rooms above the restaurant that were her apartment were almost entirely unfurnished. There were wooden crates and cardboard boxes, and several ugly lamps. And what furniture she did have—a desk, couch, dresser, and double bed—she had bought at Goodwill. She refused to spend her money on decor. She had spent it on the best possible secondhand equipment she could buy for the kitchen. Her mother had offered to furnish the apartment for her, and she had refused. All she ever did upstairs was work at her desk or sleep; she never entertained. In that respect, she was not her mother's daughter. She looked like she was camping out.

She checked on the invoices of the orders that had come in, and then went to take a shower. She forgot all about the pregnancy test she had bought until she was halfway dressed. She almost decided not to do it, and then decided what the hell. Now that Ellen had raised the question, it was better to have confirmation that she wasn't pregnant than to let it gnaw at her without knowing for sure. She followed the directions, set the test down on the counter after she used it, and finished getting dressed. She was wearing black slacks and a black sweater, with flat shoes and her hair in a braid. Her long dark hair was smooth and sleek, and she put on lipstick, looking in the mirror. And then she glanced down at the test. She picked it up then, and stared at it, and put it down again. She walked out of the room and came back and stared at it again. This couldn't be. It couldn't happen. She was on the Pill. She had only missed one, for chrissake . . . or was it two? She had been so damn drunk that night she couldn't remember. This couldn't be happening to her. It just couldn't. Not with a man she scarcely knew, and hated, who didn't even like her restaurant or understand what she was doing. It was her birthday today, for God's sake. Things like this weren't supposed to happen. But sometimes they did. She was pregnant, by a total stranger. Now what the hell was she going to do? There was no room in her life for this. How could she make such a terrible mistake? And how could life be so cruel?

She sat down on her bed in the empty room with tears running down her cheeks. This was the bed where she had slept with him. She bitterly regretted it now. This was a hell of a price to pay for one incredibly stupid mistake.

She looked panicked when she put on a black coat her mother had given her, then tied the belt tightly around her waist as though to prove that she still could. She picked up her bag and hurried down the stairs.

She didn't stop in the kitchen, which was unusual for her. She walked right into the street and hailed a cab and gave the driver the address of La Grenouille. The last thing she wanted to do now was have lunch with anyone, or celebrate with her mother. She wasn't going to say anything to her, but as they drove uptown, all April could think was that this was the worst birthday of her life.

Chapter 3

April arrived at the restaurant two minutes before her mother and was led to the table Valerie had reserved for them. Her mother went there often with friends—it was her favorite place to dine, other than April's restaurant, which she loved too. But La Grenouille was more her style. It was elegant and chic and had been fashionable for years. The flower arrangements were fabulous, the service impeccable, and April and Valerie both agreed that the food was superb, the best in the city.

April was sitting at the table lost in thought, in a state of shock, when her mother arrived. Valerie looked beautiful, and she kissed April on the cheek with a broad smile and then sat down.

"Sorry I'm late. I had a busy morning. I'm trying to lock down our Christmas show. Happy birthday! I hope it's been a good one so far."

There was no way April was going to tell her mother the truth. Maybe eventually, but certainly not now. She had to digest it first herself, and figure out what to do. Maybe she'd never tell her at all.

"It's been okay. I was at the fish market and the produce market at the crack of dawn. We're starting white truffle season tonight. They came in two days ago. You should come for dinner this weekend." She smiled at her mother. They had a good relationship, and always had, and they liked each other even better now as adults. And April would always be grateful to her for making her dream come true and lending her the money for the restaurant. It had been an enormous gift to her. "Happy birthday to you too," she added.

Valerie ordered champagne for both of them and lowered her voice as she looked at her daughter across the table. "They announced my age on the radio today," she said, looking as unhappy about it as she had been all morning, since she heard it.

"I know. I figured you'd be upset. I'm sorry, Mom. It doesn't matter. No one would believe it. You hardly look older than I do."

"Thank you for saying that," Valerie said ruefully, "but now everyone knows the truth."

"You can say they made a mistake." April tried to console her, but she was too shaken up herself to be very reassuring.

"I can't believe I'm sixty," Valerie said, as April smiled at her.

"I can't believe I'm thirty," and pregnant, she silently added. Thirty wasn't the end of the world, but getting pregnant by a man she didn't know or love was about as bad as it could get.

"You don't look it either," Valerie said, smiling at her, "especially with your hair in a braid and no makeup." She had long since given up trying to get her to wear any. April said it made no sense with her job and lifestyle. Although their features and their figures were strikingly similar, the two women couldn't have been more different. One looked as though she had stepped off the pages of *Vogue*, and the other was a totally natural beauty. With Valerie's careful attention to her appearance, they could almost have been sisters.

They sipped their champagne, and the waiter took their order. He greeted Valerie warmly and wished her a happy birthday. She told him it was April's birthday too, and he smiled. Valerie ordered crab, and April sweetbreads; she loved how they did them. It struck her then that she had had no nausea in the past two months, and not a single symptom from what had happened, just a little tenderness in her breasts, which she had assumed was because she was late. Now she knew what had happened, and it was hard to think of anything else. Impossible, in fact. She kept missing two-thirds of everything her mother said. The waiter poured her another glass of champagne and April drank it. She was trying to be in denial about being pregnant. She was feeling a little dizzy by the time lunch came. And finally, when they finished, Valerie looked at her with concern. April was looking dazed and had been worried and distracted all through lunch. And she had gotten just a little tipsy.

"Are you upset about your birthday or is something wrong?" her mother asked her gently, and April shook her head and tried to smile.

"No, I'm fine. I think thirty just hit me harder than I expected. And so did the champagne." They had been drinking Cristal, which was their favorite. April didn't carry it at the restaurant; it was much too expensive for her clients. Nor did they carry the Château d'Yquem that the waiter poured each of them after the meal as a gift. It was the best sauterne there was, and April didn't want to hurt his feelings, so she drank it.

"I'm going to be drunk when I go back to work," Valerie said, laughing, as April stared at her across the table, feeling woozy.

"Yeah, me too," April said vaguely, and then looked at her mother through a haze of wine, and said exactly what she had told herself she wouldn't. "I'm pregnant." She just blurted it out, and the announcement sat between them like an elephant on the table, as Valerie stared at her in amazement.

"You're pregnant? How did that happen? I mean . . . never mind. Who is it? Have you been seeing someone?" If she had been, April hadn't said a word to her about it. Valerie looked stunned. This was the last thing she had expected.

"No, I haven't. It was a stupid mistake I made over the Labor Day weekend. I don't even know him. I only saw him once. I just found out today."

Valerie looked at her and then touched her hand. She was as shocked as April had been when she read the test. "What are you going to do about it? Or not what, I guess . . . but when?"

"I don't know what or when. This has never happened to me before. I'm thirty years old, and this morning I was beating myself up about not being married and having kids by the time I'm

40

thirty. And now look what happened. I have no idea what to do about it, what's right, or what I want."

"Would you keep it?" Valerie looked even more shocked at the prospect. That hadn't occurred to her before, but neither had April getting pregnant by a stranger.

"I don't know. I'm not even sure I ever want a baby. But now this has happened. Maybe I should make the best of it, although it would certainly complicate my life."

"Are you going to tell the father?" These were questions Valerie had never thought she would be asking her daughter. April had always been so sensible and well behaved. And now she was pregnant by a man she didn't know. It was a nightmare for April. Her mother felt sorry for her.

"I don't know. He probably doesn't even remember me, or what happened. We were both embarrassingly drunk. I probably shouldn't tell him. I'll deal with it on my own."

"Is he a nice person?"

"I have no idea. His name is Mike Steinman, and he gave me a terrible review."

"After he slept with you? How rude!" Valerie looked shocked again, and suddenly April laughed. Confessing to her mother had sobered her a little. They decided not to have dessert and ordered coffee. April felt more coherent after she drank it.

"I'm having trouble believing that this happened. I took an antibiotic for strep throat, and my acupuncturist said that it may have canceled out the Pill. She's the one who suspected I was pregnant. I sure didn't. It never even occurred to me."

"How long ago did this happen?" Valerie asked with a worried look. She had forgotten the timing. It had been a hell of an announcement, and an enormous shock to them both.

"Two months ago. Labor Day weekend," April repeated, and her mother nodded.

"If you're going to do something about it, you'll have to do it soon."

"I know. I'll go see my doctor." But the decision was hers. And she had nothing to say to Mike Steinman, unless she decided to keep it. In that case, he had a right to know too, although she wanted nothing from him.

"What can I do to help you?" Valerie offered.

"Nothing for now. I have to figure this out for myself."

"I guess these days a lot of unmarried women have babies, especially at your age. It's not the taboo it used to be, and at least you don't have to marry someone you don't like, if you decide to keep it. But the way you work, I don't see how you could manage a child on your own."

"Neither do I," April said honestly. "This was not in my plans." It didn't make sense for April to keep it, and they both knew that, but what she decided about it ultimately was up to her. April knew her mother would support her, whatever her decision. "I'll let you know, when I figure it out. I guess this is a birthday we won't forget in a hurry. I wasn't going to tell you until I made up my mind."

"I'm glad you did," Valerie said reassuringly. "It's entirely your decision, April. Your father and I will stand behind you, either way."

"Don't say anything to Daddy yet," April said, looking upset. She couldn't imagine telling him, or Maddie. If she had a baby now, everyone would be so shocked. Or maybe they wouldn't. And did it matter? The only thing that mattered to her was what she felt was the best thing to do in the circumstances, and she didn't know what that was yet. The whole idea was still too new, and hard to wrap her mind around. She looked at her watch then, and Valerie asked for the check. "I'd better get back to work."

"Me too," Valerie said, still bowled over by April's announcement.

"What are you doing tonight?" April asked her. "Going out with friends?"

"I'm going to bed to cry over the fact that everyone knows how old I am," she said with a rueful grin.

"Do you want to come to dinner at the restaurant? We'll have the white truffle pasta tonight. I can do it for you with risotto, if you prefer."

"I think I'd rather be alone," Valerie said honestly, and April understood. At this point, with all she had to think about, so would she, but she had to work.

"I love you, Mom. Thank you for being so nice about this. I'm sorry to spring this on you on your birthday," April said gratefully as they both put their coats on.

"I'm just sorry for you that it happened." She didn't envy her daughter the decision, but she could see only one possible choice. It would be just too much for her to handle a baby and a restaurant on her own, with no one to help her. There was only one reasonable option, as far as Valerie was concerned, not two. April couldn't have the baby, and not without a father. But she respected her right to make the decision. She was sure that April would come to that conclusion too, and her mother knew that she was in no hurry to have kids.

"Happy birthday, Mom," April said sadly, as they hugged outside La Grenouille. "Thanks for being so good to me. And believe me, no one would ever believe you're sixty."

"Just don't make me a grandmother yet," Valerie said ruefully. "I'm not ready for that."

"Neither am I," April said honestly. "I never expected to be dealing with something like this."

"Well, happy birthday anyway, sweetheart." Valerie blew her a kiss, they got into separate cabs, and both of them went back to work.

When April got to the restaurant, she went upstairs to change her clothes, and was in the kitchen five minutes later, grateful for the distraction. She worked straight through the afternoon, doing the prep work herself for dinner, and it was midnight before she finally stopped and sat down. It had been the best way to spend her birthday, too busy and too tired to think.

They had sold seven truffle pasta dinners, despite the price. And the Grand Marnier soufflés had been delicious. Her staff had presented her with a birthday cake and the entire restaurant had sung "Happy Birthday." If it hadn't been for the positive pregnancy test, it would have been a nice evening. But it was impossible not to think of that. It changed everything, and April felt as though she had a thousand-pound weight on her shoulders. She felt as though she had aged ten years in a single day, facing this awful decision. She blew out the candles on her cake, praying that everything would turn out right.

In her bed that night, Valerie wished the same for her. Suddenly turning sixty didn't seem so devastating. She was worried about her daughter. And as she turned out the light, she suddenly remembered Alan's prediction about April, that she was going to have a baby. A shiver ran down Valerie's spine as she thought of it. He had been right, about the pregnancy anyway. It remained to be seen if there would be a baby. It made her think too of the new man he had predicted for her. If he'd been accurate about April, maybe he would be about that too. That would be nice for a change. But for now all she could think about was April.

Jack Adams lay in his bed, blasted on painkillers that night. He never made it to Cipriani. He had crawled home from the office and gone to bed. There was no acrobatic sex for him, and no twenty-two-year-old models to help him celebrate his fiftieth birthday. He was in bed, in agony, watching TV, thinking back on all the fun he had had for so many years, and convinced now that life as he had known it was over forever. It had been one hell of a birthday. He felt as though he was in mourning for his youth, which had ended in the arms of Catwoman the night before. He was convinced she had killed Superman for good. Fifty had turned out to be just as bad as he had feared it would be, and worse.

Chapter 4

April went back to see Ellen the same day she had an appointment with her doctor. As soon as she walked in, she told Ellen she had been right, she was pregnant.

"I'm sorry," Ellen said sympathetically. "I was hoping I was wrong. Your pulses just felt like you might be."

"You're better than you think." April smiled at her ruefully, and lay down on the table. "I was hoping you were wrong too."

"What are you going to do?" Ellen was worried about her friend.

"I don't think I have much choice," April said sadly. She had been wrestling with it all week and didn't like any conclusion she came to. It was the hardest decision of her life. "I can't manage the restaurant and a kid. I have to have an abortion. I'm seeing my doctor this afternoon."

"It's not as hard as you think, managing one kid, if you decide to have it."

"You have a husband to help you," April reminded her. "I don't. I don't even know this guy, and I probably wouldn't tell him."

"Larry's not much help with the kids. Most of the time, I pretty much take care of them on my own, and I have three. I have other friends who've done it alone. Some of them have gone to sperm banks because they wanted kids, even without a husband. The beginning is a little dicey, but after that, it settles down."

"I work twenty hours a day, most of the time, seven days a week. When am I going to find time for a baby, or a two-year-old? I don't think I could do it. Maybe I never will. The restaurant is my baby." April knew what she had to do or should. She just didn't like it.

"You'll figure it out," Ellen said quietly. "Just do whatever is right for you."

"I'm trying to decide what that is." But she had been worried and upset ever since she found out. Her mother had called her several times, trying to offer her support, but it was obvious that she didn't think April should keep it, and some of the time neither did April. The rest of the time, she wasn't sure. It was a monumental decision. She was relieved to be seeing the doctor that afternoon. April had done nothing but cry about it all week, even when she was working in the kitchen. All the kitchen staff who knew her well were worried about her. She had been unusually quiet ever since her birthday.

After she arrived for her appointment, April spent nearly an hour talking about it to her doctor, who was sympathetic and kind. She discussed April's medical options with her, and suggested that she might like to get some counseling to help her with the decision. She understood how hard it was. April explained to her that she scarcely knew the father and they had no relationship. It had essentially been a one-night stand under the influence of a lot of wine. It was hardly the way to have a baby, and not what she wanted or had ever planned. The doctor understood that too. She explained the abortion procedures to her, and they figured out that, calculating from her last menstrual period, April was now ten weeks pregnant. The doctor suggested they do a sonogram to see how things looked. It was standard procedure for a normal ten-week visit for pregnant patients. April agreed and was relieved that they had the sonogram equipment right in the office.

A nurse led her into a dimly lit room, had her drink three glasses of water, and wait twenty minutes, and told her not to empty her bladder and to put a gown on. After April lay down on the table, the technician applied gel to her belly, turned on the machine, and moved a metal wand around in the gel, as April watched the screen. And then she saw it, the tiny little being nestled deep inside her. It had the shape and look of a baby but was tiny, and its heart was beating regularly. The technician told her everything was fine, as she showed her where the head was, and the "rump," as she called it, and the little stems that were becoming arms and legs. This was a baby, not just an idea, or a mistake she had made with a total stranger. This was already a life, with a heart, and one day a soul and a mind. As she looked at the screen, April felt sick, as tears ran down her cheeks. She had never felt so overwhelmed or so alone, and at the same time so close to anything or anyone in her life. It was an avalanche of conflicting emotions all at once. She hadn't been prepared for how she would feel when she saw it. It changed everything she had thought about a baby for the past week.

"Everything is fine," the technician patted her arm and reassured her, then handed her a printout of what they had seen on the screen. April was still holding the photograph in her hand when she walked back into the office to see the doctor.

"I'm keeping it," she said in a hoarse voice, as she sat down across the desk from her again, and the doctor watched her.

"Are you sure?" she asked her, and April nodded.

"I'm sure. I'll make it work somehow." She couldn't get rid of it, and now she didn't want to.

"Then we'll see you in a month," the doctor said as she stood up, smiling at her. "If you change your mind, let me know. We still have some leeway timewise, not much, but we have a few weeks, if you decide not to proceed with the pregnancy after all." But it was no longer just a pregnancy to April, after what she'd seen on the sonogram, it was a baby. This wasn't what she had wanted to do with her life, but she was two months pregnant. Her due date was in June. She had a baby now and a due date. She walked out of the doctor's office in a daze, feeling stunned. The decision had been made. And April knew she wouldn't change her mind.

She hailed a cab and went back downtown to the restaurant, and as soon as she got there, she went upstairs and called her mother.

"I'm keeping it," she said softly. Valerie was still at work.

"Keeping what, darling?" She had just come out of a meeting and had a thousand things on her mind. "Oh my God," she said, before April could answer the question. "You are? Are you sure that's what you want to do?" She wasn't happy to hear it, and April could tell.

"I saw it on the sonogram, Mom. It looks like a baby. I can't do it. I want to have it." She was crying as she said it, and listening to her, Valerie started to cry too.

"Are you going to tell the father?" She was desperately worried about her daughter.

"I don't know yet. All I know is that I'm going to have it. I'll have to figure out the rest as I go along."

"All right," Valerie said firmly, "let me know what I can do. Thank God you're not feeling sick. I was sick as a dog with you." This wasn't the choice she had hoped April would make, but she was willing to go along with it and support her. "You're sure?"

"I'm sure," April said firmly.

"And when is this going to happen?" Valerie asked with dread.

"In June," April said, smiling for the first time in a week.

"I have to admit," Valerie said, sounding shaken by the news, "it's a bit much turning sixty and facing becoming a grandmother all in one week." She was trying to be a good sport about it. It had been one hell of a week, but surely for April too. Her thirtieth birthday had brought with it an unexpected gift. Valerie hoped that it would prove to be that and not just an intolerable burden for her daughter. It was not going to be easy. She had a demanding business to run, and her mother knew how much her restaurant meant to her. She had been willing to give up her personal life for four years in order to do it, and now suddenly she was going to have a baby on her hands too, with no man to help her. It was certainly not what Valerie would have wanted for her. "I was the same age when I had you," she said, sounding pensive. "But I had your father to help me, and he was very good with you."

"I'll figure it out, Mom. Other women do it. It's not the end of the world." And maybe, just maybe, it was the beginning of a whole new life for her, and she was willing to do all she could to have her restaurant and a baby. In the beginning at least, she could have the baby in the restaurant with her. And after that there was day care. Other single mothers did it, she told herself. So could she.

Next, April called Ellen to tell her that she had decided to keep the baby, and Ellen was thrilled for her. She promised to lend her baby clothes and a stroller. By the time she hung up, April felt reassured and a little less scared. She kept reminding herself to take it one step at a time. She still had to decide if she wanted to tell Mike Steinman, but she wasn't ready to do that yet, or anyone else. She had to get used to the idea herself first. And it was a lot to get used to. She sat staring at the photograph from the sonogram after she talked to Ellen. It still didn't seem real to her. She put the photograph in her desk drawer, then put her apron on and wrapped it around her, stepped into her clogs, and went downstairs to work. But this time, she was smiling, and everyone in the kitchen was relieved to see that she was her old self again. She was scared but excited, and she told herself all night that she had seven months to figure out how to make it work.

Valerie was thinking about her daughter that night, as she lay in bed watching TV. She was flipping through the channels, and worried about April's decision to have the baby, when she saw Jack Adams, the sportscaster, interviewing a well-known wide receiver and she recognized him from the elevator on her birthday when he could hardly walk. She watched him for a few minutes. He mentioned having injured his back recently, and he seemed to have recovered as he moved easily on-screen, but talked about how excruciating it had been.

She smiled, thinking of the condition he'd been in. He looked a lot different now on the screen, and very smooth. He appeared to be humorous and light-hearted, and he was very different from the disheveled creature who could barely walk that day, in gym clothes and rubber flip-flops. On-screen, he was a nice-looking man and more articulate than most sportscasters, and she had to admit, as she watched him, that he was very good-looking. She knew that when the network had signed him, it had been a big deal. A *very* big deal. She had heard too that he had a reputation for dating very young women. It was funny to see him on the screen, after being in the elevator with him that day. Doubled over in pain, he had looked like Rumpelstiltskin, and without thinking about it any further, she changed channels to a sitcom she watched occasionally, but a few minutes later, she turned the comedy off too. As she turned off the light to go to sleep, she reminded herself to call Alan and tell him about his accurate prediction about April's baby. She had thought he was crazy when he said that April would have one. But he was right. He certainly was good at what he did. She fell asleep thinking about him, and about April. She dreamed of her all night with a baby in her arms, crying and saying it had been a terrible mistake, and begging her mother to help her, and there was nothing Valerie could do.

Valerie woke up in the morning, convinced that April was making a huge mistake, but equally certain that she couldn't sway her. Once April made up her mind about something, she rarely changed course. She had been that way with the restaurant, dogged and persevering every inch of the way, overcoming every challenge and obstacle to reach her goal. Valerie was that way too, and always had been with her career. She was a woman who always knew what she wanted, and so did her daughter. It was a quality, not a flaw, but in this case, Valerie was convinced she was wrong. She called April to talk to her about it again that morning. She was still upset by the disturbing dream she'd had the night before.

"Are you sure this is what you want to do?" Valerie pressed her. It was still early, and April was at her desk, poring over the bills intently. She had been up since four and back at the fish market again at five that morning.

"Yes, I'm sure, Mom," April said quietly. "It's not a choice I would have made intentionally, but now that it's happened, I don't feel like there's any other option. I'm thirty years old, I don't know if I'll ever have another shot at having a baby. I haven't had a relationship in five years, not a serious one, just the kind of thing like what just happened, although it's usually not a total stranger. I work all the time. When do I have time to go out and meet anyone? I'm always working. And it's never going to be the right time for me to have a baby. I want to open another restaurant one day, then I'll have two of them and I'll be working even harder.

"If I do meet someone, I'm not even sure I'd want to get pregnant. I've never been a hundred percent sure that having children would fit in my life, or that I'd be good at it. But now that it's happened, I don't have the guts to just give it up and walk away. What if I never get pregnant again, or never meet anyone? I will have had this opportunity I threw away, and maybe I'll never get a second chance. Maybe if I were twenty-two, it would be different. But not at thirty. I'm too old to refuse a gift like this.

"And I'm not even sure I'd have felt differently at twenty. That little person with the heartbeat you see on the sonogram screen is pretty compelling. That's a baby in there, a real live human being, not just a kink in my lifestyle, or a glitch in scheduling. It's a person, and for some incredibly stupid reason, this happened to me. Now I need to rise up and meet the challenge, even if it scares the hell out of me, which it does. I'll just have to figure it out as I go along.

"And fortunately, it's no longer a big deal to have a baby if you're unmarried. People do it all the time. Women go to sperm banks and get inseminated by strangers. At least I know who this baby's father is. He's a smart, educated, employed, decent-looking guy. I may think he's an asshole, and he hates my restaurant, but he doesn't seem like a terrible person for this child to be related to. And it's what I have to work with for now. Under the circumstances, this is the best I can do, to face what happened. The responsibility here is mine."

"But you don't even know this man, April," her mother said mournfully. She was voicing all of April's own fears.

"No, I don't, Mom. I didn't pick this, and I wouldn't have. But I want to make the best of it, instead of doing something I may regret for the rest of my life, if I abort it."

"And what if you regret having it, for the rest of your life?" her mother asked her honestly, and April closed her eyes as she thought about it, and then opened them and smiled. No matter how strong her mother's doubts were on the subject, the decision had been made.

"I'll send it to live with you then. You can tell everyone it's your baby, and even look properly embarrassed about it. Then *no one* will believe you're sixty. I think that's the perfect solution."

"Very funny," Valerie said. She had already decided that under no circumstances would she admit it publicly in her professional life when she was a grandmother. Some things were just more than she was willing to endure, and this was one. She wanted to help her daughter, but not admit to grandmotherhood as part of her "image," or her age. "I just want you to be sure you know what you're doing."

"I don't," April readily admitted. "I don't have the remotest idea of what I'm doing, or what will happen when the baby gets here. I'll just do the best I can to manage. This stuff happens to people all the time. I'm hoping maybe I can get Heather to come in and help me on weekends. Or maybe I'll have to hire an au pair." She knew her mother would help her if necessary, but she wanted to try to do this on her own. It was her baby, and her decision to have it. She was a thirty-year-old woman, she had lived on her own in Europe for six years, she ran a successful business, it seemed unlikely that she couldn't manage a baby. When she tried to think about it calmly, she felt confident about it, and at other times she was as frightened as her mother sounded now. This was all very new to her. But she had seven months to get used to the idea and make plans.

"I think you should call the baby's father," her mother said, still sounding worried, and April looked pensive before she responded.

"I might. I haven't made up my mind. I've only known about this for eight days. It's not like he and I are friends. It was a stupid thing to do. A classic one-night stand, and I got him drunk because he was smart, attractive, and maybe he'd give us a good review. And look what I wound up with. A baby and a shit review. And what am I going to say to him if I do call him? 'Remember me? I'm the one you gave the lousy review to, the one who designed the overly simplistic menu, is confused about whether to serve delicacies or comfort food, and is cooking below her skill level. Well, how about sharing a kid with me for the rest of your life?' He said I should only be cooking for children, so I guess I could lead in with that, and tell him that since he thought so, I decided to have one of my own. I can't even imagine what I'd say to him, or what I want from him. I don't even know if I like him. From what I know so far, I don't think so, other than that he's cute and was pretty good in bed, if I remember correctly, but I have no idea if I'd want him to be involved with our child. Maybe he's really a jerk, or hates kids, or there are a million things I would hate about him. I just don't know."

"But you're having his baby anyway," Valerie said in a shaken voice. "This is a little modern for me," she admitted. "Maybe I'm even older than I think. I still like the idea of loving the man you have a child with, and wanting him to stick around."

"So do I. But this didn't happen that way. I'm not the first one it happened to, and at least today you don't have to marry a man you don't like, or barely even know. You don't have to hide in another city and give the baby away. And I don't have to have an abortion if I don't want to. There are plenty of women having babies today by men they scarcely know, or not at all. I'm not saying it's the best way, or even the right way, but I think I'm lucky that I live in a world, and a society, and even a city, where I can handle this any way I want. It's not going to be anyone's problem except mine, and I'm willing to take it on. I don't know if I want the baby's father helping me, or interfering with me, or maybe even getting involved in my baby's life. For now, it's my baby, not 'ours.' And the only reason I might tell him eventually is because I respect his right to know. But beyond that, I don't think I want anything from him. He never called me after we spent the night together, he never even thanked me for dinner, so he doesn't have any investment in me either. If he'd been interested in me, he would have called." Valerie realized she had a point, and April had been thinking about that all week. Since she had never heard from Mike Steinman after his bad review, she assumed he was either embarrassed or didn't give a damn. It made it that much harder to call now. It would have been hard enough if they were dating, but since they weren't, she didn't know if she should call him now, or after the baby was born, or not at all. And she had wanted no input from him in order to make up her mind about whether or not to have it. She wasn't counting on him. She was relying on herself. And her mother couldn't help admiring her for it, although the decision to have it wasn't the one she would have made, particularly not on her own. She was more than willing to admit that she wasn't that brave.

"All right, darling. I just want to be sure that you know what you're getting into." She sighed. "When are you going to tell your father?" Valerie sounded worried again. She knew her ex-husband, Pat, was not going to like it. He was very conservative and traditional, and a grandchild born out of wedlock was surely not what he had in mind for his oldest daughter. But he was also crazy about April.

"I don't know yet," April said, glancing at her watch. She had a meeting with their butcher that morning and wanted to order all the cuts she needed for the next month, and she had to see their poultry supplier for Thanksgiving. She had been letting things slide for the last week, while she wrestled with the decision about the baby. Now she had to focus on the restaurant again. She knew that from now on her life was going to be a juggling act, between the restaurant and the baby. She'd better get used to it, but at least for now she could concentrate on the restaurant full-time. "I've got to go to work, Mom. You're coming for Thanksgiving, right?"

"Of course." For the past three years, April had done their Thanksgiving dinners at the restaurant, and they all loved it. Maddie no longer had to cook Thanksgiving on alternate years, and Valerie no longer had to hire a caterer for the years it was her turn. Now her father, Maddie, her two sisters, and her mother all had Thanksgiving dinner at the restaurant with her. She served a full Thanksgiving dinner that night, and nothing else. And she did the same on Christmas Eve. They were open on holidays too, and usually jammed. She wanted to be there for lonely people or those who had nowhere else to go. Thanksgiving was three weeks away, and they were already almost fully booked. For an insane moment, she thought of inviting Mike Steinman to Thanksgiving dinner with them, and telling everyone then. It was a nice fantasy, or at least an interesting one, but it made no sense to ask Mike to join them for a family holiday, and it would make even less sense to him. If she decided to tell him, she knew she'd have to meet with him alone.

"I'll call you soon, Mom," April promised. "I have to get to work."

"So do I. We're taping our Christmas show today. I have a thousand things to do. We're covering decorations, holiday menus, doing the tree, and unusual gifts. We even have a puppy on the show. I'm giving it to Marilyn for Christmas, but she doesn't know it yet. I thought I'd do it on the show!" April knew her and liked her too. She had been her mother's assistant for four years, and she not only helped with production details, but she handled personal errands for her too. She was forty-two, had no boyfriend, and was married to her job. April thought the puppy was a great idea for her too.

Valerie was sitting in her office, wearing a red dress, gold earrings, and a string of pearls, ready to go on air while they were talking. Later that week, she was doing a segment on Christmas weddings. She had lined up some beautiful velvet gowns.

"What kind of dog are you giving her?" April asked with interest. She thought it was a sweet thing to do and she knew her mother's viewers would love it. Her mother was brilliant about things like that, adding humor, the unexpected, and something touching to her show. It was always about more than just elegance or decor. Her show had heart and its own style, which people loved.

"It's a toy Yorkshire terrier. It's adorable. I picked him out last week."

"People are going to love it, Mom. You'll probably boost sales in pet shops all over the country, or at breeders, and adoption at the SPCA." Valerie smiled at the idea. She couldn't wait to give Marilyn the gift.

The two women hung up after a few minutes, and Valerie sat at her desk and sighed, thinking about April again. This was not what she wanted for April, not at all. A baby with no father, no man to help her, no one to share this important time with her. There was no question in Valerie's mind, and there never had been, April was a very brave girl. She just hoped she wouldn't regret it for the rest of her life.

Chapter 5

On Thanksgiving Day, April got up early to do most of the cooking herself. Her assistants came in later, and handled the details. Their customers came in early that night for dinner, so she had her family come at eight, when the insanity in the kitchen had calmed down a little.

Valerie showed up half an hour earlier, as she always did, with two shopping bags full of table decorations, and while other patrons ate their turkey, stuffing, homemade cranberry jelly, and chestnut purée, she transformed the table for the Wyatt family into a work of art. People at neighboring tables loved seeing what she did. She set up silver candlesticks on the table, brought her own tablecloth and napkins with turkeys embroidered on them, and always came up with incredible decorations. Most people in the restaurant recognized her, and she signed autographs while doing the table, as April moved around the room, greeting the guests. There were always lots of children in the restaurant that night, and April gave them chocolate turkeys that she made herself. The atmosphere in the room was always friendly and festive. April in New York seemed like a perfect place to spend Thanksgiving, and many of her regulars did so every year. There were several long tables set up for families, and they accommodated as many people as they could.

The group at April's own table was the same every year. Her mother, father, stepmother, two half-sisters, and April were seated at a round table in the rear of the room. Ellen and her family came in every year at six o'clock, and were leaving just as the assorted Wyatts arrived. April had introduced the two families to each other several times, and as they left, the Puccinelli children looked drunk on food, clutching their chocolate turkeys in their hands. It was hard for April to imagine, as she looked at them this year, that in a few years she would have a child herself, and on the following Thanksgiving a baby in her arms.

She and Ellen exchanged a knowing look, as April kissed them goodbye. Ellen had been thinking the same thing about her, and was truly excited for her friend. She felt a proprietary interest in her pregnancy now, since she had been the first to guess. The two women exchanged a few whispered words before they left, and April smiled. Her mother had said nothing further about her pregnancy in the past three weeks. She had been too busy to think about it, and for the moment she preferred to have denial than focus on her coming grandchild. One thing at a time, she told herself. And April had been too busy to think about it much either. She couldn't even imagine what it would be like to be visibly pregnant, when her apron would barely go around her waist. For the moment, at thirteen weeks, nothing showed. She was three months pregnant, with six months to go.

April's father and his family arrived as she was chatting with her mother, and looking at the photographs of Valerie giving her assistant the tiny Yorkie puppy. Marilyn had cried and named him Napoleon right on the show. He looked adorable and the ratings on their show were through the roof even before the Christmas segment aired.

April was excited to see her sister Annie, whom she hadn't seen since she'd gone back to school in Boston in late August. Annie's dream was to have a job in government one day, using her extraordinary math skills. Her mother always said that she had obviously been switched at the hospital at birth, since no one in the family could add or subtract or keep their checkbook straight, although April was very competent with the restaurant's books. Annie had been a math whiz since she was six. Annie and April looked very much alike, and Annie could easily have been related to April's mother, but both Maddie and Valerie had very similar features. The entire group had a family look, and it was hard to tell who was what to whom. Maddie was younger than Valerie but looked more her age at fifty-two, and the two women could easily have been sisters. They were a talkative, congenial group. And as they sat down to dinner, Maddie was asking Valerie's advice about serving goose at a New Year's

Eve dinner that she and Pat were planning for some of his col-
leagues. Valerie was helping her construct an interesting menu
to go with it, and commented positively on the way Maddie was
doing her hair, and although she didn't say it, she thought she
should get rid of the gray. In some ways, Maddie looked older
than April's mother. Although they had similar features, she
had none of Valerie's glamour. All five women at the Wyatt table
were tall, thin, and very striking. And Pat, as the only male in
the family, was a big, burly teddy bear of a man with kind eyes
and a warm smile. He enjoyed being with what he referred to as
"his women." There had been no grandparents on either side of
the family since April was very little. April had taken a seat between her father and Heather, her younger sister, who was a senior in high school and hoping to go to Columbia, like April. At
sixty-five, Pat had been a professor there for almost forty years.

"Let's hope you stay there longer than I did," April teased
her, with an apologetic glance at her father. She knew how upset
he had been when she dropped out to study cooking in Europe.
He had had academic aspirations for her, but that had never
been what April wanted. His younger daughters were much
more likely to follow in his footsteps, and both were good students. His second family was of a far more academic, intellectual
bent than his first. But he and Valerie were still enormously fond
of each other and acted more like brother and sister than ex-
spouses. Even now he was still startled by the immensity of
Valerie's career. When he had been married to her, he had been
totally overwhelmed by her ambition and drive. He could laugh

about it now, but at the time he had felt completely inadequate and unable to keep up. It had taken them both several very unhappy years to admit to themselves and each other that he was not the man for her. He was much happier now, and for twenty-one wonderful years Maddie had been the kind of wife he needed. But he had nothing but warm feelings for Valerie and their daughter, and enormous admiration for what his first wife had accomplished. She was a legend and a star, and she looked like one even at a quiet family dinner. She had worn a soft beige angora sweater with gold threads woven through it, with beige suede pants, high-heeled sexy Italian boots, diamond earrings, and perfectly cut blond hair. Maddie had worn a very conservative brown velvet suit. There was nothing flashy about her. And the girls had worn short skirts, heels, and pretty sweaters. Pat looked proud and happy as April had him sample two of their new wines, to see which one he liked better. He was always impressed by the wines she managed to bring in from Europe and Chile, at prices her patrons could afford. She always sent him a case of whatever he liked.

The dinner April served them that night was better than ever. The conversation at the table was animated, and Heather said she had a new boyfriend. Annie had had the same one for four years, another brain, who was at MIT with her, and April was starting to wonder if they were going to get engaged and married early, although her sister denied it. Pat was always startled that there was no man in his ex-wife's life. She was such a beautiful woman, but her career had been her first priority for so long that he thought she had given up a lot for success and fame. At sixty, she was alone. He didn't want the same fate for their daughter, and worried sometimes that it could happen. April was so focused on her restaurant that, like her mother, she seemed to have no private life at all. She never talked about a man, which was hardly surprising since she worked a hundred-and-forty-hour week at the restaurant.

They were still sitting at the table at eleven, as the restaurant began to empty. Annie and Heather had gone out to the kitchen to talk to some of the sous-chefs and kitchen staff they knew, particularly an especially cute boy from France. April had just poured her three parents an extremely good Napa Valley sau-terne, which her mother said was as good as Château d'Yquem, or very close. Her father readily agreed, as he toasted their daughter, and the two older women joined in.

"Thank you for another fantastic Thanksgiving dinner." He smiled warmly at April, and leaned over to kiss her cheek.

"Thank you, Daddy," she said, smiling almost shyly.

"I think this was the best one so far," he said proudly. He was always grateful that Valerie had helped her to open the restaurant. He couldn't have done it, but could see easily how talented she was. And he was thrilled with every positive re-view he read of April in New York. He was always happy for her. There had been only one bad one in September, and the reviewer had sounded like a pill and a snob and clearly didn't know good, wholesome food when he ate it. But other than that, Pat had never read anything negative about her restaurant. All he wanted for her now was to see her with a good man in her life. He didn't want her to end up alone like her mother, having given up everything else for her job. It wasn't too late for Valerie either, he knew, but he could no longer imagine his ex-wife accommodating herself to any man, and she hadn't for him either. She was very set in her ways, and had been for a long time. She was such a perfectionist in everything she did that few men could measure up to the standards she set for herself. April was far more relaxed in her style, and less demanding, but she had no time to meet anyone either. She was always working, and owning a restaurant was a huge commitment. Unless she got involved with one of her sous-chefs, the sommelier, or a waiter, or one of their wholesale suppliers, Pat didn't see how she was ever going to meet a man. He said something to her about it again, as they finished the sauterne.

"Are you taking any time off to play and have some fun?" Pat asked her with concern. April drove herself so hard, but she seemed to thrive on hard work, just like her mother. His second wife was far more relaxed, and her priorities were different. He was a happy man.

"Not lately," April admitted. She always enjoyed working.

"Don't you think it's time? The restaurant is full every time we come here. People tell me it takes three weeks to get a reservation. You couldn't get more people in here with a crowbar." He knew the restaurant was making money, and she was making serious inroads in repaying her mother. "Why don't you take a trip one of these days? A vacation back in France? Something. You can't work *all* the time, April. It's not healthy." But they both knew that that was what the restaurant business was like, and her restaurant was a success because she was there day and night, overseeing everything, down to the last detail, and even greeting the guests whenever she had time to come out of the kitchen. She made a point of doing that every night, once or twice. April was on deck and in total control at all times. And he was right, it left no time for a personal life at all. She hadn't had a vacation in three years, since they'd opened, or even a day off, and she didn't want one.

"I will one of these days, Dad, I promise. But I really need to be here. I don't have anyone who can watch it for me if I take time off." And then she fell silent, after glancing at her mother. Valerie didn't say anything, but a look passed between them that Maddie noticed immediately, and realized that Pat didn't. She knew he didn't want to ask April again if she had "met anyone" lately. He already knew the answer to the question. It was obvious that she hadn't. Maddie knew Pat hated to nag April about it, but he worried. April was too much like Valerie in her work ethic and her drive. Her father hoped she would marry and have children, and there wasn't even a hint of that on the horizon for now, and he was afraid there never would be, as he often said in private to his wife.

"Anything new in your life?" he asked cryptically, meaning a boyfriend, and April started to say no, and then hesitated. She wanted to tell him, but just wasn't sure how to do it. She didn't want to disappoint him, or upset him, and she knew that what she was about to tell him wasn't what he wanted from her. It wasn't what she had planned to do either, but it had happened, and she wanted him to know. He was her father and she loved him. He was her role model for all things normal, and a solid, loving marriage, like the one he had with Maddie. Her mother was different, and a bright star in her heaven, but there was nothing typical or human-scale about her mother. Valerie's success had been enormous. April didn't aspire to be like her, although she admired how hard her mother worked, and tried to be like her in that way. But the life her father led with Maddie and his daughters was more her style. She had never wanted to be famous like her mother. The life that went with it would have been too much for her. It was enough for April to run a restaurant where everyone wanted to come either to eat rare and wonderful delicacies, or good, simple food, and enjoy the homey atmosphere she created. In some ways, April was more like Maddie than her mother. But most of all, she was like her father, and his respect was important to her.

"Actually, there is something new," April said quietly, as the older members of the family waited. "It's been kind of a surprise, actually. A very big surprise, and not something I planned, but sometimes life works that way." For a moment, Pat couldn't figure out if she was about to tell him about a new man in her life, a second restaurant she was going to open, or an unexpected chance to sell this one and make a lot of money. "I hope you're not going to be disappointed in me, Daddy," she said, looking at him with tears in her eyes as she touched his arm, and he put an arm around her to reassure her. He loved her, and April knew that and always had. She had never doubted it for a moment.

"You've never let me down, sweetheart. Never. I was worried when you dropped out of college, but it worked out fine for you in the end. That's all I care about. I just want you to be happy. So what's this big surprise that happened to you?" He hoped it was a man, and not another restaurant that would eat up more of her time. She already had none as it was now.

April waited for what seemed like an interminable moment, and then glanced at Maddie and back at her father. She wanted to include her stepmother in her announcement too. She had always loved Maddie, who had treated her like a daughter even before she had her own. "I'm pregnant," she said softly, looking into her father's eyes, hoping he would forgive her for the sloppy way it had happened, and not hold it against her child. But that wouldn't have been his style.

Pat was silent for a long moment, not sure what to say to her, or understanding what went with it. "You are? I didn't think you were seeing anyone. Are you getting married?" He looked a little hurt that she hadn't said anything to him sooner. He liked to think that he was closer to her than that. He glanced quickly at her mother, but Valerie had lowered her eyes and said nothing, as Pat looked back at April and Maddie watched.

"No, I'm not getting married, and I'm not seeing anyone. I would have told you," she said with a sigh, leaning against him for comfort and support. She needed it to tell him the rest of the story. She knew he wouldn't be happy. But her father had never failed her, and she didn't think he would this time. She hoped not, although she wouldn't have been pleased about it as a parent either. And her mother had been nice about it too. "It was an accident," she said honestly, "with a man I hardly know. I saw him once. I had too much to drink. We wound up in bed, don't ask me how, I don't even remember. And I just found out I'm pregnant. I haven't spoken to him since it happened. I don't know if I'm going to tell him. I don't even know if he's a nice person. He's a food critic, and judging from the review he wrote, and the fact that he never called me, he probably doesn't even like me. But I'm thirty years old, I don't know if I'll ever have a chance to get pregnant again, and I'm going to keep the baby. I want to," she added, so that her father would understand that this was a choice she had made, even knowing all the risks, headaches, and problems she was willing to sign on for. "I didn't want this to happen, and to tell you everything, I'm on the Pill, but I think I forgot one, and I was on an antibiotic at the time, and it made my Pill just ineffective enough so I got pregnant. Maybe it was destiny. Whatever it was, I'm having the baby." She looked at him cautiously, with no idea what his reaction would be. He was visibly shocked but trying to digest it. He glanced across the table at Maddie, who was worried for her stepdaughter, and then he looked back at April, with his arm still around her shoulders. He had loosened his grip for a moment.

"That's quite a story. Are you sure you want to have the baby? That's a lot to take on, on your own. A lot of responsibility, with no one to lean on. You have me, and Maddie and your mother of

73

course, and we'll do everything we can to help you, but single motherhood isn't easy. I see a lot of my students do it, for various reasons, some of them by choice, and some because it just happened, but it's never easy. Will you give up the restaurant?" he asked, and April quickly shook her head.

"Of course not. I don't see why I have to do one or the other. I can do both, work and be a mother." Her mother always had, and she was her role model. And Valerie's career had been far more demanding, but April had always had her father too. This baby wouldn't. All this baby would have was its mother, three grandparents, and two aunts. It didn't sound like a bad start to April, and it was all she could provide.

"I know you can do it," her father said quietly, trying to absorb what she had told him. He would never have expected this from April, neither the one-night stand nor the decision to have the baby. He wondered if turning thirty had been an important part of the decision for her and made her feel that it was now or never. He knew that more and more women were deciding to have babies alone these days, so it didn't totally surprise him. But it seemed completely out of character for April. "I just hate to see you take on something so difficult all by yourself. I think you should talk to the father. He may be a nicer guy than you think and want to help you and be involved. It's his child too. And you're going to need all the help you can get. It's going to be a hell of a juggling act for you, particularly if you keep the restaurant and continue working as hard as you do. That's going to be really rough on you." Much rougher than he wanted for his daughter. He had always hoped she would marry and have children, in that order. What parent didn't? And April appreciated the fact that so far he hadn't condemned her for what had happened, and he didn't look like he was going to.

"I've been thinking about calling the father. I just feel kind of stupid, and I don't know what to say to him. 'Thanks for the bad review, and remember the night we spent together when you got drunk at my restaurant on Labor Day weekend?' If he'd called me after, it would have been different. Or easier anyway."

"I think I saw his review. It was nasty and sarcastic," her father said, sounding angry. Pat's loyalty to his children was fierce, and he expected others to be too. Mike Steinman, the food critic April had mentioned, clearly hadn't liked the restaurant, and hadn't been afraid to say so.

"That's the guy." Steinman's critique of their food and April's efforts had been demeaning and disdainful. It didn't bode well for the future, or the news she was going to tell him. And his silence for the past few months didn't encourage her either. He obviously hadn't wanted to see her again, for whatever reason. It made calling him that much harder. "Remember me? I'm having your baby." She couldn't imagine him being thrilled to hear that piece of news. She hadn't been either. But she was adjusting to it now. And it was no longer "bad news" to her, it was a baby.

"Well, this is certainly important," her father said, smiling at her, trying to be supportive. "I have to admit, it's a surprise, and it's not how I would have wanted things to happen for you. But if you're determined to go ahead with it, Maddie and I support you." He glanced at Valerie then, and she was nodding with tears in her eyes. "And your mother does too, I think. So it looks like we're going to have a baby," he said, as he waved to the sommelier who arrived at the table quickly to serve them. Pat asked them for a bottle of champagne. "When is it due?" her father asked as the waiter went to get the bottle he had ordered.

"In June," April said, as tears spilled down her cheeks and she put her arms around her father. "Thank you, Daddy. Thank you, all of you," she said, looking at her family, as she reached out to touch her mother and Maddie, and both women smiled at her and were crying. "I'm sorry I did this so stupidly. Thank you for being nice to me about it. I promise I'll do a really good job of it, and try to be a good mother like both of you."

"Don't worry, darling, you will be," her stepmother said kindly. "I don't doubt it for a moment, and it will be nice to have a baby in the family. Do you know what it is yet?" Maddie asked with interest, holding April's hand across the table.

"I won't know till I have another sonogram in February." She was young enough not to need any invasive tests to check about defects or genetics, which was a relief to her. At thirty, the process was routine.

The sommelier returned with the champagne then, and poured it just as Annie and Heather returned from the kitchen, and he poured each of them a glass too and left with the empty bottle. He could tell that something emotional was going on at the table, and didn't want to intrude on his employer. He was the sommelier who had just come to her from Daniel Boulud. His name was Jean-Pierre, and he was from Bordeaux. He had learned about wines since he was a very young boy, and he had been a great addition to the restaurant.

"What are we celebrating?" her sisters asked as they sat down.

April looked at them, embarrassed, but there was no point in hiding it now, they had to know sooner or later. "I'm having a baby," she said, looking at both of them as they stared at her in amazement.

"You have a boyfriend?" Heather looked astonished, and a little hurt not to be told sooner as April smiled.

"No, I don't. Just a baby."

"How did you get pregnant then?" she asked her older sister, and this time April laughed.

"The stork brought this one, I'm afraid, and I decided to keep it. So you're both going to be aunts in June," she said, looking from Heather to Annie, who looked at her and smiled, as their father raised his glass.

"I am proposing a toast to the new member of this family, who will be with us at this table next Thanksgiving. And actually, I think I should thank April for not burdening me with a son-in-law whom I may not have liked, who might have dragged me to football games in the freezing cold, or expected me to play softball with him, which I hate. I don't have to impress him. All we have to do here is love April, and welcome this new member of the family into our midst." They all raised their glasses as

April started to cry again. She didn't sip the champagne, since she wasn't supposed to drink, and passed her glass to her dad. She hadn't had a drink of anything alcoholic since she'd made the decision to have the baby, and only two glasses of champagne on her birthday before that.

"Thank you, everybody, for your support. I love you," she said softly, looking at each of them gratefully. And a little while later they left, and she went out to the kitchen to see what was happening there as the dishwashers cleaned up. It had been a beautiful Thanksgiving for her, and her unexpected announcement had gone over surprisingly well. Her father had been wonderful, her stepmother as loving as ever, Valerie seemed to be adjusting to the idea a little, as long as no one called her "grandmother," and both of her sisters had promised to help. She couldn't ask for more than that. And with a sigh, she finally took off her apron and went upstairs. She was exhausted and felt emotionally drained as she fell into bed. She had a lot to be grateful for, she knew, her family, the restaurant, and now this baby, which was a mixed blessing of sorts, but maybe it would work out for the best. She hoped so, as she closed her eyes and fell asleep as soon as her head hit the pillow. It had been a long and important day for her.

Chapter 6

April woke up early the day after Thanksgiving. She sat in the kitchen, drinking a bowl of café au lait. No one had come in yet, and she had the restaurant to herself, which was rare. The staff had left everything in good order the night before, and the tables were already set for lunch. She was thinking about what her father had said and his loving toast. And she finally made the decision she had been wrestling with for weeks. She went upstairs to her office and looked for the number he had given her when he called about reviewing the restaurant. She had his office number and a cell phone. She called Mike, and he answered on the second ring. His voice was deep and sexy, but he didn't sound happy to hear from her when she said who she was. It wasn't an encouraging beginning, but she decided to get it over with anyway. She didn't want to tell him on the phone, but he had a right to know, so she invited him to dinner at the restaurant, and he instantly sounded hesitant and almost stern.

"It's too soon for me to write another review," he warned her, and then his voice softened a little. "I'm sorry about the one I wrote. I just think you could reach higher than you are." He could tell from the dishes she had prepared that her skills were worthy of a much more important restaurant, and he knew from her CV that she had worked in some. Other than the selection of delicacies on the menu, he had no idea why she wanted to serve food that anyone could make at home. He had missed the whole point of April in New York, but April no longer cared. She didn't want another review, or a better one, she only wanted to tell him about their child. And if they never saw each other again after that, that was fine with her too. She had no illusions about having a relationship with him, since he had never called her. And she didn't need anything from him, nor did her child. She had her family's support now, and she could take care of herself *and* a baby, hopefully. Knowing that made it easier to call him, no matter what he thought her motivations were. They were very different than he thought.

"The restaurant seems to work," she said casually, not wanting to get into it with him. They had entirely different points of view, and she could tell from other reviews of his she'd read that he was a snob about food. She wasn't. "People like it, and this is what I always wanted to do. A restaurant like this was my dream. It's not for everyone, I guess, but it works for us. And I wasn't calling for another review," she corrected him. "How was your Thanksgiving?" she asked, sounding pleasant.

"I don't do holidays. And I hate turkey anyway." They weren't off to a very good start. And then he sounded awkward for a moment as he broached another subject, one that they were both uncomfortable about. "I'm sorry I didn't call you after that night. It was great, but I figured you'd be mad at me once you read the review, so I didn't call. It's a little strange writing a harsh review about a restaurant, and then inviting the owner out. I had a really good time though, and I'm sorry if I was rude not calling afterward." At least he knew enough to be embarrassed about it, and to acknowledge that the review was harsh. He wasn't totally without manners or brains, even if he didn't have a heart, which seemed to be the case. He sounded chilly on the phone.

"Don't worry about it," April said easily. "I just wondered if you'd like to come to dinner. It's not a date, and I'm not trying to butter you up, or ply you with wines this time." They both laughed at her admission.

"The wines were great," he conceded. And he had mentioned that in his review too. It was the only positive thing he had said, that she had a remarkable wine list of obscure, excellent, and inexpensive wines. He had looked down his nose at the food, but not the wines. That was something at least. "And you were pretty goddamn great too," he said, warming up a little. "What I remember anyway. I don't think I've gotten that drunk in years. I had a hangover for three days." He laughed about it now, but she

81

suspected he wouldn't be laughing when he heard what else had happened that night. And the aftermath of their fling was going to last a lot longer than three days, more like the rest of their lives, or hers, since he didn't have to be involved.

"Yeah, me too," she admitted. "I don't usually do things like that. The wine went to my head" and other parts. He had been younger and better looking than she'd expected. He was thirty-four years old, single, and sexy as hell. He had been hard to resist with all that wine under their belts.

"That's what people always say," he teased her about their one-night stand, which was embarrassing for them both, but they were handling it pretty well on the phone. She was glad that she had called. Her parents were right. He didn't sound like a bad guy, for a food snob and a one-night stand who had never called her afterward.

"How about an easy dinner tonight?" she persisted, and he was flattered. She was a beautiful girl, and there was nothing he could do for her, since he had already told her he couldn't write another review of the restaurant this soon, which was true. "We're fully booked, but if you come around nine, I can save a small table in the back. And I won't serve you turkey since you hate it. How does lobster sound?"

"Excellent. I'll try to get to an AA meeting first," he teased her. He had a sense of humor, which was something at least. She tried not to sound seductive on the phone, or even interested in him as a man. She didn't want to mislead him about the reason for their dinner. She tried to make it sound like she just wanted to be friends. Even that would be a stretch, but it would be help-ful since they were going to share a child. "Thanks for asking me," he said easily. "See you at nine." He was impressed that she had called him after the bad review he'd given her, but they had slept with each other, which wasn't entirely negligible. He had liked her a lot, but thought it politically incorrect to call her since he had bashed her as a chef, and her restaurant. He almost hadn't written the review so he could see her again, but in the end decided to be true to himself as a journalist. He owed that to his paper. So he had given up on her instead, which he was sorry about at the time. He was glad she had called him out of the blue and invited him to dinner, although he couldn't imagine why. But he had to admit, the sex had been great, for both of them, even though they were drunk at the time. It had obviously im-pressed her too. Enough to call him three months later. And he was glad she had. He was looking forward to that night.

Mike showed up at the restaurant a few minutes after nine. He was even better looking than she had remembered. He had both a serious look and a boyish quality about him. Her heart skipped a beat when she saw him. He looked sexy, appealing, and casual in jeans, hiking boots, and an old fisherman's sweater. She remembered that he had been a journalism major at Brown. He had wanted to be a war correspondent, and write from danger zones, and had told her that a bad case of malaria had sent him home from his first assignment, and it had taken a year to get over it. And by then he'd been assigned to food and wine and become a restaurant critic. He didn't love it and would have preferred to do something more exciting, but he had a reputation now and a solid job. It accounted for some of the acerbic comments in some of what he wrote. He had a certain disregard for some of the restaurants he covered, and many of the chefs. But the paper liked his tough comments and often tart remarks. It was his style, and he had been doing restaurant reviews now for ten years, and people responded to what he wrote, so he was locked into his job, whether he liked it or not.

He looked around the restaurant for April as soon as he arrived, and the headwaiter led him to their table, in a quiet corner in the back. April came out of the kitchen in her apron shortly after, wiping her hands on a cloth, which she handed to one of the busboys. She stopped to greet people at several tables, smiled when she saw Mike, and finally sat down. She certainly hadn't dressed for a date, he noticed. Her dark hair was piled on top of her head in a wild ponytail pulled up in an elastic, she had no makeup on, and she was wearing clogs with her traditional black and white checked pants, and white chef's jacket, covered with spots from the food she'd prepared that night.

She was a little fuller in the face than he remembered, but it suited her, and she was even prettier as she smiled at him. She had deep hazel eyes that looked slightly worried as she smiled and thanked him for coming. She ordered a bottle of Chilean wine for them, he stuck with the lobster she had suggested, and she offered him some of the last remaining white truffles on pasta. It sounded like a perfect meal to him, and much better than the meat loaf, roast chicken, or steak tartare she was famous for. His tastes were more refined and his palate more critical, but she knew that about him now. And the wines Jean-Pierre suggested for the meal were even better than the ones he had had with her before.

"See what I mean?" he said, savoring the pasta, and the lobster afterward. "You're better than what you usually do. Why would you want to make hamburgers, when you could be in Paris earning three stars for your restaurant, or doing the equivalent here? You're underachieving, April. That's what I was trying to say in my review." It had come out harsher than he had intended it to sound, which he was slightly sorry for now, but he believed that the essence of what he had said was true.

"How often do you think people want to eat food like that?" April asked him honestly. "Once a month, every couple of months, for a special occasion? No one can eat that way all the time. I can't, and I don't want to. Maybe you do, but most people don't. Our customers, our regulars, come here once or twice a week, some more than that. I want to make the best possible version of what they want to eat every day, and the occasional exotic treat, like truffle pasta or escargots. That's the kind of restaurant I always wanted. I can still do special things, and we do. We offer that too, but most of the time I want to offer real food to real people for real life. That's what this restaurant is all about," she said honestly. It had been her theory behind it since the beginning, and it had worked. The tables had been jammed around them all night, and people were still coming in close to midnight, begging to be seated and eat her food. Mike had noticed it while he chatted with her about restaurants in France and Italy that they both loved. And as he had noticed the first time he met her, she knew her stuff, and also about wines.

"Maybe I missed the point," he admitted. "I just figured you were being lazy and going for an easy shot." She laughed at what he said. Lazy she was not, and anyone who knew her knew that wasn't the case.

"I want to serve people's favorite foods, whatever they are, fancy or simple. I want to be the restaurant they wish they could go to every night. My mother and I love La Grenouille, but I can't go there every day, although my mother does, or close to it. Maybe I'm a simpler person than you are and she is. I need comfort food sometimes. Don't you?"

"Sometimes," he confessed sheepishly. "I go to a pancake house when I want that, not a top-notch restaurant. When I go out to dinner, I want a great meal," he said, savoring the last of the lobster. It had been absolutely perfect as far as he was concerned, four star, and would have won a flawless review from him if he'd been writing about it, which he wasn't.

"That's my point," April insisted. "You can get fantastic pancakes here, or waffles, or mashed potatoes, or mac and cheese. You should try my pancakes sometime," she recommended seriously, and he laughed at the intense look on her face. She really believed in what she was doing. He hadn't fully understood that before. Maybe he'd been too drunk. But that had been her fault, she had absolutely buried him in wines that had been too good to resist. He was more careful tonight, he didn't want to drink too much again and make an ass of himself. He liked her, and her passion for her restaurant.

"Okay, I'll come back for pancakes the next time I'm feeling sorry for myself."

"You're welcome anytime. The pancakes are on me."

"It was nice of you to invite me here tonight. I figured you hated me after what I wrote about the restaurant."

"I did for a while," she said honestly, "but I got over it."

"I'm glad you did. The meal was fantastic tonight." He was beginning to understand that she was trying to do something for everyone, the more refined palate as well as the simpler one, and even food that children loved. There was a certain merit to her theory, although it had escaped him before. "So why did you ask me here, since I can't write a review this soon, and you said it wasn't a date? Burying the hatchet in lobster and white truffle pasta?" he asked with an amused look, and she smiled at him, wondering if their child would look like him, or her, or a combination of both. It was strange to think about that.

"I have something to tell you that I just figure you should know. I don't want anything from you. I don't need anything. But I figure you have a right to the information too." She didn't beat around the bush. She wanted to let him know. That was all. She was having his baby and he had a right to decide how and if he wanted to deal with it, or not at all, which was fine with her too. She had no expectations of him. "I was on an antibiotic for strep throat when we saw each other in September. I didn't realize it could do that, but it screwed up the Pill I was on, and to be honest, I got so drunk that night that I forgot to take the Pill. I'm three months pregnant. I'm having a baby in June. I found out four weeks ago, and I decided to keep it. I'm thirty years old, and I don't want to have an abortion. You don't have to have anything to do with me or it, if you don't want to. But I thought you ought to know, and at least give you the choice." It was as direct and honest as she could be with him, and he looked across the table at her as though he was going into shock. He looked pale. His hair was as dark as hers, he had dark brown eyes, and his face was as white as the tablecloth when he spoke.

"Are you serious? You're telling me that now? You invited me here to dinner to tell me *that*? Are you crazy? You're having it? You don't even know me. You don't know if I'm an ax murderer or a lunatic or a child molester, and you're having a baby by a guy you slept with once? Why aren't you having an abortion? Why didn't you ask me how I felt about that before it was too late to do anything about it?" He looked furious as his eyes blazed at her across the table. For a moment, she was sorry she had told him at all.

"Because my decision to keep it is none of your business," she said just as harshly. "It's my body and my baby, and I'm not asking you for a goddamn thing. You don't ever have to see me again, if you don't want to. And frankly, I don't care either way. You don't ever have to see the kid. That's up to you. But if there were a child wandering around who was mine, I'd want to know about it, so I could decide if I wanted to be part of its life or not. That's the opportunity I'm giving you, no strings attached. You don't have to support me or the baby, or contribute anything. I can manage by myself, and if not, my parents are willing to help me, which is nice of them. But they thought, and I agree, that I owe you at least the information that you're having a baby in June. That's all. The rest is up to you."

She glared back at him then, and he fumed silently at her for a minute. He had to admit, she was being decent about it, but he did not want a baby, with her or anyone else. He had been clear about that all his life. And she was screwing up everything for him. Now he had to decide if he wanted to be a father or not. Because like it or not, and without even consulting him about it, she was having his baby, because they had both been stupid enough to get drunk and sleep with each other and her birth control had malfunctioned. How romantic was that? But she didn't look sentimental about it either. Just honest and practical, and she was trying to be fair to him. But he didn't like it anyway. He was sorry he had come to dinner and found out about it, and even sorrier that three months before he had slept with her.

"And who are your parents, that they're being so noble about this?" She looked startled by the question. It was hard for him to imagine parents of a thirty-year-old woman who were willing to be so supportive of her. He didn't even know parents like that, and surely not his own, whom he hadn't seen in ten years and didn't want to see again.

"My parents are perfectly nice, normal people," she answered him directly. "My father is a medieval art professor at Columbia, my stepmother is a speech therapist and a wonderful woman, and my mother is Valerie Wyatt, she talks about home decorating and weddings on TV." She said it as though she had a job like everyone else as he stared at her.

"Are you kidding?" he said. "That's who your mother is? Of course ... Wyatt ... why didn't I think of that? For chrissake, your mother is the arbiter of everything that happens in the home, or at a wedding. What do they think of this? Don't they think you're crazy to have this baby too? How are you going to manage a restaurant and a kid all on your own?"

"That's my problem, not yours. I'm not asking you to show up and change diapers. You can visit it if you want to, but if you don't, that's fine too."

"What if I want more than that?" he said angrily. He was furious at her now, for what she and fate had done to him. He realized it had happened to her too, but she had decided to keep it. He never would have. And her plan to have it sounded utterly stupid and wrong to him. It wasn't fair, in his opinion, to bring a child into the world with parents who didn't know or love each other. But it seemed even worse to her to get rid of it, so she was having it, whether he liked it or wanted to participate, or not. "What if I *want* to be a father and want joint custody, for instance? I'm not saying I do, and I don't. But what if I did? Then what would you do, since you're so independent about it? Would you share the child with me?" She looked stunned by the idea. She hadn't thought of that possibility at all.

"I don't know," she said quietly. "I guess we'd have to talk about it, and come to some agreement." She didn't like the sound of it. She didn't know him well enough to know if she'd trust a child with him, or a baby, but he had a point. He was one of the baby's parents too.

"Well, you're off the hook on that one. I don't want children. I never did. My childhood was a nightmare, with alcoholic, abusive parents. My parents hated each other, and me. My brother committed suicide when he was fifteen. And the last thing I want in this world is a wife and children. My own childhood was screwed up enough, I don't want to fuck up someone else's. A month before I met you, I broke up with a woman I was in love with. We were together for five years, and she finally put it to me. She wanted to get married and have babies, or find someone else who would. I gave her my blessing, kissed her goodbye, and left her. I don't want a baby, April, yours or anyone else's. I don't want to be responsible for anyone else hurting the way I did as a kid. I don't feel suited to be a parent, but I don't want to abandon someone either. If I don't see this child, or involve myself in its life in some way, it will always feel that I rejected it. It's not right that you're doing this to me, or the kid. It's fine for you to say you'll manage on your own and your parents will help you. But how are you going to explain the father that walked out on you and him or her? What's that going to do to a child? Did you ever think of that when you decided to keep it? It may sound cruel to you to have an abortion, but there's nothing between us, and there never will be. It's not fair to bring a child into this world with only one parent who wants it, and another one who never did."

"What if we loved each other and were married, and you died? Then what, should I kill the child then too because you wouldn't be around?" She had a point, but he wouldn't concede it. He was adamant on this subject, and had given up a woman he loved over just these arguments. She had had two abortions for him in five years and refused to have any more. She wanted kids, and he didn't.

"That's different and you know it," Mike fumed at her, squirming in his seat. It had turned into a miserable evening. The lobster dinner hadn't been worth it, and he never wanted to see her again. She was always plying him with something, with some ulterior motive and scheme, but as far as he was concerned, this was the worst of all. Feeding him exquisite food in order to tell him about the baby she was having that he didn't want was far more serious than getting him drunk to get a good review.

"Mike, lots of people have only one parent. And these days, lots of women have babies without men. They go to sperm banks, they get gay men friends to donate sperm for them so they know who the father is, single gay men and women adopt babies. I'm not saying it's ideal, but people alone have babies. Sometimes people who even love each other, if one of them dies or disappears. I saw this baby on the sonogram, its heart was beating, it looked like a baby, it's going to be a baby one day, a person. I didn't want to have a child either, it's not in my scheme of things right now, and it won't be easy for me. And you're right, I don't know who the hell you are, or if you're a decent person. But I'm not going to kill this baby, my baby, our baby, because your parents were shitty to you. I'm sorry as hell about that, and those things shouldn't happen, but sometimes they do. But now that it's there and it happened, this baby has a right to live, so I'm giving it that opportunity, even if it's not convenient for me. I'll do the best possible job I can. And I have three parents and two sisters who will love it too.

"If you want to step up to the plate and be its father, terrific. And if you don't, it'll be okay too. This was an accident that happened to both of us. I'm trying to make the best of a tough situation, that's all we can do." She was being very sensible about it, but he shook his head miserably. He had had the same conversation with his previous girlfriend before her second abortion. He had managed to convince her, but he could see that April had made up her mind. He was screwed, or he felt that way at least.

"This is an accident that can be fixed, if you'll be reasonable about it," Mike said quietly but intensely, still hoping to deter her. "If you want kids, find some guy who wants them too. I'm not that person. I never will be. I don't want children. I don't want to be married, to anyone, April, and I don't want this baby." She didn't want him either, but she was still going to have his child, and nothing would convince her otherwise. He could see it in her eyes.

"I wasn't looking to have children," she said clearly. "I'm not after you. I want nothing from you. But I'm going to have this child. Whether you want to be involved or not, or even see it, is up to you. I'll let you know when the baby is born, and you can decide then."

She could see that he was very angry with her, but more than that, he was scared. She had faced him with something he had done everything to avoid until now, even giving up a woman he had truly loved. He told her that she was already seeing someone else, and hoping to get married soon. She was thirty-four years old and felt she didn't have time to waste if she wanted kids. Mike said he had been willing to let her go rather than do that with her. And now April had just sprung a baby on him that was already in the works. It was just too cruel, as far as he was concerned.

He stood up finally, still looking furious. "Thanks for dinner," he said coldly. "I'm not sure it was worth it, given the acute indigestion at the end of the meal. I'll call you when I figure out what I want to do about this."

"There's no rush," she said quietly, standing up and facing him. She was beautiful, but he didn't care about that now. All he could think about was what she had just told him. "The baby's not due till June. Thanks for coming to dinner. I'm sorry it's such bad news for you." He nodded and said nothing, and walked out of the restaurant with his head down, without ever looking back at her. The waiters and sommelier could see that they'd had an argument, and they knew who he was, the critic who had given them the bad review three months before. It was obvious that he wasn't going to be giving her a good one anytime soon.

Chapter 7

April told both her parents about her meeting with Mike Steinman the next day. Valerie was sorry to hear about it, and her father was furious. He thought Mike could have done a lot better than that.

"He doesn't want kids, Dad," April said calmly, although she was upset about it too, but there was nothing she could do. "He broke up with a woman he was crazy about rather than have children with her." She was trying to be reasonable about it, although she had found Mike's position both harsh and extreme, just like his review. It was apparently who he was. And it was not a trait in him she liked, despite his obvious brains and good looks. He had apparently been severely mistreated as a child. She felt sorry for him, but she thought it was a poor excuse for the way he was behaving now.

"You didn't want a child either," her father reminded her, "but you're making the best of it. Why can't he?" He had a point.

"He doesn't want to, Dad. Don't worry. I'll be okay."

"I think he's a total jerk."

"He has a right to be upset," she said quietly. She was being adult about it, or trying to, but she'd shed tears over it the previous night. Mike had been pretty nasty.

And she was utterly stunned when he walked into the restaurant kitchen the next day after the last lunch customer had left. April was in the kitchen, discussing new wine purchases with Jean-Pierre, the sommelier. He disappeared as soon as Mike walked in. He looked stormy, but calmer than he had on Saturday night when he left. It made the sommelier wonder what was going on between them. This looked more personal than business.

"Can I talk to you for a minute?" Mike said tersely. He looked like he hadn't slept in two days, and he hadn't shaved. He looked utterly tormented and deeply unhappy, but less angry at her.

"Sure," she said calmly, and led him upstairs to her office. She pointed to a chair, but he didn't sit down. Everything in her office was ancient, ugly, battered, and had been secondhand, in order to save money.

He stood looking at April intently. "Look, I'm sorry I got so upset the other night, and was so tough on you. I just didn't expect this to happen. It's my worst nightmare come true. I respect what you're trying to do, and that you're stepping up to the plate. And I'm sorry I'm not doing the same. I wish this had never happened to either of us. I don't want a kid, but I also don't want to be someone who deserts a child and creates even more problems. I wish you'd have an abortion, but if you won't, I need to consider this. Give me some time to think, and I'll get in touch with you. That's the best I can do for now." She looked at him and appreciated that he was at least wrestling with it, she could see how hard it was for him. He wasn't an asshole or a bad guy probably, he was someone who had been very badly hurt, didn't want to hurt anyone else, and just didn't want to have children. He looked as though he rued the day he had come to the restaurant at all.

"Thanks for thinking about it, Mike," April said quietly. "I'm sorry this is so hard, for both of us. It shouldn't be like this." No child deserved to come into the world with grief-stricken, devastated parents. At least she didn't feel that way now. There were times when she was even excited about the baby, and she knew that when she finally saw it, she'd be happy. It seemed very obvious now that Mike wouldn't. He was too frightened by it to ever enjoy it. But he was trying to be responsible, and she respected him for that.

"I'll call you," he said miserably, looked at her for another moment, and then hurried back down the stairs and vanished. He was gone by the time she walked back into the kitchen. She had no idea when she'd hear from him again. Maybe not until the baby was born, if then. She was certainly not going to pursue him. And if she never heard from him again, that was just the way it was. She wasn't in love with him fortunately, he was "just" her baby's father. It didn't get much more serious than that.

She told her mother about his visit when they spoke that afternoon.

"At least he's trying," April said generously.

"He's lucky you're not suing him for support," her mother reminded her. "Another woman would have."

"Whatever. I'm not counting on him in any way. It might be easier if he's not involved." She had thought that from the beginning, and had only contacted him to be fair. She'd done her part now, and whatever he decided about it was up to him. She had no expectations or illusions about him.

For days after Mike had last seen April at the restaurant, he could hardly think straight and couldn't concentrate on his work. He had reviews to write of three new restaurants, and he couldn't think of a word to say. He didn't remember the meals he'd eaten there, everything around him had become a blur. He was sitting, staring blankly at his computer at the newspaper, when his longtime friend Jim stopped at his desk and grinned at him. Mike hadn't shaved all week, and he looked as discombobulated as he felt. His expression was a combination of desperation and grimness.

"It can't be as bad as all that," Jim said, leaning against Mike's desk.

"Actually, it's considerably worse." He looked at Jim miserably. They had shared a cubicle at the paper for five years, and had been friends even before that. Mike considered him his best friend, and had been thinking about telling him about the horror that had happened to him, but he was still too upset to do even that. Talking about it would have made it seem all too real and irreversible.

"You look like the roof fell in." Jim knew he wasn't getting fired, their editor loved the reviews Mike wrote, and he hadn't had a girlfriend in a while, so he hadn't broken up with anyone. Jim couldn't imagine what had happened to make him seem that upset.

"It did," Mike confirmed with a desolate expression, as Jim sat on the corner of Mike's desk attentively. "Last weekend."

"Something happen to your parents?" Jim asked sympathetically. He knew Mike had had an unhappy relationship with them for years.

"Who knows? They never call me anymore, and I don't call them either. The last time I did, my mother was so drunk she didn't even know who I was. I figured they wouldn't miss the calls." Jim nodded. He had heard it before.

"So what gives?" Mike seemed unusually reluctant to spill the beans about whatever was bothering him. Most of the time the two men confided in each other about everything.

"I reviewed a restaurant over Labor Day weekend," Mike began as Jim listened quietly. "I hated the food ... well, actually that's not true. I liked the food, but I thought the chef was underachieving with the menu. It was diner food, prepared by a first-rate chef who is capable of a hell of a lot better. I gave her a lousy review." He looked mournful about it now.

"So she's suing you?" Jim volunteered, and Mike shook his head.

"No. Not yet anyway. But in time, she could," he said cryptically, and Jim smiled. If that's what it was, he knew Mike had nothing to worry about. There were no grounds for a lawsuit in a bad restaurant review, if what he had essentially said was that he didn't like the food.

"She can't sue you for that. Hell, if that were true, you'd be sued three times a week." Jim laughed.

"She could sue me for child support," Mike said bluntly, as Jim's face grew serious and he looked long and hard at his friend.

"Would you mind elaborating on that for me? I seem to have missed something here." Now Jim looked worried too.

"So did I apparently, my self-restraint," Mike confessed to him, and felt foolish as he did. "She had a terrific wine list, and I must have tried a half a dozen different wines. We got drunk together, and she's a hell of a good-looking woman. I don't remember exactly how or when it happened, but I know that eventually we wound up in bed, and what I do remember was pretty impressive. It would have been memorable, and I would have seen her again, except I decided to write the review I did anyway. I thoroughly dumped on her restaurant, so I thought it would have been tasteless to call her. I never heard from her either, until last week. She invited me back to the restaurant for dinner, as some sort of peace offering, I thought. It turns out that she asked me to dinner to tell me she's pregnant." Mike looked almost ill as he said it, and Jim looked stunned.

"And she wants money?" That much he could figure out, but the rest of what had happened was a little fuzzy.

"No, not a penny," Mike said grimly. "Her mother is a well-known TV personality, and the restaurant is successful, in spite of what I wrote about it. She doesn't want anything from me, nor did she ask me to participate in the decision. She has decided to have the baby, and all she wanted was to inform me." Mike looked miserably at his friend, who was staring at him in consternation. "I'm screwed whatever I do in this. Either I stay away from her and the baby, and then I'm an asshole who is ruining some innocent kid's life. Or I get involved, and then I'm up to my neck in a situation I would do damn near anything to avoid. I don't want a child, ever. I promised myself years ago, after my own childhood, that I would never have children. And now this woman I don't even know does this to me. I can't goddamn believe it. And nothing is going to sway her. Believe me, I tried. She is absolutely determined to have this baby, and she doesn't give a good goddamn if I participate or not. I think she'd almost prefer it if I didn't." And in some ways that was true. He could sense it in the way she had told him. She expected nothing from him, which somehow made the situation even harder for him. She was being so gracious about it that it made him look even worse for his violently negative reaction. It was visceral for him. He didn't want the baby.

"Does she seem like a nice person?" Jim asked with interest. He was still stunned by what Mike had just told him.

"Maybe. I think so. All I can focus on is this baby she's foisted on me."

"If she's not asking you for anything, it doesn't sound like she's doing much 'foisting,'" Jim pointed out fairly.

"Not financially, but she's sticking me with the responsibility of fatherhood for the rest of my life if she has this baby," Mike said, looking angry about it again.

"Maybe that's not the worst thing that could happen to you," Jim said thoughtfully. He was two years older than Mike, had been happily married for fourteen years, and had three children he was crazy about. He had been telling Mike for years that he should find a nice woman, get married, and have children. Mike was always adamant when he said no. "Since she's going to have the baby anyway, why don't you spend some time with her and get to know her, and see how you feel about it then? It's hard not to fall in love with your own children," Jim pointed out to him. He had been there when each of his were born, it had been a life-changing event for him, but he had never had the resistance to having children that Mike very obviously did, and Jim loved his wife.

"Funny, my parents seem to have managed not to fall in love with me," Mike said with a rueful grin. "I don't think parenting is for everyone. That notion is probably the only thing I have in common with my parents. They never wanted children, as they say at every opportunity, and I'm smart enough not to try."

"Destiny seems to have decided otherwise," Jim said as he stood up, and went to sit in the chair at his own desk, only a few feet from Mike's. He was the paper's leading art critic, and like Mike, he had a number of gallery show critiques to write. He often invited Mike to go to openings of art shows with him, and whenever he could, Mike took Jim along when he went to check out a new restaurant to review. He was sorry he hadn't taken Jim with him the first time he went to April in New York. If he had, none of this would have happened. "I think you ought to give this some very serious thought," Jim said carefully. "This could turn out to be the best thing that ever happened to you. There's nothing more miraculous in life than having a child."

"Whose side are you on?" Mike asked, looking irritated as he tried to concentrate on his computer screen again and ignore everything that Jim had said.

"I'm on your side," Jim said quietly. "Maybe this happened for a reason," he said cryptically. "God moves in mysterious ways," he added smugly as Mike almost snarled in response.

"This has nothing to do with God. It has to do with two very drunk supposed adults, who had way too much wine and got into a hell of a mess of their own making," Mike said, willing to take responsibility for the mistake and the dubious behavior, but not the child.

"Don't be so sure," Jim said, and then concentrated on his own computer screen, and for the rest of the afternoon, neither of them said another word.

* * *

April didn't hear from Mike for the next three weeks, and didn't expect to. She told Ellen that it wouldn't surprise her at all if she never heard from him again. He so much didn't want the baby that his solution to the problem might be complete denial, of her and the child. She was startled in fact when the week before Christmas he called her on her cell phone. It was midmorning, and she was getting ready for the lunch crowd. They were booked solid straight through the holidays for the next four weeks. She had even decided to keep the restaurant open on Christmas Day and New Year's, for their regulars, who wanted a place to go.

"April?" He sounded somber and tense when she answered.

"Hi. How've you been, Mike?" She tried to keep it light. He sounded so unhappy.

"I've been fine." He sounded busy. "I'm sorry to call you with news like this. But I was just turning in a story, and all hell is breaking loose here. I thought you'd want to know. It'll be on the news in a few minutes, and I wanted to give you a heads-up. There's a hostage situation going on at the network where your mother works. They think it's been taken over by half a dozen men. No one seems to know yet how it happened, or who they are. The screens have gone blank over there, and your mother was on air when they did." She did a morning show several times a week, and an evening show. April glanced at her watch as he

104

said it, and realized that he was right. She was right in the middle of the morning show.

"Is she okay? Did something happen to her?" April sounded panicked, and he felt sorry for her. He had realized during his dinner with her how close she and her family were, even if it was hard for him to understand.

"I don't know. The screens just went blank. I think they're holding two floors, and the building is full of SWAT teams on other floors. They haven't moved in on the hostage-takers yet. And they've managed to keep it off the news for the last half-hour, but the story's about to break. I didn't want you to see it on TV." He sounded sympathetic and worried about her.

"Thanks, Mike," she said, fighting back tears. "What am I going to do? Do you think I can go over there?"

"They won't let you near it. Stay put. I'll call you if I hear anything. Turn on your TV. I think the story's coming on now."

"Thank you," she whispered, and hung up, panicked by what was happening to her mother. She turned on the TV in the kitchen immediately, and the report was alarming. Six armed gunmen had taken over the network building an hour before. It was hard to believe they could pull it off, but they had. Once they took their first hostages, they kept gathering more, on two floors of the building. The report said that they were heavily armed with machine guns and automatic weapons, were of unknown nationality and origin and could have been from the Middle East or even American terrorists, and they had sealed two

105

floors of the building. All the hostages were being held on those floors and no one had dared to try to free them yet for fear that the hostages would be killed. The broadcaster mentioned which floors were being held, and April realized instantly that one of them was the floor where her mother did her show. Her show had gone dark right after the introduction, as had several others. There were a number of studios on those two floors.

As she kept her eyes glued to the screen, April quickly dialed her stepmother and told her what had happened. She told her to turn on her TV, and five minutes later, her father called her, in tears. He was as frightened as April was. It reminded them all of 9/11. This wasn't as dramatic, but the potential risk was huge. It had occurred to everyone that they might blow up part of the building in a suicide bombing and take hundreds of people with them, in a major public statement. Or there was also the possibility that they wanted to use the network to disseminate their message. No one knew yet. But everyone feared that the hostage-takers were extremists of some kind to attempt such a desperate act.

Within five minutes, responsible Middle Eastern governments and religious groups had denied all association with the attack. Their assessment was that it was possibly a fundamentalist splinter group, and there was no question, the risk factor was major to everyone in that building and possibly within blocks around if they had enough explosives on them to do major damage. No one knew for sure if that was the case. April was sitting with her eyes riveted to the screen, her heart pounding as she listened to the broadcast, and she turned when she felt a hand on her shoulder, not sure who it was. She was stunned to find herself looking at Mike. He had come to the restaurant to be with her. Their vigil lasted all day, as crisis teams tried to make contact with the hostage-takers. By six o'clock that night, the building was still under siege. A few people had trickled out from one of the two floors, when the gunmen moved everyone to a single floor so they could control them better. The SWAT teams had since taken over the abandoned floor, to get closer to where the hostages were being held on the floor above. And those who had escaped said that several people had been shot. There were two bodies in the corridors on the floor that the SWAT team reclaimed, but their identities had not been announced. April prayed her mother wasn't one of the victims.

There were SWAT teams on the roof, on the floor below, and the lobby and none dared make a move so far, for fear of endangering the hostages further. Neighboring buildings had been evacuated, as the street below swarmed with crisis teams, equipment, firefighters, and police, waiting for something to happen.

And through it all, Mike sat with April and held her hand. The restaurant opened for business, and she never left the kitchen. She had sat in the same spot for hours, praying for her mother, while Mike sat with her in silence, and once in a while he tried to get her to eat something or handed her a glass of water. He felt desperately sorry for her. April's face was deathly white, and he wondered if she'd lose the baby from the shock, but he didn't dare think about that now. He just wanted to be there for April. Whatever disagreement they had about their accidental child paled in comparison to this major drama. It seemed inevitable that more people were about to be killed, when the SWAT teams moved in to liberate the hostages. And the hostage-takers were threatening to shoot their victims.

April had no idea how her mother was faring. There was no communication with anyone on the floor where the attackers were holding them captive. Helicopters were whirring overhead, and several had already landed on the roof. No one dared to rush the floor in question for fear that the hostage-takers would kill them all.

Their first clear message came just after seven o'clock that night. They were a desperate group of Palestinian extremists, willing to die themselves and kill Americans, in protest of recent Israeli commando attacks on the Palestinian-Israeli border. They said they wanted Americans to know how it felt. The Palestinian government denied any association with them, and knew nothing of them. They were protesting the ongoing plight of their people and seeking world attention, even if it meant killing innocent people to do it. Their willingness to die made it difficult for negotiators on the scene to reason with them. By then, all of the responsible Middle Eastern governments were outraged by their actions, and offered any help that was needed. Several delegates came over from the UN to try to assist with the negotiations, and translations if nothing else. They came as a gesture of their good faith, and explained that the group was acting on their own without their own government's knowledge or blessing, and was being severely criticized by them as well. No one in any government wanted the hostages to get hurt, while the hostage-takers frantically insisted that they were prepared to die for their cause, and take as many victims as possible with them. They appeared to be beyond reason. Their attack on the network had been disorganized but frighteningly effective.

April just sat there and cried as she watched. She talked to her father and Maddie frequently on her cell phone, and Mike never left her for a minute. He said little, but he was steadfastly there with her and had been all day.

The scene in the street outside the network building was one of organized chaos and extreme tension. The hostage-takers claimed that they had enough explosives on them to blow up the building, and intended to do so. There were vehicles and men in uniforms of every kind everywhere, SWAT teams, crisis units, the office of emergency services, firefighters, police, police captains, fire chiefs, and there was talk of a National Guard unit being brought in. And UN diplomats were scattered everywhere, looking grim and feeling helpless. For the moment, they all were. The SWAT teams were poised to attack, but it had to be impeccably done, with speed and precision, and even then there was a good chance that all or most of the hostages could be killed. No one wanted to take that chance with a bungled attack that was badly orchestrated or premature. It was kept out of the news, but a small team of Israeli commandos who normally protected their ambassador had come to advise them, although their presence would have enraged the hostage-takers even more. It seemed like half the Middle Eastern security from the UN was there to help. No one wanted to be associated with the attackers, or to see another 9/11 happen. The tension in the air was palpable, and a command center had been set up a block away, teeming with experts, CIA, FBI. There had been no warning of the attack. It had just happened, and so far, no one dared to make a move, for fear of making the situation worse.

By sheer coincidence, Jack Adams had been on his way into the building when it happened. He realized he had forgotten his cell phone in the car and had gone back out, and by the time he returned five minutes later, the building was shut down, and he had stuck around to help. All of the police and SWAT teams recognized him, and were impressed that he stayed all day. He looked over building maps with them and conferred with network security, who were as helpless as everyone else. Unless they were willing to risk the hostages, their hands were tied. And at six o'clock, the heads of assorted units were formulating a plan to come up the vents from the floor below and take the hostage-takers by surprise. Jack was listening carefully to the plan with the others and being given VIP status by being allowed to be there.

The estimate was that close to a hundred people were being held hostage. The terrorists had released no one in the nine hours they had held the building, and given the frantic quality of the hostage-takers' messages, it was becoming clear to everyone that there was a possibility that they could all be killed. They were impossible to reason with. There was no way of knowing how many had already died. No one was sure, and the terrorists weren't telling. The captain of the SWAT team had finally established ongoing radio contact with them at four o'clock, and UN interpreters were translating, but so far their messages consisted mainly of threats, and lengthy diatribes about the situation in their country. Several UN negotiators from Middle Eastern countries attempted to talk them down to no avail.

By eight o'clock that night, there was no doubt in anyone's mind that the only way to free the hostages was not by negotiation with the terrorists, but by force. And the captain of the SWAT team didn't want to wait much longer. Other members of the SWAT team and the New York police chief were going over maps of the building in detail, as Jack Adams listened. They were studying the air vents and crawl spaces closely. Even the architect of the building was on the scene. The CIA and FBI finally made an executive decision to send the SWAT teams in by nine o'clock, and the governor and president were being kept closely informed. The mayor was on the scene, along with assorted diplomats and a UN task force, and the whole country was watching. It was all too reminiscent of 9/11.

A clumsy attempt by the terrorists to broadcast was made at 8:15, with hand-held cameras. They rambled on at length, and said they were going to blow up the building. You couldn't see them clearly, but as the hand-held camera bounced crazily, you could see hostages in the background huddled together. The hostage-takers looked like a rough group. There were only six of them, but they appeared to have an arsenal of weapons that no one knew how they had gotten in.

April looked intently at the screen when the message came on, but she didn't see her mother. She had no idea if she was dead or alive by then. All they could do was wait to find out. Mike said nothing, but stood behind her and rubbed her shoulders. She looked up at him and thanked him. It had made a difference, having him there with her all day. Her staff didn't quite know what to make of it. They all knew she didn't have a boyfriend, but clearly there was some kind of bond between the well-known restaurant critic and their boss that they had never known about before. It was hard to believe that it was new to April too. But she'd been grateful for his company all day, and for his warning of what had just happened before it hit the news.

By eight-thirty the plan to attack the hostage-takers was in place, although it was dangerous for all concerned, both liberators and hostages. It was almost inevitable that some people would get killed.

All the buildings in the surrounding area had been evacuated hours before, and all traffic had been stopped in case the hostage-takers followed through on their threat to blow up the building. Only emergency vehicles and crisis units and eventually the military were on the scene, and a handful of advisers.

Jack Adams was hanging in, talking to them whenever possible. No one was sure if he was there as a journalist, or just a very concerned person, with friends and co-workers in the building under siege. But because of who he was, they let him stick around. The CIA and SWAT teams chatted with him, and whenever appropriate, he joined in their discussions. He wanted to go in with one of the SWAT teams, but they declined. There was no way he could. It was a risk they couldn't take. This was a tight, highly professional operation.

And finally, the SWAT teams prepared to make their move. The electricity in the building had been cut off shortly before, and a few minutes before nine a group of forty highly trained men went in through the basement. Others had landed on the roof, and still others were crawling up the air vents in a carefully orchestrated strategic plan. The men were carrying oxygen tanks and wearing infrared goggles, had on bulletproof vests and the overalls of the SWAT team. They were carrying automatic rifles and machine guns as Jack watched them leave.

It was nine minutes after nine when they reached the floor where the hostages were being held, gleaned from reports of the few people who had escaped, disappearing down back stairways while no one was looking. The few who got out did so only on a fluke, but had given them valuable information.

The leading SWAT team had come up an air vent from a lower floor in total darkness, with suction devices on their gloves and shoes.

They came out of the vent into an empty hallway, but they

could hear voices nearby. The voices were speaking English, and by sheer luck, the men from the SWAT team found a room of sixty women, with only two men guarding them near the door. The lead marksmen of the SWAT team took the guards out instantly in silence, as the women watched in amazement, and miraculously no one screamed. They signed to the women as best they could not to make a sound, and to follow them. As quickly as possible, they were taken through three sets of doors, and led down two stairways, handed from man to man. Many of them had lost their shoes and were barefoot. All looked frightened but were brave, as they hurried down the stairs. They were all stunned that no one had stopped them, as their liberators wondered exactly where the male hostages were being held.

Jack was standing in the lobby with one of the commando units waiting for news from upstairs, when the women came through a fire door and began running across the lobby, sobbing and in bare feet. No one had radioed to say they were on their way and that they had been freed. Most of the members of the SWAT team had stayed upstairs to find the men. And suddenly it was pandemonium as sixty women ran through the lobby and front doors of the building with a handful of men directing them, and the commandos in the lobby sprang into action to lend a hand, as did Jack. A woman near him stumbled, nearly fainting, and he picked her up and carried her outside. A reporter took his picture as he handed her to the nearest fireman and rushed back inside.

The women were still coming down the stairs, and he suddenly saw Valerie emerge from the fire door, and she looked startled when she recognized him. He was heading toward her and several others, when they all heard a shot. No one knew where it had come from, and within seconds, all hell had broken loose.

A lone sniper had come down another stairway when he found the women missing and opened fire on them. Two women dropped to the floor, and a commando was shot in the arm before anyone could react, and by then the sniper was darting through the crowd with a mask on his face. The commandos didn't dare shoot at him, for fear of killing any of the women, who were screaming and running toward the doors.

Jack had reached Valerie by then, who was kneeling next to a woman who had been shot in the head. And without thinking, Jack grabbed Valerie, pulled her to her feet, shielded her with his body, and led her to the doors, where a policeman pulled her out. Just as he did, four of the commandos took careful aim at the sniper and killed him on the spot. He lay in a pool of blood facedown on the marble floor near the two women he had killed.

Jack was staring at the scene in disbelief as the faces of the women swirled around him, and he heard a man's voice say something to him. The words he heard were a blur, as Jack saw legs around him and wondered what had happened, and as he did, everything went black. He passed out without a sound.

The women were out of the building as the remaining commandos knelt over Jack. The sniper had shot him in the leg and hit an artery before the SWAT team took the sniper out. They had Jack on a gurney and rushed him to an ambulance, as

Valerie and the other women were being tended to, covered with blankets, and shepherded into the hands of medical units that had been waiting for them for hours. Valerie saw the ambulance leave but didn't register who was in it. She hadn't seen Jack fall.

In the lobby, firemen and police were covering the three bodies with tarps. It was a grisly scene, and the white marble floor was covered with blood.

There was no further news from upstairs yet, but within seconds their radios came to life. The male hostages were safe. Three were killed during the operation to free them, and four had been shot before their rescuers arrived. In total, eleven people had died in the attack. It was more than anyone wanted, but better than they had feared. The remaining terrorists had tried to detonate a bomb, which the SWAT team had been able to deactivate immediately. It was a small, amateurish bomb, and all of the hostage-takers had been killed by the commandos. Their weapons had been rough and their plan crude but astonishingly effective.

The men who had been taken hostage were brought downstairs, taken past the grisly scene in the lobby, and turned over to medical units, just as the women had been. Several units of the SWAT team were still upstairs checking for bombs.

Valerie left the scene in a police car, with siren screaming, as many of the vehicles in the area began to back up and leave. More police units were brought in for the clean-up, as Valerie borrowed a cell phone from one of the policemen to call April at the restaurant.

April burst into tears the minute she heard her mother's voice. She was sobbing incoherently in relief. Valerie said they had to be debriefed and examined at the hospital, and she would call her as soon as she got home. She didn't think it would be for several hours. As she hung up, April melted into Mike's arms.

"She's okay," she said to him, blowing her nose in a tissue someone handed her. "She didn't have time to tell me much else. She'll call me later. I'm okay, if you want to go." She looked at him apologetically, and he shook his head. He was staying till the bitter end. She called her father then to tell him that Valerie was okay, and he burst into tears too. The day had been agonizing beyond belief for them all. The tension had gone on for nearly twelve hours. It was hard to believe that six gunmen had taken over the network building, and that they had gotten in, while the whole free world watched what they were doing on broadcasts in every country.

By eleven o'clock, it was confirmed that in total eleven people had been killed, all network employees, although their names hadn't been released, until their families could be notified. The only one Valerie knew about for sure was her assistant Marilyn, who had been one of the two women the sniper shot in the lobby. Valerie had seen it happen. When April was talking to her father, Valerie was at Bellevue being examined, and Jack Adams was at New York–Presbyterian Hospital, in the trauma unit, critically injured.

There was a rapid mention of it on the news, which April saw at the restaurant. The report said that Jack Adams had been shot at the end of the hostage situation, while helping the freed women from the building. A sniper had shot him and hit an artery in his leg. They identified him as the former NFL quarterback turned sportscaster and said he had been at the site all day, talking to the SWAT teams and other crisis units at the scene, and offering any assistance he could.

The restaurant was closed by then, and April finally left her vigil in front of the television. She and Mike both looked exhausted and as though they'd been there themselves. She could only imagine how her mother felt and was still waiting for her call when she was allowed to leave the hospital. April wanted to go to her, but Valerie had said she couldn't. It was too chaotic.

Valerie finally called at 2:15 in the morning, and said that she was in a police car, on her way home to her apartment. It was over, the building was secure, the terrorists were dead. Eleven hostages had been killed, but it could have been infinitely worse. It had been terrible for all of them, but it wasn't 9/11. Six amateur terrorists had actually taken over a network, and accomplished only chaos and death, and nothing for their cause. Even their own government was horrified by what they'd done.

The network had already set up broadcast capability on other floors so they could resume programming in the morning, and get back to some semblance of normalcy, or at least the appearance of it.

"I'll be there in five minutes," April promised her mother. She was going to spend the night with her and was grateful that that was possible. Valerie could just as easily have been one of the victims as the survivors. They all could. April was shaken to her core, and the only thing that had gotten her through it was Mike. "I don't know how to thank you," she said as she locked the restaurant and took a deep breath of cold air on the sidewalk. "This has been the worst day of my life . . . and the best . . . since she lived through it." She couldn't bear to think what would have happened if the terrorists had killed her mother. She was so relieved they hadn't. "Thank you for being here, Mike." He had been wonderful to her, and she had seen a side of him she couldn't have imagined, and would never have seen otherwise. A side of humanity, tenderness, and compassion, so unlike his sometimes direct, cold, and aloof side.

"I'm glad I could be here," he said gently as he hailed a cab. He was exhausted too. "That's too bad about Jack Adams," he added as they shared a cab uptown. He was going to drop her off at her mother's to spend the night. "He was my hero when I was a kid. I always wanted to be just like him. I hope he makes it. I've always heard he's a good guy, and it sounds like he was a real hero, helping people out. He didn't have to do that." April nodded. All she could think of now was her mother, although she felt sorry for Jack Adams.

Mike dropped her off at her mother's building on Fifth Avenue, and he was taking the cab back downtown where he lived. April offered to pay for the cab, and he laughed at her.

"I think I can manage it," he said, teasing her. "You pay for our kid's college education, I'll take care of the cab." She smiled shyly up at him at the mention of their unborn child. It was the first time the subject had come up all day. They had had other things on their minds.

"That's a deal," she said, smiling at him. She wasn't sure she'd have heard from him by then, if it wasn't for her mother, and he wasn't sure of it either. He needed time to think about what had happened, and what was facing them. He still hadn't decided if he wanted to be part of it or not. But he had been happy to be there for her today. He couldn't let her face this agony and terror alone, and she reached up and hugged him. "Thanks, Mike. You were a hero for me today, and whatever happens after this, I love you for it. I couldn't have gotten through today without you."

"Just take it easy. Get some rest. And I know you probably won't, but you should take the day off tomorrow. Today was one hell of a day."

"Yes, it was." She nodded as he got back in the cab. She waved, and he drove off a minute later, as he laid his head back against the seat and closed his eyes. He had never been through anything this hard, and he admired April enormously for her calm grace and self-control.

April walked into the building only moments after her mother had arrived. Valerie was still wearing the red slacks and sweater she'd worn for the show that day, and the slippers they'd given her in the hospital when she arrived without shoes on. She was still shaking when April put her arms around her, and she had a hospital blanket around her shoulders. She had never seen her mother look like that, disheveled, frightened, and so profoundly shaken.

"I love you, Mom," April said, crying as she held her. All Valerie could do now was nod and sob as her daughter held her. The terror of it had been awful, waiting to be shot or die in an explosion at any moment. She had been sure none of them would come out of it alive, and many of the experts on the scene agreed with her, although they hadn't said that to the public. "Come on, let's put you to bed," April said as her mother just shook harder and expressed her sadness about Marilyn again.

April led her into her bedroom, like a child, and undressed her. She tucked her into bed and turned off the lights, and lay beside her, still dressed, on top of the covers. She held her mother tight, and finally Valerie drifted off to sleep. They had given her a tranquilizer at the hospital, and April lay awake for hours, watching her and stroking her hair, so grateful that she had survived it. She couldn't help thinking about Mike too, and their baby. At least she knew now that her baby had a decent father, he had a kind heart, even if he didn't want children. Having almost lost her mother that day, the baby seemed like even more of a gift now. Destiny moved in strange ways. Her mother had been spared, while others died. And she was having a baby with a perfect stranger. All she knew as she hugged her mother that night was how relieved she was. And as the sky turned to pale gray on a cold December morning, April fell asleep peacefully beside her mother.

Chapter 8

Thanks to the pill they'd given her at the hospital, Valerie didn't wake up the next morning until eleven. April had called the restaurant and told them that she wouldn't be in until later, and she was sitting quietly in the kitchen, drinking a cup of tea and reading the paper, when her mother wandered in, in her nightgown, still looking pale and shaken. Pat and Maddie had already called early that morning to see how she was, and April promised to have her mother call them when she woke up.

"How do you feel, Mom?" April asked her, still looking worried. But however she felt, she had survived it. That was all that mattered.

"Like I lived through a nightmare," she said as she sat down at the kitchen table and glanced at the paper. There were photographs on the front page of when the women had been freed and came running out of the building. There were other shots of when the male hostages had been brought out, looking panicked, with the SWAT team all around them. Valerie looked at a photograph of Jack Adams, and remembered his shielding her from the sniper to get her out of the lobby. There were details about his injuries, and the paper said he was still in critical condition, but stable for now.

"It was a nightmare," April confirmed, still shaken by it herself. "It was the longest day of my life, waiting to find out if you were alive."

"I'm sorry. How awful for you. Where were you?"

"At the restaurant. I spent the whole day glued to the TV in the kitchen. Mike Steinman was with me. He called to warn me before the story broke. He heard it at the paper where he works. He came over, and stayed with me until we knew you were safe. He dropped me off here last night."

"Well, that's an interesting development," her mother said with a raised eyebrow. "I didn't think you'd heard from him in a while."

"I hadn't. But he called to tell me about you. And then he showed up after that. I guess, despite all his craziness and neurosis about not having kids, and hating my restaurant, he's a nice guy. He was very decent yesterday. It's nice to know he's a human being, even if I never hear from him again."

"I'm sure you will," her mother said with a sigh. Every inch of her body was aching. The stress of the day before, and the trauma, had taken an enormous toll. She felt a thousand years old. "Do you know what happened to Jack Adams?" Her mother looked worried when she asked.

"I haven't listened to the news. I didn't want to wake you. By the way, Dad and Maddie called you. I said you'd call when you got up." Bob Lattimer, the head of the network, called shortly after that. He wanted to make sure Valerie was all right. He told her they were going to try and get back to normal programming the next day, if she was up to it. They were devoting most of that day's broadcasts to special reports on the news. It gave them a chance to clean up the two floors the hostages had taken over, and the lobby.

After talking to him, Valerie walked into the living room and turned on the TV. There was news on every channel, special reports, and as she flipped through the channels, she saw the footage of Jack Adams being taken away by ambulance, and then a live feed of him sitting up in bed, looking weak but smiling. He insisted that he hadn't been a hero but just did what he could, which he said wasn't much. He said the leg was doing fine, although there was a nasty rumor going around that he might not be quarterbacking anymore that season. He insisted the rumor wasn't true, and the interviewer laughed. Once they went back to a shot from the studio, the anchor said again that Jack had been a hero helping to get the women out of the building. They quipped for a minute that it wasn't surprising that Jack Adams would be the one to escort the women out, since it was no secret how much he liked women and what a womanizer he had been during his NFL career, and perhaps still was. Everyone in the studio laughed, and Valerie was pleased to know that he had survived. He really had been a hero with her, trying to protect her from the sniper in the lobby. She wanted to send him flowers or champagne, or something to thank him, and wondered what hospital he was in. She called the network a few minutes later, and they told her he was at New York–Presbyterian Hospital.

She said something about it to April, who had a better idea. "Why don't you send him some decent food? He's been to the restaurant quite a few times, I can find out what he likes. If I remember correctly, I think he loves our meat loaf. We can send him some chicken too, and mashed potatoes. They can heat it up in the microwave for him." It sounded like a great idea to both of them, and April called the restaurant to arrange it.

After that, Valerie called Marilyn's family to express her sympathy. They were devastated. It made the horrors of the day before even more real to her, and her own survival seem even more miraculous, to both of them. Marilyn's mother tearfully said that she had gone to her apartment to pick up the little Yorkshire puppy Valerie had given her on the Christmas show, and she was going to keep her. Marilyn's tragic death was going to make the segment agonizingly poignant.

Valerie spent the rest of the day at home, in a bathrobe, relaxing and resting, before going back to work the next day. There was no reason for her not to, since she hadn't been injured, but she was still looking very shaken and sad about Marilyn when April left her to go back to the restaurant. She promised to bring her mother some food too. And a waiter had already taken a cab to New York–Presbyterian Hospital with the food for Jack, and a message from her mother. The two women hugged before April left the apartment. She hated to leave her mother for even a minute but needed to check on things at the restaurant.

She called Mike from the cab. He sounded busy when he answered.

"Bad time?" she asked cautiously.

"No. I'm just on deadline, and the newsroom is nuts today. You can imagine it after yesterday."

"I just wanted to thank you again for being with me." Her voice was gentle, and he smiled.

"I'm glad I could be. How's your mom today?"

"She's pretty shaken up, but so am I, and I wasn't even there. Her assistant was among the casualties, and she's very upset about that too."

"Are you feeling okay?" He didn't inquire directly about the baby, but she knew what he meant.

"I'm fine." He was sorry for what they'd all gone through. It had even been emotional for him, and he didn't know her mother. It was shocking to hear that eleven people had died.

April had an idea then, but she didn't know how he'd feel about it. "My family comes to the restaurant for dinner on Christmas Eve. You're welcome to join us, if you'd like to. I don't know if that's something you'd like to do, or not." She didn't want to push him, but she felt closer to him now, and brave enough to ask, after the time they'd shared the day before, waiting for news of her mother.

"I told you, I don't do holidays. They were such a nightmare in my family when I was a kid, with my parents drunk and beating each other up, I'd rather pretend they don't exist. But thanks anyway."

"I understand," she said quietly. She couldn't even imagine growing up in a family like his. It was not surprising he didn't want kids. Being one in his world had been bad enough.

"I'll call you after the holidays," he promised, "or before that, if I need comfort food," he said, and laughed. He had begun to understand her restaurant and why it was so popular. It wasn't Alain Ducasse or Taillevent, which she might have been capable of replicating, but in some ways it was something even better, and he could see the merit of it now. What she offered met a real need for her patrons. It was real food for real life, as she put it, and the best of its kind.

"Just call if you need pancakes," she reminded him. "In emergencies, we deliver." She told him they had just sent food to Jack Adams from her mother. "Apparently he helped her on the way out. That's when he got shot."

"I gather he got hit pretty badly," Mike commented. It seemed incredible to both of them that Valerie had escaped without getting injured. She had been severely traumatized certainly, and the news reports said the hostages had been warned that they might suffer from post-traumatic stress for a long time, but at least physically, she was fine. "I'm glad your mom is okay," Mike reiterated, and then said he had to go back to work, before he missed his deadline. He said he'd call her sometime soon, and she had no idea if he would. At least it felt as though they were friends now. That was something at least, given the situation. It was hard to believe they had ever been lovers, even for a night.

It felt good to get back to the restaurant, and be involved in her familiar world again. The day before had had such a nightmarish quality to it that it was hard to believe it had really happened. Everyone asked about her mother, and April confirmed that the food had been sent to Jack Adams at the hospital. The waiter who had taken it to him said he had been thrilled, and still looked pretty rocky. He had been getting a transfusion, but told the waiter that April's meat loaf and mashed potatoes were worth ten of them, and laughed. He had been surrounded by doctors and nurses, and a news team had been there, but they had let her waiter in anyway. And she knew her mother would be glad.

"We can send him some more tomorrow," April told her kitchen staff, and then got back to work, organizing her kitchen. They were low on produce, and she had to go to the fish market in the morning. And she had Yule logs to make in a few days for Christmas, and plum pudding. It was going to be a busy week for her. She forgot all about Mike, the baby, and even the hostage crisis of the day before as she raced around the kitchen, checking everything at full speed. She was in good spirits and happy to be back. She called her mother late that afternoon to check on her, and she didn't answer. April wasn't worried, she assumed her mother was sleeping. It was good for her, and then she got busy cooking dinner for the restaurant. April in New York was in full swing.

* * *

Valerie was feeling shaky when she dressed in jeans, a sweater, and a big down coat and left the house that same afternoon in a cab. She had planned to stay home and take it easy, but the more she thought about it, the more she realized that she wanted to thank Jack Adams personally for what he'd done. She wasn't exactly sure when he'd been shot, but she remembered him shielding her from the sniper to get her to the front door and out of the building. She still looked pale when she got out of the cab at New York–Presbyterian Hospital, and she had worn very little makeup, which was rare for her, but she looked pretty anyway.

Alan Starr, the psychic, had called her that afternoon, and apologized for not seeing the terrorist attack in her cards. He said that sometimes that happened, but like everyone else, he was grateful she had survived.

Jack was in a suite on the private VIP floor of the hospital, and just to be on the safe side, there were police guards outside his room. There had been no threats against him, but the police chief wanted to do everything he could for him, and had come himself to visit that morning. Jack had signed autographs for the chief's kids and grandchildren, and thanked him for saving his life the night before when his artery was hit.

He was resting and there was no one in his room when Valerie knocked. One of the cops at the door had recognized her immediately. He said his wife was addicted to her show and had all her books, but he didn't dare ask her for an autograph. He knew she had been a hostage the day before. She still looked pretty shaken.

"Hi," she said cautiously, as she peeked around the door. Jack was watching TV and looked half asleep. They had given him a shot for pain not long before, but he was awake enough to recognize her. He smiled as soon as he saw her face. "Can I come in, or is this a bad time?"

"No, it's a fine time. Thanks for the food," he said, struggling to sit up a little, and she told him not to, to just stay where he was. She promised not to stay long. "I didn't realize April was your daughter. It's my favorite place to eat," he said, and meant it.

"Mine too. How do you feel?"

"Not so bad. I hurt my back two months ago, and that was worse. I just feel a little woozy from the drugs. The leg isn't so bad." And the painkillers were strong. "How about you?"

"I'm fine. Just a little shaky. It was a terrifying day. I came to thank you for helping to get me out. That was a brave thing for you to do and I'm sorry you got shot." She said it admiringly, and he smiled. He had been hearing it all day, and all the nurses on the floor had been fighting to take care of him. He was in good hands.

"That's okay. I'll be fine," he said, trying to sound light-hearted. He changed the subject then. "The day I saw you in the elevator, I didn't know it was your birthday till I saw it on the news. I was feeling pretty sorry for myself that day. It was my birthday too, and I was a mess with my herniated disk."

"Your back looked pretty bad. I felt really sorry for you. How is it now?"

"It's fine. I'm going to be on crutches for a while for the leg. Shit, ever since my birthday, I've been falling apart." He laughed again. "I hit fifty, and it's been downhill ever since." He had heard how old she was on the news, so he knew she was older, but she didn't look it. He thought she looked great, and not nearly her age, and old enough to have a daughter as grown-up as April. Even after the events of the day before, and with very little makeup on, he thought Valerie looked terrific.

"Don't talk to me about birthdays. I've always kept mine quiet, and they had it all over radio and TV this year. I nearly had a heart attack when I heard it." And then she sighed. "Somehow after yesterday, it doesn't seem important. We're lucky to be alive." They were both sobered by the reality that so many others hadn't survived it. "Today I don't even care how old I am." And she meant it.

"Yeah, me too, and I figure if I can survive a sniper, I should be okay from now on. The night of my birthday, I figured I was all washed up."

"So did I." She smiled. "I don't want to wear you out," she said politely, and he looked tired. There were dark circles under his eyes, two IVs going into his arms, and a machine next to him to self-administer pain medication. He was no longer on the critical list, but he was by no means recovered yet, and he had nearly died the night before. "I just wanted to thank you in person."

"I really appreciate that, Valerie," he said, saying her name

131

for the first time. And as she stood up, she realized how long his legs were in the bed. He was a tall, powerfully built man. "Thanks again for the food. Why don't we have dinner at April's sometime? They're sending me home in time for Christmas, in a few days."

"I'd offer to cook for you," she said, as she approached the bed, and he smiled at her, "but I set a great table, and I'm a rotten cook. April is the chef in the family, I'm not."

"I'm a pretty good cook, if I can stand up when I get out of here. I think April's is our best bet. I'll call you in a few days. Thanks for coming by."

"Thanks for saving me," she said, with a serious expression and tears in her eyes. "I thought we were going to die." He reached out and took her hand and held it in his own with an equally serious expression.

"I wasn't going to let that happen to you, or the others, if I could help it, once I had you in my sights in the lobby. You're all right now," he reassured her, and she nodded and brushed the tears off her cheeks. She was still very emotional after the day before, and the death of her assistant. And Jack was upset about Norman, the young assistant producer of his show, who had been one of the eleven who died. It had all hit very close to home. To them, the casualties weren't just names, they were people they had cared about and known.

"I'm sorry. I'm still kind of shaken up after yesterday," Valerie said with a trembling voice.

"Yeah, me too," he said, and smiled at her again. There was something about him that was very reassuring. "Take care of yourself," he said, sounding genuine and concerned.

"I will. You too. Would you like more food tomorrow?" It was all she could offer, although there were flower arrangements everywhere. Dozens of others had been sent to other wards and rooms.

"I'd love it. I'm addicted to April's apple pie, if she has any. Waffles, fried chicken." His appetite was healthy, and he was smiling at her. "Thanks for coming, Valerie. Take it easy. Don't go back to work too soon."

"Are you kidding?" She laughed. "I'm taping again tomorrow. I have another Christmas episode to do, for my evening show."

"I'm off till the Super Bowl now. Dead or alive, they want me on air for it in Miami." It was always the high point of his year as a sportscaster, just as it had been when he played football.

"You rest too," she said, and walked to the door with a smile. She was grateful to him, and felt as though they had a special bond. She owed him her life. And she felt now as though she had a new friend. He was an easygoing guy, and she felt comfortable with him. He wasn't seductive or romantic, not with her. He was just friendly and warm, and nice to talk to. "Take care, Jack," she said with a wave as she left the room, and he lay thinking about her after she left. She seemed like a nice woman, and different than he had expected her to be. From all he had heard about her and seen on TV, he had expected her to be prissy and uptight and she wasn't. She was funny and witty, and unpretentious, in spite of her fame. And she was prettier and much more down to earth than he would have expected.

Valerie had always heard that he was a Lothario and womanizer, and he hadn't come off like that either. He just seemed like a big, cuddly teddy bear, with a great sense of humor, and more guts than anyone she could ever imagine. And as Valerie went back uptown to her apartment, and he went back to sleep, they both thought about how nice it was to have a new friend, however unexpected. The events of the day before had formed a bond between them like no other. They had both survived something unimaginable.

Valerie called April from the cab and told her what to send him the next day. April was surprised that she was out, but Valerie told her that she had wanted to thank Jack Adams in person, which April thought was nice of her. It didn't surprise her, her mother was always very thoughtful. After they hung up, Valerie wondered if he would actually invite her to dinner at April's. He probably had lots of other things to do, and women backed up for miles, waiting for his attention, but she liked him, and she hoped he'd call her. It would be fun to have dinner with him. And even if he didn't call, she was grateful to him anyway. She owed him and the SWAT team her life, as did so many others. Every second seemed precious now, and the world had never looked better to her, as she got out of the cab, after giving the driver a big tip. She smiled at the doorman, and went back to her apartment, which looked doubly beautiful to her now. She appreciated everything, and saw life through new eyes. Having survived the day before had given her a new lease on life. She felt about fifteen years old, no matter what her driver's license said. The numbers seemed completely irrelevant now. She was alive!

Chapter 9

The morning of Christmas Eve, Valerie went to a memorial service for Marilyn. There had already been a number of them for others who had been less fortunate than she and Jack. It made the events that had happened all too real.

Jack hadn't been able to attend the service for Norman Waterman, the young production assistant he had liked so much who had also been killed. But he had sent a long and heartfelt letter to his family about what a fine man he had been and how much he admired him and what a huge loss it was for them all.

Valerie was brooding quietly about Marilyn when she got home after the service, thinking about how wonderful Marilyn had been and how much Valerie would miss her. It was hard to believe that people they knew were gone. It cast a pall over her all day.

And much to Valerie's surprise, Jack did call her when he got out of the hospital. They sent him home that morning, and he called her in the afternoon to wish her a Merry Christmas and thank her for all the meals from April's. He said his son was home from college, and staying with him, and he also had a nurse to help him. He was still on crutches but said he was getting around okay. He invited her to dinner at April's the day after Christmas. He asked if there was anyplace else she'd prefer, and they both agreed it was the best food in town, and a nice relaxed atmosphere that suited them both. He told her he'd see her in two days, and would pick her up to go downtown. They discovered that they only lived a few blocks from each other, and he said he'd pick her up at eight. She was delighted when she hung up.

And April was stunned to hear from Mike three hours before her family was due at the restaurant for Christmas Eve dinner. They had a lot to celebrate this year!

"This probably sounds crazy, and very rude," Mike said, sounding embarrassed, "but I get depressed over the holidays. I think I need comfort food." Spending the day of the terrorist attack together and his support had opened a door of friendship between them. And he didn't know how to say it to her, but more than comfort food, he wanted to get to know her now as a friend.

"Do you want me to send you something?" April said, smiling at what he said. "What would you like?"

"I was actually thinking about your invitation to have dinner with your family. I'd like to come, if I can have pancakes for dinner." She laughed at the suggestion, and told him she'd be delighted if he joined them. "I'd like to meet your mother, after spending a whole day with you worrying about her. Do you think they'd mind my being there?"

"Not at all," she said easily, not wanting to tell him that they were desperate to get a look at the man who had fathered her baby but wasn't involved with her. It was a crazy situation. She wanted to remind her parents not to say anything embarrassing to him. She thought it was actually brave of him to come, comfort food or not. There was nothing comfortable about meeting the parents of a woman you had gotten pregnant but didn't love or have a relationship with, or want the child. She was impressed, and curious about why he had really called. "Are you serious about the pancakes?" she inquired, not sure for a minute if he was kidding.

"Totally," he said. "I usually get in a fetal position on Christmas Eve, and stay that way until New Year's Day. This is a big break with tradition for me. I don't want to shock my system too badly by eating Christmas food too. So don't waste it on me. I'm the original Grinch. Pancakes would be great."

"Your wish is my command, Mr. Steinman. A stack of my best buttermilk pancakes will be on your plate. No plum pudding for you!"

"Good. What time?"

"Eight."

"Thanks for letting me crash your family dinner. I guess I'm curious about them. I assume they know about me," he said cautiously, sounding a little nervous.

She didn't want to lie to him. It was obvious that they did.

"They do. But they've been pretty cool about it. No one's going to give you a hard time."

"That's decent of them. I would in their shoes," he said honestly.

"I guess they just figure we're a couple of shameless alcoholics who got what we deserved," she teased him, and he laughed. There was a lot he liked about her, and he liked the night he had spent in bed with her, what he remembered of it. He may have been drunk, but he wasn't blind or stupid. She was a smart, sexy, beautiful girl, and better than that, she was nice, even if she had gotten pregnant. He hadn't forgiven her for that yet, or the fates, but it would be good if they could be friends. She didn't seem to want more than that. And for now, that worked for him, even if nothing else did. He wouldn't let himself think about the baby yet, and maybe never. That was too much for him to deal with. One thing at a time. First April. Then he'd see about the rest. He was touched by the fact that she wanted nothing from him and was being independent and gutsy about her circumstances. It was one of the things he liked about her, and he was beginning to think that her idea of having comfort food on the menu was not such a bad idea. It was exactly what he wanted now, not dinner at a three-star restaurant. He loved the idea of having pancakes on Christmas Eve, and so did a lot of people for whom the holidays were hard. He had finally gotten her message. Better late than never.

April called both her father and her mother before they arrived, to warn them that Mike would be there, and not to say anything to him about the baby, or their situation. Both her parents thought his coming to dinner was a hopeful sign of some kind of involvement on his part, but neither of them dared to comment. They knew how sensitive April was about it, and they didn't want to upset her. But they were both anxious to meet him, and see what they thought of him. Pat warned Maddie and the girls on the way to the restaurant to be careful too. They all promised they would be.

Pat and his contingent were the first to arrive, and Valerie a few minutes later. She looked better but still tired after her shocking ordeal. Pat and Maddie hugged her and told her how happy they were to see her, as did their daughters. They could have been having a very different Christmas, if she and the other hostages hadn't been rescued. There had been services that day for many of those who hadn't survived it, and there would be all through the coming week. It was sobering to still see it on the news.

The whole group was in great spirits as they sat down at the table, and just as they did Mike arrived, wearing a blazer and tie, and looking very serious and respectable. He had correctly guessed that he needed to show up looking proper for dinner. Valerie was the first to hold her hand out to him with a broad smile.

"Thank you for keeping April company for that awful day." Mike returned the smile, and was stunned by how beautiful she was and how young she appeared, even more so than on TV. She looked like a real star, and he could easily see the resemblance to

April, despite their different styles. He preferred April's natural look, but her mother was a lovely-looking woman too.

"I'm just glad you're okay. That was one hell of a day," Mike said with obvious sympathy, and then shook hands with Pat and Maddie, who greeted him warmly, and he said hi to the girls. April had seated him between herself and Annie. She thought it might be too intense to seat him next to either of her parents, who might not be able to resist asking him pointed questions, in spite of her request. But Mike seemed totally comfortable in their midst. They were kind people and put him at ease.

He talked to Annie about MIT, and Heather about the colleges she had applied to. He got into an interesting discussion with her father about medieval history, which Mike seemed to know a lot about, and he and her mother chatted amiably, and he spoke to Maddie on several topics, and everyone teased him when his pancakes arrived instead of the roast beef and Yorkshire pudding they were all eating. And he liked his pancakes so much that he ordered a second stack and ate them all. And as usual, the wines Jean-Pierre picked out for them were excellent. By the end of dinner, everyone was in high spirits, and Mike decided to have one of her Yule logs and ate all of that as well. He had made a total pig of himself, and thought her family were the nicest people he'd ever met. Her father even scolded him for the bad review he'd given the restaurant, and Mike admitted that he was deeply embarrassed about it.

"I was a total jerk," he confessed readily. "I just didn't get what she was doing. I could tell what a great chef she is, and how well trained, from her CV, and I thought she was underachieving. Instead her idea is sheer genius. Look at what I just ate." He had waved at the crumbs of the pancakes dripping in maple syrup as he said it. It had been all he had craved for dinner, and he admitted that her mashed potatoes and white truffle pasta were the best in the world. "I'll make it up to her one day," Mike promised her father, who looked mollified as they drank champagne with dessert. Some of them ate her Yule logs, and the others had plum pudding, delicately lit. And both girls ordered s'mores.

Jean-Pierre offered her father a glass of cognac after dinner, and Mike accepted one too. The two men got along much better than April had expected, and her mother put an arm around her shoulders and hugged her and whispered "I like him," and April whispered back, "Me too." And when he went to the bathroom, both of her sisters agreed that he was cute. That didn't mean that they'd wind up together, but at least her judgment hadn't been totally off when she'd gone to bed with him, it had just been premature.

The entire group left the restaurant after midnight, and they weren't the last to leave. Mike thanked them all for allowing him to join them, and he didn't say it, but it had been the best Christmas Eve of his life. He liked them all. And before Valerie got into a cab, April told her mother that Jack Adams was coming to dinner the day after Christmas, so he must be doing all right.

"I know." Valerie smiled at her daughter. "I'm having dinner with him here. He called me today. He's still on crutches, but he says he's feeling fine. He attributes it to your mashed potatoes and meat loaf." She laughed, and April looked surprised.

"He invited you to dinner? That's nice of him." She didn't tell her mother that he usually showed up with girls half his age or younger. The two were obviously becoming friends after he rescued her from the terrorists. Once everyone had gotten into cabs, April went back inside. Everything was under control in the kitchen, so she went upstairs.

Mike called her on her cell phone just as she was getting into bed. He sounded relaxed and happy, not like a Grinch at all.

"Thank you for a wonderful evening. And I think your family is great. Everyone was really sweet to me, and they didn't have to be. They could have been really pissed."

"They're not. And they liked you too," she said honestly. "Heather thinks you're 'hot,' " she said, and he laughed out loud.

"I think your mom is 'hot.' She looks incredible." He suspected she'd had a little help, but the results were great. She looked fifteen years younger than she was. And he liked Pat and Maddie too. He liked them all. They were intelligent, interesting, loving to one another, and they obviously had a great time together. It was easy to see why April loved them as much as she did, and they just as clearly loved her. And they had warmly welcomed him into their midst. "Would you like to have dinner one of these days?" he asked out of the blue, and April was surprised. "The only problem is that yours has become my favorite restaurant, so I don't know where we'd go. Do you like Chinese?"

"I love it," she said, sounding delighted.

"I'll figure something out. Or maybe Thai. We'll see. How about next week?"

"Anytime you like."

"Perfect. Good night, April. Merry Christmas," he said, and meant it for the first time in years.

"Merry Christmas, Mike." She smiled as she hung up. It was funny to think about, she was almost four months pregnant with his child, and he had just asked her out for their first date. And she was thrilled.

The day after Christmas, at the appointed hour, Jack showed up at Valerie's building in a Cadillac Escalade SUV, with a driver. He was sitting in the backseat, and she hopped in beside him. He was wearing a big shearling coat and a turtleneck sweater, and she had dressed casually too. He had warned her that dressing was still difficult for him. They had both worn jeans, and she was wearing a short fur jacket. One of the nice things about April's restaurant was that you could wear whatever you wanted.

She and Jack chatted easily on the way downtown. He said that he had spent Christmas with his son, who had left to go skiing with friends that morning. He said he was on good terms with his ex-wife, who had remarried shortly after their divorce sixteen years before and had three young boys. Valerie said she was on great terms with her ex too, whose second wife she liked immensely, and they had two daughters.

Jack admitted readily that he hadn't been a great husband. "In fact," he said, looking sheepish, "I was awful. Too much temptation. And I was way too young. We were married for ten years, and I have no idea why she stayed as long as she did. It's heady stuff being a quarterback at the top of your game. I thought I was hot stuff, and I guess back then I was. I had way too much fun, and I have to admit, I have since then too. This last birthday kind of got me thinking. Could be it's time to get out of the fast lane and slow down. The night before my birthday damn near killed me."

She smiled at the memory. "You looked pretty bad when I saw you."

"I thought I was dying. I was in bed for two weeks with that disk. That never happened to me before. I figured it was some kind of message."

"And what would that be?" she teased him. He looked in good spirits despite his recent injury, and he didn't look like he was slowing down to her. He was out for dinner less than a week after he'd been shot.

"I'm not sure what the message is," Jack said, smiling at her. "Get thee to a monastery maybe. Or at least slow down. I've been raising hell for a long time. I was thinking about it in the hospital too. We could have all been killed. I think I want to put more thought into how I spend my life, and be a little more selective about *who* I spend it with." The models he went out with were beautiful, but essentially he knew better than anyone that they were just a string of one-night stands. He hadn't had a serious relationship in years. He was beginning to think he was ready for one now. He knew he hadn't met the "who" yet, but the rest was coming clear, since the terrorists had taken over the network.

They arrived at the restaurant, and when April saw them getting out of the car, she came out to meet them and helped Jack in. She had given him a table with easy access, and was happy to see her mother. Together they settled Jack on a banquette, with his injured leg on a chair. He said it worked, and Valerie sat next to him on the banquette. It was a cozy table, but everyone in the room had recognized him when he walked in. Even on crutches, he was a striking man. He was six four and still weighed 240 pounds. Her mother was a tall woman, but she was dwarfed beside him, as was April. And of course people had recognized Valerie too. They always did.

April had gained a little weight recently, and she was losing her waistline, but in the apron she wore constantly, so far no one had noticed. It would be a while still before the baby showed. She knew she would have a lot to explain then. No one had any idea what was coming.

Jack ordered all his favorites that night for dinner. He had crab salad, and hot, fresh Maine lobster. Her mother had a cheeseburger, which she said she had been craving for days. And they shared a double order of April's delicious French fries. And after serious debate between a chocolate soufflé and a leftover Yule log, they decided to share a hot fudge sundae instead. Each of them was delighted with what they ate, and spent ten minutes praising April.

"So tell me about your show," he said to Valerie, as they dove into the hot fudge sundae. And April had left a plate of home-made chocolates on their table for good measure, with truffles and delicate butter cookies she had learned how to make in France. "How did you get to be the authority on everything in the home?"

"God knows. I was a decorator for a few years, and I always had lots of ideas about how to set a beautiful table, and what a home should look like. We didn't have any money when we started out, and I was always figuring out how to make things pretty on a budget, and making things myself. Friends started asking for advice, and how I could help them. I did a couple of weddings. I wrote some books, wound up on the network, and presto magic, I became the guru for gracious living." She made it sound a lot simpler than it was. She had put a huge amount of thought into her work over the years, and was always trying out new things and doing careful research even now. And she was willing to work harder and longer than anyone else, and make whatever sacrifice she had to. That had been an important part of her success. She was extremely disciplined about her work.

"Yeah, like I wound up in the Hall of Fame." He laughed at what she had said. "I kicked a couple of balls around a football field, made a couple of touchdowns, and there I was. Valerie, no-body knows better than I do that it's not that easy. I worked my ass off in the NFL, and everybody tells me you work like a dog. Just like your daughter, look at her, she hasn't sat down all night. In the end, I think we both know that hard work wins the prize."

Even as a sportscaster he had worked hard, and the interviews she had seen him do recently were good. The ratings loved him. "Let me ask you something: How many football games have you been to in your life?" She was embarrassed at the question. She knew nothing about sports. "Honestly. Don't lie," he warned her with a smile. "I'll know."

"Honestly? Two." And she had never seen him play, although she knew he was a legend.

"Pro or college?"

"College. When I was in college myself."

"We have to do something about that." He thought about it for a moment. It was a very different move for him, but why not? They had both just gotten a new lease on life. "How would you like to come to the Super Bowl with me? You can have your own room of course," he reassured her. "I have to work, but Super Bowl's about as good as it gets. You might have fun. I'm going to Miami for it in four weeks. I just hope I can get around better by then. But whether I can or not, I have to go. They want me back on deck for that."

Valerie hesitated for only a fraction of a second and then laughed. "I'd love to. I'll try to take some kind of crash course before I go."

"You don't have to. I'll explain it to you when we're there."

She laughed out loud then. "I've been telling people how to do Super Bowl parties for years. You're going to make me an honest woman."

"It's about goddamn time. My son always comes down with

me. I hope you don't mind. He's a great kid. He probably knows even less about football than you do. He hates sports, probably thanks to me. But he thinks the Super Bowl is fun. He used to come when I played. I guess it was pretty rowdy for him. And it still is. Every time I go, I wish I were still playing. It's hard to give all that up. I played in four winning Super Bowls. It doesn't get sweeter than that. I'm glad I retired when I did, but I still miss it sometimes. Who wouldn't? Being a sportscaster is great, but it's not like being in the game."

"Sometimes I feel that way," she admitted to him, "when I see young women just starting out on their careers. It's hard to get older." They both looked at April as they said it. To them, she looked like a child, and in some ways she was.

"I used to tell myself I was still young, but this last birthday kind of brought me up short," Jack admitted.

"So did mine," she said, laughing ruefully, "especially when they announced it on the radio. I was ready to kill someone when I saw you in the elevator that day, except I felt so sorry for you, all hunched over."

He laughed now when he thought of it, his night with Catwoman and the disastrous result. "I think that was my last fling with youth. After that, I figured maybe it was time to grow up. Living through the terrorist takeover at the network was an epiphany for me about what matters and what doesn't. Some of the things I've done were pretty dumb. Basically, I destroyed my marriage in order to show off." What he said struck a familiar chord for her, she had done some of that herself, although Pat had been nice about it. Her day as a hostage and the lives lost had sparked an epiphany for her too. And she realized now that most of her decisions while she was married to him were about what was good for her and her career, not him or their marriage. She couldn't help wondering now if she'd been wrong, and regretting some of it.

"I pretty much wrecked my marriage in order to build my career," she confessed ruefully, but with her usual honesty about herself. "Although I was married to the wrong man. It never really worked. He's a wonderful person, but we were much too different. He admits now that I scared him to death. He wanted more children, and now I wish I'd had them. But I wanted to build an empire, and I did. You sacrifice a lot for that, and I'm not sure it's worth it. I love my work, and I still have a good time doing it, but that's not all there is. It's taken me this long to figure that out," Valerie said with a candor and openness that impressed Jack.

"Yeah, me too," Jack admitted. "Life isn't just about having fun. Or that's all you wind up with. A lot of good-time Charlies hanging around to cash in on you, and a lot of very pretty empty-headed girls who're there for a free ride. That gets old. Maybe I did myself a favor on my birthday when I threw my back out. The two weeks I spent in bed feeling sorry for myself gave me time to think."

"I've thought about it a lot in recent years, but by now I don't know what else to do," Valerie said quietly. "My marriage has been over for twenty-three years. April's all grown up and doesn't need me. Now all I've got left is work, and it's what I do best." Jack looked at her thoughtfully as she said it. What she said made sense to him too.

"I think what you need in your life now, Valerie, is football," he teased her again. "We'll get you a total immersion course in Miami next month. In exchange, you can teach me how to set a table." But even though he was being playful with her about it, he had enormous respect for the career she had built. Hers was a name that absolutely everybody knew. She was truly the world authority on gracious living. There wasn't a girl in America who planned her wedding without one of Valerie's books. It was easy to pooh-pooh it, but she was an industry unto herself. She was a business, a star, an icon, and a legend all her own, just as he was and had been. In their own way, they were both in the Hall of Fame, but in the end, they had both figured out that as exciting as it could be at times, it just wasn't enough. Pat had figured that out when they split up and he married Maddie, and went on to have more kids with a woman whose greatest joy in life was their family and marriage. They talked about things the way he and Valerie never had. Most of Valerie's decisions had been unilateral based on what was good for her career. At the time, it had been heady stuff. It was too late to go back and turn it around, and she wasn't sorry she'd done it. But some of the sacrifices she'd made, and the choices, no longer made quite as much sense.

Jack Adams was in a similar situation to hers. He had opted for a lifetime of fun, and he didn't regret it, but at fifty, there was no one important in his life, except his son. And he had never slowed down long enough to marry again and have more children. He had told himself he would one day, and the women he went out with were young enough that he could still marry and have more kids. Lots of men had second families at his age and older, particularly successful ones. But he wished that he had done it when he was younger. When he saw his ex-wife's three other boys, he knew that somewhere along the line, he had blown it. It was hard to play catch-up at fifty. And even harder at Valerie's age. One day you woke up and you were alone, and you wondered how it had happened. In Valerie and Jack's case, they both knew how it had.

"Would you do it differently if you had it to do all over again?" he asked her, and she thought about it before she answered.

"Maybe. Maybe not. I probably should have tried harder to stay married, but Pat and I didn't want the same things. He wanted an academic life and I didn't. I didn't care about medieval history, or his tenure at the university, or his students. I was much too interested in my own career and where it was going. I was on an express train all by myself. I didn't even notice that no one else was on it, and I probably didn't care back then, although I do now. I'd like someone on that train with me, and it's not going quite as fast. It's going at a good clip, but there's room for someone else on board. There never was before. Probably what I regret most now is that I didn't put any time and effort into finding someone else after Pat. I was too busy. But one day you wake up, and you're all by yourself, and there's no one in the station wanting to get on the train anymore. You've been flying by too fast. I don't want to end up alone one day, when I'm really old, but it could happen. I didn't stop at enough stations and let anyone else on board before now. And by the time you figure that out, it's probably too late to change it. You have a life, a show, a career everyone envies, a history, but if you're all alone, I'm not sure the accomplishments mean that much."

"It's not too late for someone to get on that train with you," Jack said quietly, and meant it. "You're a beautiful woman, Valerie. You just have to slow down long enough for someone to get on board." She nodded, and she could tell that he knew exactly what she meant, and had done the same thing himself, in his own way.

"I'm trying," she said honestly. "Some people say you can't have everything, a successful career and a relationship. I always thought you could, although I didn't put much effort into it myself."

"I think you can have both. People have said that to me too. I think it's bullshit. I think people who say that are jealous, and they don't like the idea that you can have it all. You can, you just have to moderate what you want. I've probably been out with every airhead in the country for the last twenty-five years. That's fine if what you really want is airheads. If you want more than that, at some point you have to get off that train too. I forgot to get off that train. I fell off that train recently, and I'm starting to think that's a good thing. It woke me up." She nodded. There was definitely a choice to be made about the kind of women he wanted.

It had been an interesting conversation, as April walked over to them with a smile. She had been on her feet, in and out of the kitchen, and greeting people, all night. Valerie worried about her staying on the career train for too long too. This baby was going to do her good. It was going to put something real and human in her life, not just a restaurant to love, but a person, a child. The one thing in her life Valerie didn't regret was April. She had been the greatest gift of all.

"How are you two doing?" she asked as she observed the remains of the hot fudge sundae. They had made heavy inroads on the chocolate truffles and butter cookies too. There was only one of each left.

"I'd say we've done very well, and had a terrific evening. Your mother is telling me all about how to set a table, and I've been explaining about field goals and incomplete passes." April laughed. They were obviously having a nice time.

"Just don't let her teach you how to cook."

"No worries. We have you. The lobster was delicious." April was pleased to hear it.

Jack paid the check after that, and Valerie could see that he was tired. The leg was probably still hurting more than he wanted to admit, and it had been a little too soon for him to go out. He seemed slower on his crutches when they left, although he claimed that it was all that food weighing him down. But he looked exhausted, and Valerie suspected he was in pain.

She thanked him for dinner when he dropped her off at her building. He said he had had a wonderful time, and so had she.

"I'll have my secretary call you about Miami. I'll give you the name of the hotel and the dates. See if they work for you. We don't need to book a flight, the network will send us down on the company plane." It was a nice way to travel. He was definitely a star, and the nice thing was that so was she. They were on equal footing. He was going to be a wonderful friend to have.

"Try to rest a little over the holidays," she reminded him.

"Look who's talking," he said, and laughed. "How many days did you take off after the hostage incident? Remind me, was that one or two?" She laughed in answer. He had a point. They had both spent their lives pushing as hard as they could, doing as much as possible, and there were a lot of good things about it. It had gotten them where they were. But at this point in their lives, they were both questioning how high the price had been for that fast ride. And for different reasons, they both wanted to slow down, not totally, but just enough to let someone else on the merry-go-round with them. They had both been honest and open about it that night. It would be interesting to see if they could do it, or if they ever would. She was looking forward to going to the Super Bowl with him, if she had the time. She had never done anything like it. It sounded like fun, and she liked the idea of doing something so different.

Jack kissed her on the cheek as she got out of the car, and she waved as she walked back into the building. She had had a really good time. Who would ever have guessed that they would wind up friends?

Chapter 10

Mike picked a tiny Chinese restaurant in Chinatown near Canal Street for their first date. It looked like a hole in the wall, but the food was delicate and exquisite. He had been there before, so he knew what to order. April was fascinated by the combinations they served. They did some wonderful things with shark and lobster. He had ordered Peking duck when he made the reservation, and it was cooked to perfection. They had fragrant paper-wrapped chicken, shark's fin sauté, and some vegetable dishes that they both tried to analyze and guess what spices had been used. There was a meat dish she wanted to figure out for her restaurant, but the owner just laughed at her when she inquired about it.

"They're not going to tell you their secrets," Mike said with a grin. He was glad that she had liked the food so much.

"Tell the truth," she said to him over delicate green tea ice cream. "Isn't this more fun than reporting from war zones?"

"Sometimes," he admitted, "but only when the food is this good. You don't know how many bad meals I eat, while writing reviews. A lot of chefs have no imagination, and their food is just no good."

"Is that what you thought when you gave me the bad review?" she asked with a wistful look. He was still embarrassed about it, and hoped to make it up to her one day.

"No, I thought the food was terrific, but I thought you weren't trying hard enough with the menu. You made a convert of me with the pancakes on Christmas Eve, and even before that. I dream about your mashed potatoes now, and I even love your mac and cheese." She had made him try a mouthful of both on Christmas Eve.

"I have to admit, they're not as good as this. I've always wanted to go to China, and take a serious class on how to do their food." There were so many things she still wanted to do. But her life was about to become infinitely more complicated in June. She wasn't going to be traveling anywhere anytime soon.

They were leaving the restaurant when she cautiously asked him a question, wondering even before she said it if it was a mistake.

"I'm going to the doctor tomorrow for my four-month visit. Any chance you want to come see it on the sonogram or listen to the heartbeat? My feelings won't be hurt if you don't want to, I just thought I'd ask, if it's something you want to do." They both knew he didn't, but she asked him so nicely that he suddenly thought he should. He felt as though it weren't his baby, only hers. He had no relation to it. It was still hard for him to believe that it even existed. It was hers but not yet his, and maybe it never would be. He could see now just the slightest roundness of her stomach. But the baggy sweaters she wore when she wasn't working, and her chef's jacket and apron at the restaurant, hid it most of the time. But he knew it was there, just waiting to destroy his life forever.

"Sure. Maybe. What time are you going?" he asked vaguely, looking uncomfortable as he said it.

"Four o'clock." She told him where the doctor's office was, and he nodded. He could do that, he told himself, it was no big deal. How much damage could one visit do?

"I can meet you there," he confirmed, and she looked up at him with a gentle smile that made his heart ache, and he didn't know how to tell her that he was afraid of what he'd see and how real it would make the baby seem to him after that. What if the baby turned out to be like him, whom his parents had blamed for everything, or his brother, who couldn't face their constant fights and accusations, and killed himself at fifteen instead? Things like that didn't show on a sonogram and were more devastating than deformities or anomalies. And if he let this child into his life, and her with it, would they break his heart, or find him inadequate later? He couldn't take the chance. With a family like hers, she had no concept of the kind of childhood he'd had. And what if he was as bad as his own parents? That would be even worse. What if bad parenting was hereditary, locked somewhere in his genes? She had three solid role models to draw from, and Mike knew he had none.

He took her back to her apartment over the restaurant, and remembered all too easily what had happened there four months before. There were moments like tonight when he was tempted to reach out to her again, and do it right this time, because he cared about her and respected her, not because of the wine. But he thought it was too late for a fresh start. His baby was already growing in her belly. He had done enough damage. They had both made a terrible mistake. He didn't want to make another one by starting with her all over again. He kissed her on the forehead, and left her on the stairs to her apartment. He seemed overwhelmed with sadness when he left. She wondered if he'd actually show up at the doctor's appointment the next day. But at least now they were slowly becoming friends. She had thoroughly enjoyed her evening with him.

She saw Ellen for acupuncture the next morning, who commented that the baby was turning into a good-sized bump. Neither of them could guess what sex it was, although Ellen said she might be able to tell from her pulses later on. April said she hoped it was going to be a girl. If she was going to be alone with it, a girl would be easier for her. Mike had stated no preference, since he didn't want the baby at all.

They had a full house at the restaurant that day for lunch, and a problem with one of their refrigerators, which had almost

159

made her late. The repairman was just walking in when she left. She got to the doctor's five minutes after four, and Mike wasn't there. She was almost certain he wouldn't come. They were just weighing her, when she heard someone asking for her at the desk. It was Mike. She came out to the waiting room to meet him with a smile. She had gained ten pounds in the last four months. She was allowed to gain twenty-five in the next five. She was going to start gaining real weight from now on.

Mike looked pained as they sat in the waiting room with other women with enormous pregnant bellies. By the time they went in to see the doctor, he looked pale and as though he were about to bolt. April introduced him to her doctor, who was pleasant and easygoing, and she agreed to do a quick sonogram so Mike could see the baby for himself. April hadn't felt it move yet, although the doctor explained that she would in the next few weeks. But Mike had never put a hand on her stomach, and April doubted he ever would again. She told herself that he was there not so much as the baby's father, but as an interested friend.

The doctor left April and Mike with the technician, and after emptying her bladder, April came back into the room wearing a cotton gown. She got onto the table so they could put the gel on her, and she saw that Mike looked away. Nothing was exposed except her long legs and her gently rounded belly, and then once the machine was on, the technician rolled the wand around on her abdomen, and the baby appeared on the screen. Mike was staring at it with total fascination. It looked like a baby, was curled up, but you could see its head, its back, its arms and legs, its hands and feet. And the rhythmic thump of the heart beating was equally clear. They could hear it through the microphone. He looked at April with amazement, then went back to staring at the screen. She was smiling at him, feeling the wand move around her belly in the cold gel, so he could see the child that was growing in her. The baby they had conceived together as an accident had never seemed more real, not only to her, but now to him.

Mike didn't say a word as this time the technician handed him the picture to take home with him. He didn't ask any questions, he just stared at it as April followed him out of the room. She was glad he had come with her, and somehow she was hoping he would be less angry and frightened about it.

He followed April into the exam room, dropped the photograph from the sonogram into the wastebasket, and looked from April to the doctor. April thought that he looked sick, and there was a thin film of perspiration on his face.

"I'm sorry," he said hoarsely, looking at April, "I can't do this. I just can't. This is a terrible mistake." And then without another word, he left the room. April followed him. He had already crossed the waiting room with long strides, and the door closed as she stood there in the gown, and she then ran back into the exam room and burst into tears. She apologized profusely to the doctor, who reassured her that these things happened. Some men were too shaken up by the responsibility facing them to easily embrace the idea. But April knew it was more than that. It was raw terror, and an absolute refusal to have anything to do with this baby. He just couldn't, and she had the sudden feeling that she would never see him again.

The doctor examined her quickly so she could leave. She told April that everything was fine. Ten minutes later April was crying as she walked down the street. She took a cab back to the restaurant, and she was still crying when Mike texted her. She knew that taking him to the doctor had been a huge mistake. His text to her said, "I'm sorry. I just can't." He wanted to tell her she should never have decided to keep it, but there was no point saying that again. It was too late to change that now, and she wouldn't anyway. She didn't when she had the chance. He felt totally betrayed by her and this hideous quirk of fate. And April had the overwhelming sensation that he would disappear this time for good.

She went back to the restaurant looking shaken and depressed, and more frightened than she'd ever been. It was clear that Mike wanted no part of this. She hadn't counted on him in the beginning, but the worst part now was that she realized she was falling in love with him, maybe in part because of the baby, but also because she really liked him. Losing him now suddenly really mattered. And she knew there was absolutely nothing she could do about it.

Chapter 11

Jack called Valerie the morning after their dinner at April's and asked her if she would like to see a movie with him on New Year's Eve. He wasn't feeling up to going out again, he admitted, but he had a full-scale movie theater in his apartment, and had an assortment of films currently in the theaters that he thought she might like to see. It sounded like fun to her, and she had nothing else to do. April would be working that night, as she always did, and Valerie didn't like going out on New Year's Eve. Staying in and watching a movie with Jack sounded like the perfect way to spend the evening. And he was looking forward to it too. He said he'd have food brought in for them. Something a little more elaborate than April's this time, just to make the evening more festive. But he told Valerie to relax and come in jeans. They didn't need to show off, they could just spend a quiet night at home. She loved the idea. She didn't say anything to April about her plans for that night. It wasn't a big deal.

When Valerie showed up at his apartment, the nurse he still had to assist him let her in. Jack was on his crutches in the kitchen, organizing dinner, and doing surprisingly well getting around, considering what he'd been through.

He looked up, happy to see her. He had decided to cook for her himself. He had ordered caviar, oysters, and cracked crab, he was making pasta to go with it, and had made a huge salad, which was sitting in a bowl. It looked like a real feast as he poured her a flute of Cristal champagne and handed it to her. He looked pale but well.

"Well, you've been busy," Valerie said, smiling at him. "What can I do to help?" It looked like he'd already done everything. The food was already on platters.

"Your daughter says you're a menace in the kitchen," he teased her, and she laughed. "Maybe you'd better just sit down." He was hobbling around, but managing well despite the crutches, and once in a while, he hopped from place to place on his good leg to take the pressure off the bad one.

"Why don't you let me do something, at least hand you things if you don't trust me? You're going to hurt yourself." Valerie looked worried about him, and he grinned. He was used to taking care of others, not having women take care of him, but he liked her motherly look of concern, which was new to him.

"I'm fine," he reassured her. "You can set the table if you want."

"Ah, now that's something I'm good at," she said confidently, as he pointed to a cupboard where the placemats and china were kept. He had assorted colors and motifs, and she picked gray linen mats, and napkins with silver threads in them, and put them on the round glass table at the far end of the kitchen, in front of the view of Central Park. It was a huge room, with a fabulous view, even better than hers. He was a few blocks north of where she lived, but on a much higher floor. He could see east and west to both rivers, and all across Central Park. It was a perfect bachelor pad. He walked her into a wood-paneled office a few minutes later, after she set the table, to show her shelves of trophies and awards covering one wall. He looked like a kid when he proudly pointed at them, and she was bowled over by how many there were.

"The rest of them are in the safe," he said vaguely, as she looked at them with interest and read what they were for. They covered some of the high points of his career and he assured her there were many more, with a childlike grin. It was kind of a "Look, Ma! See what I did!" She found it both impressive and endearing. She realized that was who he was, a man of major accomplishments, with a boyish heart, and she liked that about him.

"You're a very important man," she said, as she turned to smile at him. There was an innocence about him that touched her, even though he was bragging and they both knew it.

"Yes, I am." He grinned, looking boyish and happy with himself. "But so are you, Ms. Wyatt. You're as important as I am."

165

Their budding friendship was an even match in many ways. He had always gone out with women who were impressed with who he was, but had accomplished nothing much themselves. They were too young to have done anything yet, except in some cases model. That was the problem with going out with very young women. They didn't provide much of a challenge or bring anything to the table except their looks and their bodies. Valerie was far more interesting, and he didn't mind the ten-year gap in their age. He didn't feel as though she were any older, and she didn't look it. They looked roughly the same age. He wouldn't have admitted it to her, but he had had his eyes done and got Botox shots too. Maintaining his youthful looks was an important part not only of his career as a sportscaster but of his dating life too. It was one thing to be older than the girls he went out with, but he didn't want to look it. Or not too old anyway.

He walked Valerie back to the kitchen then, and she finished setting the table. She put silver candlesticks on it, and lit the candles, and selected plates with a wide silver band. Everything he had was elegant but masculine, and of the best quality that was made. While going through the cupboard, she had noticed that his candlesticks and flatware were from Cartier, and the plates were from Tiffany and had been made for him in Paris and had his name on the underside. He was a man who liked expensive things and the best of what life had to offer, and he had style and taste. He had come a long way from his early days as a football player, and had acquired a patina of sophistication, but he still had a natural simple side to him too. It was what women loved about him. He was very smooth but still real.

He hobbled over on his crutches and checked out the table, and nodded with approval. "You set a lovely table. Not everyone can say that Valerie Wyatt set their dinner table. I'm honored," he said, and she laughed and took another sip of the champagne. She was enjoying her evening with him, and he looked happy to be with her, and very much at ease.

She took the platters he had filled and set them around the table, and a few minutes later he turned down the lights and put on some music, and they sat down. The nurse had disappeared as soon as Valerie arrived, and she realized that she felt completely comfortable with him, which was surprising since they barely knew each other. He was a very pleasant man, and an interesting person of many contrasts. Success hadn't spoiled him. If anything, it had widened his horizons, and opened his eyes to the finer things in life. He enjoyed what wealth could give him, but he cared about people too. And he talked a lot about his son, who was in college. It was obvious that he was crazy about him, and he said he spent time with him whenever he could.

They talked about art during dinner. He had a good eye for that too, and she had noticed an impressive Diebenkorn painting when she walked in, which she knew was worth a fortune. There were two Ellsworth Kellys in the kitchen, which added color to the room. One was a deep slash of blue, and there was a red one next to it. She liked them both. They chatted easily as they ate dinner. It was a perfect New Year's Eve for two friends. It was easy more than romantic, which she liked. She had the feel-ing he was trying to get to know her, not seduce her, which ap-pealed to her. She knew he could have all the women he wanted and didn't need to add her to the collection, nor would she have wanted to be one of his flock of "girls."

The food he had set out was delicious, and the pasta he had made was surprisingly good. He had even made the salad dress-ing himself from scratch. They ate the caviar and oysters, and Valerie helped herself to some of the crab. And then he served her some of the pasta. It was hard to believe that after what they'd both been through recently, they were relaxing in his kitchen now, enjoying the minor luxuries and indulgences of life.

"It's weird, isn't it?" he commented. "Ten days ago I was get-ting shot in the leg by a sniper, and now here we are, as though nothing ever happened, eating oysters and pasta and talking about life." She glanced over at his crutches as he said it and raised an eyebrow. Getting shot didn't seem like "nothing" to her. "People have an amazing capacity to bounce back from the worst disasters and tragedies. One minute everything is a sham-bles, and then it all seems normal again," he said, looking re-laxed. None of the trauma he'd been through showed in his eyes as he smiled.

"I can't say I feel entirely normal," Valerie confessed, looking at him in the candlelight. "I've had nightmares every night, and I got off very lucky." They both thought of the assistants and col-leagues they had lost, the eleven who had died. And all of them had been traumatized in a major way, including him, whether he acknowledged it or not.

"We were both lucky," Jack said gently. She was impressed that he felt that way. And their friendship had resulted from that single horrifying event. She still remembered him helping the women out of the building. The sounds and smells of that lobby still haunted her and maybe always would. It was hard to erase it from her mind, although she knew that in time it would fade. But for her, it hadn't yet. And probably not for him either in spite of what he said. He was just happy to be alive, regardless of the pain in his leg.

He told her funny stories about his days in football then, to distract her. He could see in her eyes that she was still pained by the memories of that terrifying day. At least for him, he had no memories from the time he had been shot. After that everything was a blank. Valerie knew there had been talk of his receiving an award for heroism. The mayor had called him personally to thank him several days before, and Valerie had heard about it at the network too.

He talked about his marriage then, the things he regretted, the things he still missed about it, the moments he had loved. He said that the high point of his life had been when his son, Greg, was born. It touched her to hear that it wasn't winning the Super Bowl or being inducted into the Hall of Fame. It was when his only child had come into the world. It said something about him that she liked.

"I feel that way about April too." It would have been the

perfect time to tell him that her daughter was having a baby, but she didn't. Talking about it made her feel old. It was bad enough being sixty and single. She didn't have the heart to tell him she was going to be a grandmother, or even admit it to herself. She hadn't made her peace with it yet. Pat seemed more relaxed about it, but he was happily married and a man. And he was undisturbed about his age. Jack and Valerie had that in common, the fact that they were both struggling to accept how old they were and what it meant in their current lives. And both of them worked and lived in a culture based on youth. It wasn't easy getting older surrounded by people half their age who were itching to step into their shoes, and waiting for them to slip in some way. Valerie was constantly aware of it in her work, and Jack was too. They had more similar experiences, far more than she'd ever had with Pat, or even more recent men in her life. And Jack had nothing in common with the girls he dated. They were just more trophies on his wall. There was rarely one he could even talk to. His only bond with them was sex. And what would happen when that went downhill? He worried about that now.

"My age didn't use to bother me," he admitted to her over ice cream he scooped into crystal bowls and set down on the table for them, after she helped him clear the remains of their dinner. "I never thought about it. I was always the youngest guy in the room. And then suddenly one day I realized I wasn't. All of a sudden, I was the *oldest* guy in the room, and I was trying to convince myself it couldn't happen to me. Now all of a sudden I'm fifty. *Fifty!* And I'm competing on screen, and at the network, and in the bedroom with guys twenty years younger than I am, or half my age. It doesn't matter that I was a star quarterback, or I have a room full of trophies, or I look good for my age. I still am what I am, and they know it, and so do I. It's pretty scary, Valerie, don't you think?" She was smiling at him somewhat ruefully, as they ate their ice cream. It was the most honest he had ever been with anyone about how he felt about it.

"To tell you the truth, Jack, these days fifty sounds pretty goddamn good to me." As she said it, he laughed. She was candid with him too.

"I guess it depends on your perspective," he said. It was relaxing and pleasant being with her. He didn't have to work as hard as he did with younger women. He wasn't trying to impress her. They could eat in his kitchen in jeans, and speak the truth. She was as successful as he was, or more so, and faced the same problems every day. In some ways, it was a little strange for him being with a woman as important as he was, but there was an equality to it that he liked and had never encountered before, nor sought out. He didn't have the feeling she was older than he was. He felt like they were equals of the same age. They looked it, and both of them seemed youthful and looked at things in similar ways. The same things were important to them. They loved their children. They had even made some of the same mistakes, in their desperation to get ahead and establish who they were when they were younger. And without even really meaning to, they had become superstars when just being successful and good at what they did would have been enough. Instead, they had overshot the mark by quite a lot. Success was a faucet that was hard to limit or turn off, and so was fame.

"You're a much bigger star than I am," Valerie commented, without sounding bothered about it. In some ways she liked it, but Jack denied it vehemently.

"That's not true. There are plenty of people who don't know who I am," he insisted. "You're a household word. You're synonymous with elegance and lifestyle in every way. I'm about football and nothing else."

"Should we argue maybe about who's the most famous?" she suggested, and then giggled. She sounded like a kid when she did. He was having fun with her. It was the nicest New Year's Eve he'd had in years.

She mentioned to him too the recent news she'd heard at the network, that he was due to be given a citation for bravery by the mayor. And as soon as she said it, he looked embarrassed and brushed it off, saying that the police department and their SWAT teams deserved it, and he didn't.

After they'd finished eating, Valerie put the dishes in the sink. She offered to put them in the dishwasher, but he said that someone would be in to do it in the morning, and after they put the leftovers in the fridge, they went upstairs to his study, which had an even more spectacular view. They stood looking at it together for a moment, as the lights sparkled around the skyline of the city, and then Jack pressed a button and blackout shades came down over the windows, so they could watch a movie. He had a screening room too, but said this was more comfortable and cozier. They sat in two big armchairs side by side and he stuck a bag of popcorn in the microwave. He offered her several choices of films, and they picked one that neither of them had seen yet but wanted to. Valerie said she hadn't been to a movie in months. She never had time. She often worked on her books and shows at night.

"You work too hard," he reminded her, and she agreed readily. "I play more than you do," he confessed. "Or at least I used to. I haven't been out for two months, since Halloween." He didn't go into detail about it, and didn't want to, but she knew something drastic had happened, since she had seen him the day after in the elevator at work, on their birthdays. He had said it was an accident, but she sensed there had been more to it than that. He wouldn't have admitted it to Valerie, but he had only had sex once since, with one of his more sedate younger dates, but he had been so nervous about injuring himself again that he had barely dared to move, and it hadn't been good for either of them. He was terrified to rupture the disk, and hadn't dared to try it since, with anyone. The night before his birthday had changed his life, maybe forever, he was afraid. In an odd way, he and Valerie were at opposite ends of the spectrum, but with the same end result. He had a flock of women around him, she had no one, and in the end, both of them were alone, in all the ways that really mattered. It hadn't occurred to either of them, but it was true. They were both lonely, in their own way, and worried about the future, although for all intents and purposes, to anyone looking at them from the outside, they had golden lives.

They happily munched the popcorn while watching the film they had selected. It was a romantic comedy about an actor with a million girlfriends who falls in love with his snooty leading lady, who is disgusted by him and wants nothing to do with him. Throughout the film, he tries to convince her that he's a decent person, while the women he's been involved with drop in, drop by, run into them, show up, climb in windows naked, and show up at his house, while the leading lady loathes him more and more. Some of the incidents portrayed in the movie were truly funny, and they both laughed loudly. The film particularly resonated for Jack, who could see himself easily in the role of the beleaguered actor if he ever truly fell in love. It was light fare and they both enjoyed it as they guffawed and giggled at the leading man's discomfort and ate the popcorn. It had a happy ending, of course, which pleased them both. It set just the right tone for their friendly New Year's Eve as buddies, recovering from their recent trauma, and trying to keep things light.

"I loved it!" Valerie said, looking delighted, as Jack switched some soft lights back on. They were cozy in the big chairs, and he had handed Valerie a cashmere blanket to snuggle under since he liked keeping the apartment cooler than most women liked. She hated to get up, she was happy where she was as he turned on the lights. "I hate sad movies, or violence, or anything about sports," she said without thinking, and then laughed out loud, and apologized to him.

"Okay, I heard that!" he said, referring to her comment about sports. But it didn't surprise or offend him. He watched movies with women all the time, and they felt much the way Valerie did. He watched the violent ones on his own, and the guy films about wars and sports. "I like happy movies too. I'm kind of a softie and I like chick flicks with happy endings. Life is tough enough without watching films that depress you for three days after you see them. I hate that stuff," he said, and he meant it.

"Yeah, me too," she agreed. "I like thinking that things can turn out okay."

"What does 'turning out okay' mean to you?" he asked with interest. He often asked himself the same question, and had a relatively clear idea of what he wanted out of life. He just hadn't found it yet, and the goal shifted slightly year by year. His version of a happy ending had been different at thirty and forty than it was now. So was hers.

"Happy, peaceful, no big drama in my life," she answered his question, looking thoughtful. "Sharing my life with someone, *if* it's the right person, not if it isn't. I don't want to do that anymore. Good health obviously, but that's kind of an old fart answer. Mostly just being happy and peaceful, loving someone and being loved by him, and feeling good in your own skin."

"That sounds about right to me too," he said, and then he chuckled. "And don't forget good ratings for our shows, please God." She laughed in answer.

"Yes, but I have to admit I don't think about that when I'm making a wish list for my personal life."

"Do you do that often?" He looked surprised. "Make a wish list for your personal life?"

"Not really. I do it in my head sometimes, when I think about what I want. Most of the time, I just roll along, doing what I have to. I think I do it on my birthday, or on New Year's, those milestones always get me. I think about what I should have and be doing, but it never matches up, so I try not to anymore. Life never happens on the schedule you want, and I think I'm kind of past all that now anyway." She looked sad when she said it, but she had felt that way for months now. This last birthday had hit her hard.

"What's that supposed to mean?" He looked puzzled, as though he didn't understand what she meant. And she took a breath before she answered. They were friends now, and she felt like she could be honest with him. She wasn't a candidate for romance with him anyway, and she knew he had no interest in that with her, or any woman her age. They were friends, and that was enough.

"Let's face it, women my age are not a high commodity on the market. Men my age want to go out with women like the ones you go out with. No one's looking for sixty-year-old women, except maybe ninety-year-old guys. The eighty-year-olds are taking Viagra and looking for twenty-five-year-olds. Most men would rather go out with my daughter than with me. That's simple fact. Add success and fame to that mix, and what you get is a guy screaming out the door, or who never shows up in the first place. I don't have a lot of illusions left about it. I used to, but I don't anymore."

She didn't tell him that she hadn't had a real date in three years and couldn't remember the last time she'd had sex. It had begun to occur to her that maybe she never would again, which seemed sad to her. But you couldn't invent a man out of thin air, and no even remotely possible dates had crossed her path in a long time. She had given up on the terrible blind dates people used to fix her up with, with men who were severely damaged, very angry, or had a chip on their shoulder about who she was and what she had accomplished and were sometimes even nasty about it. Meeting them was always depressing and disappointing, so she didn't bother anymore.

And there was nothing else and hadn't been in a long time, despite the Botox shots, good haircuts, well-toned body thanks to her trainer, and expensive wardrobe. Old was old, and she was, or so she thought. "I have this psychic I talk to a couple of times a year. He's been telling me for years now that I'm going to meet a terrific man. I think he says it to give me hope. It never happens, or hasn't in a hell of a while. I'd been to see him that morning I saw you in the elevator, doubled over with your back."

"He must have fangs," Jack teased her, remembering it perfectly, despite the pain he'd been in. She was very striking, and had made an impression on him. "Your face was bleeding."

She hesitated and then laughed again, not worried about what she said to him. "I had just had Botox shots *after* I saw him. My dermatologist has fangs, not the psychic." He was touched that she was so open with him. She was a surprisingly honest woman, given who she was.

"I get them too," he admitted, equally honest. "So what, if it makes us look good? I don't usually advertise that, but shit, we both make a living on screen, and with high-definition video now, you need all the help you can get."

"Isn't that the truth? You can't lie to the camera anymore, although God knows I try." They both laughed at their reciprocal confessions, which didn't seem so shocking. Even schoolteachers and younger women were getting Botox shots now. It was not just for the very rich or movie stars. "The vanity of it is a little embarrassing, and I think my daughter thinks I'm pretty silly. She doesn't even wear makeup, probably in reaction to me, but I also make my living, or part of it, based on how I look, and so do you. And it makes me feel better if I look a little younger. It's not fun or easy getting old." They both knew that was the truth, and had been wrestling with it for the past two months, each in their own way, since their birthdays.

"You're not old, Valerie," he said kindly, and meant it. "We all feel that way past a certain age. It always annoys me that I think I'm falling apart. I hate having my picture taken, and then five years later I see the same picture and think I looked pretty good back then, but like hell now. I don't know why we're so obsessed with age in this country, but we are. It's hard to live up to at any age. I know thirty-year-old women who feel old.

"And I agree with your psychic. I think someone great is going to turn up one of these days. You deserve it. Forget the ninety-year-old guys. *And* the eighty-year-olds. They give me a run for my money too, if their bank account is bigger than mine. That's pretty screwed up." But those were the kind of women he dated, girls who were after money and power, which was why they liked him too. He didn't kid himself about that. "Have you ever thought about a much younger guy? I mean like thirty-five. A lot of women do that now. I think Demi Moore set the trend. I know a fifty-year-old woman who has a twenty-two-year-old boyfriend. She says she loves it. That's pretty much what I do. It's fun a lot of the time."

Valerie looked at him and shook her head. "I'd feel stupid. I've never seen a boy that age who appealed to me. I like grownups, and I think that would just make me feel older. I don't want to sleep with a man young enough to be my child. Besides, I want to share common life experiences, similar points of view and concerns. What do you have in common with someone that age? That's really about sex, not love. I may be old-fashioned, but I'd like to have both. And if I were going to sacrifice something, it would be sex, not love." For the moment, she had neither, but she was true to herself and always had been. Jack could sense that about her. She was a woman who knew who she was and what she wanted, what she was willing to sacrifice and what she wasn't. But it wasn't easy finding the right person, for anyone. He hadn't found it either, so he settled for sex and a lot of fun, and a herniated disk when he had a little too much fun.

"I don't think it's easy to find someone at any age. Look at all the people in their twenties and thirties trying to find dates through the internet. That tells you something, that it's not as easy to find people as it used to be. I don't know why, but I think it's true. People are better informed, more particular. They know themselves better through therapy. Women don't just want a guy to pay the bills, and they're not willing to put up with anything to get it, they want a partner. That narrows the field considerably. And there are always guys like me out there, who throw the balance off, dating twenty-year-olds, which leaves the fifty-year-old women with no one to go out with, except some Neanderthal who's watching TV and drinking beer, never had therapy, and doesn't know who the hell he is or care."

"So what's the answer?" she asked, looking puzzled. He seemed to understand the problem perfectly, but had no more solutions to the problem than she did.

He grinned, as he switched the music on the stereo to something more lively. "Sex, drugs, and rock and roll," he teased. It was five to midnight, almost New Year's, and the evening had flown by. "I don't know what the answer is. I suspect you probably find the right person by accident one day. And it's never who you thought it would be, or what you thought you wanted. Kind of like real estate. I was looking for a brownstone in the East Sixties, and wouldn't look at anything else. This apartment came on the market, and my realtor dragged me here kicking and screaming. I fell in love with it, and you couldn't get me out of here now. I think we have to stay open to what comes along. I think *that* is the real secret to youth and a good life, staying open, interested, excited, learning about life, trying new things, meeting new people. And whatever happens, you have a good time, and if the right person turns up while you're doing that, terrific. If not, at least you're having fun. I think it's when we start to shut down, give up, and limit our options that life starts to be over. I don't ever want that to happen to me. I want to keep opening new doors till the day I die, whenever that is, whether it's tomorrow, or when I'm ninety-nine. The day you stop opening doors, and give up on those new opportunities, you might as well be dead. That's what I believe anyway."

"I think you're right," she said, looking hopeful. She liked the way he looked at things, and his philosophy about life. He was fully alive and excited about whatever he did. It was why he wasn't sitting there clutching his leg and moaning about the trauma he'd been through and the near-death experience. Instead he was ready to move on, and having a good time with her, getting to know a new person, and making a new friend. She liked the way he thought, and it was an inspiration to her.

Jack looked at his watch then, and flipped on the TV to the ball in Times Square where a crowd of thousands was waiting to see the New Year in. He started counting. They were almost on it. Ten . . . nine . . . eight . . . seven . . . He was smiling and so was she . . . and when they reached "One!" he put his arms around her and looked into her eyes.

"Happy New Year, Valerie. I hope it's a great year for you in every way!" He kissed her lightly on the mouth then, and hugged her.

"You too, Jack," she said, and meant it as they held each other, as they both thought at the same time that it was already a great year. They were both alive!

Chapter 12

Valerie had lunch with April right after the New Year. She had sent a bottle of Cristal and a note to Jack to thank him the next day. The note said, "Best New Year ever! Thank you! Valerie," and she told April about it over lunch. They both agreed that he was a genuinely nice guy, in spite of the showy twelve-year-olds he went out with, as April put it. Most of them looked like gold-diggers when he brought them to the restaurant, but he didn't seem to mind.

Valerie told her he'd invited her to come to the Super Bowl, and April was stunned to hear that she was going.

"But you hate sports, Mom, and you know less about football than I do, and that's not much."

"You're right. But he said something on New Year's Eve that I think is true, about staying open to life, doing new things, meeting new people, opening new doors. I think that's the antidote to getting old and shriveling up. I may hate it, but I might have fun. Why not try it? He invited me as a friend, not a date, with my own room. Why not do something different for a change? I don't want to get stuck in a rut." Her daughter was impressed by her attitude, and Valerie herself had noticed that since surviving the terrorist attack on the network, she had been more open to everything, and more grateful for her life. She could easily have been killed like some of the others, and instead she had gotten another shot at life. As terrifying as it had been, it had freed her in some important ways. The little aggravations seemed less important, and everything seemed like a gift, especially a new friend like Jack, and a chance to go to the Super Bowl with a retired football star. Why not? Maybe that's what getting older was all about, she said to April. Maybe it was about "Why not?" Even April was taking a huge chance, being willing to have and embrace a baby she hadn't planned. Life was about living, Valerie realized now, not huddling in a corner, too frightened to move or try anything new, or too tired and disenchanted to bother. April's had been an enormous decision, and although she worried about her, Valerie admired her for what she had decided to do. Even if she didn't want to be a grandmother. *That* she was not ready for, and wasn't embarrassed to say so to her daughter.

"The baby will have to call me Aunt Valerie or Mrs. Wyatt," she said to April as they both laughed. "If it calls me Grandma, I'm going to deny it immediately, and act like I don't know either of you. I'm not ready to be anyone's grandmother yet! My vanity won't allow it." She was more than willing to admit it, and still looked faintly outraged about it. "How's it going, by the way? How do you feel?" April looked well, but her mother could see sadness in her eyes. She was afraid that this was harder than April had thought. Having a baby alone was far from easy, and being pregnant without the baby's father was sad, or at least Valerie thought so anyway, although people did it more and more these days. But it had been such a sweet time for her and Pat, waiting for April to arrive. She was sad that her own daughter didn't have the benefit of that experience and a man to love and care for her. Instead, she was working as hard as ever, at the fish market by five every morning, meeting with commercial fishermen, and fighting with wholesale butchers for better prices, working a twenty-hour day with no one to love her or rub her back. It seemed like a hard road to her mother.

"I felt the baby move a few days ago. It felt so sweet, like a butterfly. I thought it was gas or indigestion at first, and then I realized what I was feeling. It's happening a lot now." She looked deeply moved but still sad. Her mother knew her well.

"How's Mike? Have you seen him?" Valerie hoped so. She liked him. And maybe something could work out between them, despite an inauspicious start. Stranger things had happened. But April shook her head.

"No, I haven't. He disappeared. I did something stupid, I guess. We had a nice evening over Chinese dinner, and I invited him to the doctor's visit, to see the baby on a sonogram. And he freaked. He walked out, and texted me after that he just can't. I guess he had a pretty awful childhood, and doesn't want to be part of anyone else's. He broke up with a girlfriend a few months ago, because she wanted to get married and have children. I guess he's one of those damaged people who is never going to be able to commit to anyone." She saw that now, and Valerie looked annoyed.

"That's all very nice to cry about your childhood. But this baby exists now, and so do you. You didn't ask for it either, and you thought you were being careful. It's not like you threw caution to the winds. It happened to both of you. He can't just walk away from it because it makes him uncomfortable. So what? How comfortable are you? Not very, I would guess. You're running a business and pregnant all alone with a baby you didn't want. I think he owes you more than just running away and hiding. That's a little too easy. I thought he was better than that." She sounded disappointed, and although she didn't say it, so was April. For a crazy minute, when he had agreed to go to the doctor with her, she had hoped he would get involved. But that was obviously not going to happen. She hadn't heard a word from him since he walked out of the doctor's office and sent her the text. And she wasn't going to call him and try to force the baby or herself on him. She knew that would be a huge mistake. She had to let him go, if that was what he wanted. It was her baby now, not his.

"I decided to have it, Mom. He didn't. It was my decision. I didn't consult him about it. I told him. He doesn't want this child." April was as firm about it as he was, and realistic. No matter what she felt for him, if he didn't feel the same things for her, or the baby, she couldn't beat her head into a brick wall, and she wouldn't try.

Valerie was still worried about her, when she left her after lunch. April wandered out to the kitchen, looking wistful. She enjoyed seeing her mother, but had been down ever since the last time she'd seen Mike. They'd had such a good time at dinner. It had made her hopeful about a possible relationship between them, which she realized now was impossible. She would always be the woman who had forced him to have a baby he didn't want, and he would never forgive her for it. Their relationship had been doomed from the beginning.

Jean-Pierre the sommelier was watching her as she helped herself to an orange, and sat down at the counter to look at some bills. There had been some irregularities in their butcher bills recently, and she wanted to stay on top of it and make sure they hadn't been cheated. She had already spotted a charge for a leg of lamb they'd never gotten, and several pork loins. She didn't like that at all.

"Can I make you a cup of tea, April?" Jean-Pierre asked her, and she nodded, distracted by the bills she was poring through with infinite precision.

"That would be nice, thank you," she said, and when he handed the cup to her, she looked up and smiled. It was a cup of the vanilla tea that she ordered from Paris and their customers loved. And it was decaf, which was even better.

"How are you feeling?" he asked quietly. She had told no one about the pregnancy yet. It didn't show as long as she kept her apron on, although she knew it would any day. And if you looked closely, there was a noticeable bump. Those who had observed it just thought she was gaining weight. Her face was rounder too. But nothing else had changed.

"I'm fine," she answered the sommelier, and thanked him for the tea. He had added a cookie to it, which she ate.

"You work too hard, April," he scolded gently.

"We all do," she said honestly. "That's what it takes to run a good restaurant. Constant attention to detail and being on deck at all times." She did both, and she really liked the way he worked with the customers and the suggestions he made. He already had a deep respect for her ability to buy great wines at good prices. He thought she was brilliant at what she did, and he loved the atmosphere of the restaurant, and her theories about it, and passion. He thought she was a remarkable woman. And he hadn't seen a chef he respected more, since France, and he had worked with some very good ones. He had a strong case of hero worship for her, and they were the same age. He had grown up and trained in Bordeaux, and had been in New York for five years. His English was surprisingly good, and he had married an American and gotten a green card, which was important for April. He and his wife had just gotten divorced. They had a three-year-old little boy. She had left Jean-Pierre for someone else, a waiter in another French restaurant, this one from Lyon.

"I know you're not telling anyone," he said softly, as April sipped her tea. "But I've noticed the changes lately."

"In the restaurant?" She looked worried. She didn't think

anything had changed. That was never a good sign, when the staff saw that things were slipping before you did. She was panicked by what he said. What did he mean? Theft? Taking money from the cash box? Poor service? Sloppy food or presentation?

"I meant the changes in you." He pointed to her belly, and she was instantly relieved. "You look sad, April," he said boldly. "This can't be an easy time for you." She didn't know what to answer him. She didn't want to admit to it, but if she denied the pregnancy, in a few weeks he and everyone else would know it anyway.

"I guess I just have to look at it as an unexpected gift," she said with a sigh. "Please don't say anything to anyone yet. I didn't think it showed. I don't want to tell them for a while. Nothing's going to change here, but it'll worry them anyway. Maybe they'll think I won't care as much about the restaurant, but I will." She tried to reassure him, but he looked sorry for her. He was a nice man, and a good employee, but she had no other interest in him than that. She never got personally involved with her staff, and didn't intend to start now. And she could sense that he was personally interested in her. She didn't welcome it from him.

"And who is going to care about you, not just the restaurant?" he said pointedly.

"I can take care of myself." She smiled. "I always have."

"It's not so easy with a child, especially now." She nodded, not sure what to say to him, and uncomfortable with the conversation. "The baby's father?" he asked, and she shrugged.

"He's not involved."

"I thought so." He had also guessed that it was Mike. He had seen the way she looked at him, and he had come to dinner with her family on Christmas Eve. He also knew that he hadn't been back since, which wasn't a good sign. And the sadness in her eyes said the rest. He knew she was alone, and he felt sorry for her.

"If there's anything that I can do for you, I'd like to help you," he said gently. "I think you're a wonderful person, and you're very good to everyone. We all love you." He didn't tell her that he did, but he could have gotten there with ease, with a little encouragement from her, which she was careful not to provide. She didn't want to mislead Jean-Pierre. She wasn't interested in him. And with his divorce, he was vulnerable now too, and probably lonely without his wife and child.

"Thank you," she said simply. "I'm fine," she reassured him, and wanted to get off the subject. She tried to make that clear to him.

"I'm here if you need me," he said again, and then disappeared into the wine cellar. He had said enough. He had let her know that he cared about her as a person, and would be happy to as a woman, if she let him. She didn't seem to be open to it now. He hoped she would be one day. Maybe when the baby was born. He wasn't going anywhere, and it touched his heart to know that she was pregnant and alone. He was a good man. But April didn't want him that way. Right now, she wanted Mike or no one. She couldn't think about getting involved with anyone while carrying someone else's child. That was too complicated for her. It was convoluted enough as it was, without adding someone else to the mix. She was better off alone now anyway, she told herself. She had enough on her mind.

Jack called Valerie in her office that afternoon. She sounded busy, and said she was interviewing someone and would call him back. He assumed it was for her show, but as she hung up, she was sitting across her desk from a young woman the Human Resources office had sent her as a possible assistant to replace Marilyn, and Valerie didn't know whether to laugh or cry. Her name was Dawn. She had a nose ring, and a diamond stud just above her lip. Her hair was dyed jet black with a royal blue streak in it and spiked with gel, and she had colorful tattoos of cartoon characters up and down each arm. She also had tattoos of a red rose on the back of each hand. Other than that she was neatly dressed in jeans, high heels, and a short-sleeved black sweater. She sounded intelligent, had gone to Stanford, and she was twenty-five years old. She was a far cry from the beloved assistant Valerie had worked with for years.

Dawn said she had been working in London since she graduated, first at British *Vogue* and then at a decorating magazine, but life in England had become too expensive, so she had come back to New York. She had never worked in television before, but her mother was an interior designer in Greenwich, Connecticut, and Dawn had worked for her in the summer all through high school and college, so the world of decorating wasn't unfamiliar to her. She had been assigned to the Home section of British *Vogue,* and had eventually moved to *The World of Interiors.* She had majored in journalism in college, and Valerie could see she was a bright girl. She tried not to focus on the way Dawn looked, although the diamond stud above her lip kept catching Valerie's eye. She certainly didn't look like a girl from Greenwich. But she answered everything Valerie said, directly and intelligently. By the time the interview was over, Valerie couldn't think of a reason not to hire her, other than the way she looked, which she knew was not politically correct or a valid reason, but it made her miss Marilyn more than ever.

"I'm sorry about your assistant," Dawn said quietly as she stood up. She had good manners, as well as being bright, and seemed very poised. Valerie would have loved her if it weren't for the pierces, tattoos, and hair. "It must be hard for you to change after working with her for so long."

"Yes, it is," Valerie admitted with a sigh. "The whole thing was terrible and very sad. We lost eleven." Dawn nodded respectfully and shook Valerie's hand as she was preparing to leave. Her handshake told Valerie that she was confident but not forceful. She liked the fact that Dawn seemed sure of herself without being overbearing, and Valerie wondered. Maybe it didn't matter how she looked. She was clean and neat, although her style was as far from Valerie's as you could get.

"I don't mind working long hours, by the way," Dawn volunteered. "I don't have a boyfriend. I live in the city, and I love to work. Weekends are okay too." She was very appealing in a lot of ways. She was quick, bright, and willing, even if Valerie thought she looked weird. She wondered what April would think about her, and suspected she might like her. But April could afford to have someone who looked like that in her kitchen, a lot more easily than Valerie could, meeting guests on her show. But if Valerie liked her, which she did, maybe others would too. She was trying valiantly to be open-minded about it, and told Dawn that the Human Resources office would let her know. Valerie made no commitment to her before she left. She needed time to think about it.

Half an hour later, Valerie picked up the phone with a sigh and called HR.

"So, what did you think?" the head of HR asked her. Dawn was the first candidate Valerie had seen, but she had to admit she was a good one. And her work credentials and references were excellent.

"I think she's smart as a whip even if she looks like a freak. I hate the pierces and the hair, and the tattoos."

"I know. I figured you would. She's about as opposite from Marilyn as humanly possible. But I liked her too. I figured you wouldn't take her, but I thought I'd give it a shot. She's everything you want, just the wrong look." It was true. She was young and fun and dying to work. She had watched Valerie's show before the interview and made intelligent comments about it. "Don't worry about it, Valerie. I'll tell her no. She knew it was a long shot too, and said it to me. Not everyone wants an assistant with cartoon characters up and down their arms, although I thought Tweety Bird and Tinker Bell were pretty cute."

"She'll be sorry about those when she's fifty," Valerie said sensibly, and then stunned the head of HR. "Hire her. I'll take her. I like her. She's smart. I can live with Tinker Bell and Tweety Bird. I need someone who can do the job, and I think she can. She knows nothing about weddings and entertaining, but she knows decorating. I can teach her the rest." She had taught Marilyn everything from scratch—she had been a schoolteacher before she went to work for Valerie, and had been the best assistant Valerie had ever had till now.

"Are you serious?" the surprised head of HR asked, impressed by Valerie's decision. It showed an openness to new ideas she didn't know Valerie had.

"I am," Valerie said firmly. "When can she start?"

"She said tomorrow if you want. If you don't mind, I'd rather start her next week, so we can process her and get all the paperwork done."

"That's fine," Valerie said easily.

"I think you made a good decision," the head of HR complimented her.

"I hope so. We'll see," Valerie said optimistically, and she called Jack back the moment she hung up, a little shocked herself by her decision. Jack apologized for having interrupted her earlier.

"It was fine," she reassured him, as she leaned back in her

chair and sighed again, trying not to think of Marilyn and miss her as much as she did. "I was interviewing a new assistant."

"That must be hard for you," he said sympathetically. "They're interviewing here for Norman's job. We haven't found anyone yet. It's too depressing even thinking about it."

"I know. I hired her," Valerie said, and then she laughed. "She's right out of a sci-fi movie, with pierces all over her face and blue hair. *Brave New World.* I figured what the hell, she's a Stanford grad, she's got great references, and she's willing to work long hours and weekends. She's got tattoos of Tweety Bird and Tinker Bell on her arms in living color and didn't even wear long sleeves to hide them. You have to give her credit for that."

Jack laughed at the description. He couldn't imagine Valerie with an assistant like that. "Good for you. She might turn out to be terrific."

"I hope so," Valerie said, and then he invited her to see another movie at his apartment that night. It was one she had wanted to see but had missed in the theaters. She was enjoying the time they spent together, and had seen him only three days before.

"I'm off until the Super Bowl and I'm bored stiff," he complained. He still had trouble getting around on his crutches, and he was supposed to stay off the leg, at least for a few weeks. He said he felt like a shut-in and had been watching soap operas and agony talk shows all day.

"You may be bored," Valerie said to him, "but I'm working my ass off here. Christmas is over, but we're already working on our Valentine show, and I start working on weddings right after the new year. We're busy as hell."

"Does that mean no?" He sounded disappointed. He had had a good time with her and wanted to see her again. She hesitated, and then shook her head. It was about opening those doors to a new friend, and making time. He was right.

"No, it just means that I'm whining about all the work I have to do. I just had lunch with April. She said to say hello to you," and had commented on his ten million young girlfriends, which Valerie didn't say to Jack. He was more than willing to admit to them himself.

"Say hello to her from me. I need to go in for some of her magic healing mashed potatoes. Maybe I should just spread them on my leg." He never complained about the pain, which Valerie thought was brave of him, although she knew he had been used to some pretty brutal injuries during his football career.

"I can have her send you some, like she did in the hospital," Valerie suggested.

"If I sit here, watching TV and eating mashed potatoes and mac and cheese for the next three weeks, I'm going to weigh four hundred pounds by the Super Bowl, and I won't look so good on air. It's driving me nuts that I can't do any exercise, but the doctor says not yet." He was normally a very active man, although the herniated disk two months before had slowed him down too. He worried about getting fat. "So how about dinner and a movie?"

"I'd love to. Can we make it a little bit late?" She had been planning to work at home that night, but if she stayed late enough at the office, she could get a lot done. Sometimes it was hard juggling a social life and work, and her priority was always her job. "Does eight-thirty work for you?"

"That sounds fine. I was going to suggest that anyway. I have a physical therapist coming at seven to work on the leg."

"Perfect. Do you want me to pick something up for dinner?" she offered.

"Don't worry. I'll order in. I'm good at that." He laughed. "See you later," he signed off, sounding happy, and so was she. It was fun having a buddy to spend time with. She knew a lot of people, but they were busy too. And normally, he had a very active social life, but now that he was housebound he had more time on his hands than usual, and after what he had done for her, she was more than happy to visit him while he convalesced. It seemed like the least she could do. And she enjoyed his company.

She picked up some magazines and a book for him at a newsstand, leaving work. She didn't have time to go home and change. And she arrived at his apartment promptly, looking slightly frazzled and a little bit out of breath. She hadn't combed her hair or put on lipstick since noon. She hadn't had time to think of it all day. She was wearing casual slacks and a sweater, a parka, and flat shoes, since she hadn't been on air that day. She'd been at her desk since early morning, except for her lunch with April. It had been a full day of making decisions and plans for future shows, selecting samples, guests, and topics they wanted to cover. She always did that at this time of year, mapping out the shows. It was going to help her a lot when Dawn started the following week. Valerie just hoped she'd be as efficient as she had seemed in the interview.

Jack opened the door, perched on his crutches in sweatpants and bare feet. The nurse didn't seem to be around. And odors of something delicious were wafting from the kitchen. He had ordered Indian food, spicy for him, and mild for her in case she preferred it.

"Something smells great," she commented as she took off her jacket. He had music playing on the stereo, and she followed him into the kitchen as she had on New Year's Eve. He had ordered a ton of food, and it was still warm enough to eat. So they sat down at the kitchen table quickly after she set it.

"I'm beginning to feel like I live here," she teased him, since she knew where everything was now. And they talked about her day and what she'd done. He told her about a football scandal he'd been following all day. He was planning to do a show about it once he was back on his feet. It was a lively exchange. Then they discussed network politics, which were always complicated. There were rumors that the head of the network was leaving, which was a concern in terms of the impact it could have, but both of their situations were secure. No one was going to get rid of Valerie Wyatt, and he was the biggest sportscaster on TV. But nothing in television was ever totally sure.

There was a lot of talk too about the recent terrorist attack. It was still all over the news. Official groups all over the Middle

East were in an uproar about it, and wanted no association with it. They were furious over the damage it had done to their image and worried about the impact on their relationships with the U.S. They had all expressed sympathy over the lives that had been lost. And the president and governor were trying to reassure the public that nothing like it could ever happen again, but they knew it could. No one was safe anymore. And hardest for those who had lived through it were the friends and co-workers they had lost, like Jack and Valerie with their assistants.

By the time they finished dinner, both of them were tired and relaxed. They walked up to his den, and forgot about the movie as they talked. There seemed to be a thousand topics they were interested in and had opinions on, and they watched a few minutes of *Monday Night Football* that he had recorded, and he explained some of the plays to her, in preparation for her trip to the Super Bowl.

"You're still coming, right?" he asked, looking worried, and she smiled at him.

"I wouldn't miss it. April was impressed that I'm going. I like your idea about continuing to open doors and explore new things. I told her about it at lunch." She was tempted again to tell him about the baby, but didn't. She just couldn't bring herself to admit to being a grandmother yet. Maybe when she saw the baby she'd feel differently. But right now all it was to her was an assault on her vanity, a confirmation of her age, and a worry for her about April. "She's juggling an awful lot these days," she said cryptically to Jack, without saying more.

"She always does. She's an incredibly competent young woman. She runs that restaurant like a Swiss clock. I suspect she learned that from you." He smiled at Valerie. He already had a sense of how organized she was. He was a little more haphazard about how he approached things, but he got a lot done too. Except for now. He was going stir-crazy being stuck at home. He had worked hard with the therapist in the gym in his apartment. The bullet had done more damage than he thought, and the leg was still painful and very weak.

They were both surprised to discover that it was midnight by the time they stopped talking. Valerie put on her parka and bundled up. It was cold outside and had started snowing during the evening. It looked like a Christmas card, and Jack looked forlorn as she got ready to leave, although she could see that he was tired.

"I'm sorry I can't walk you home." He would have liked to, but there was no way he could. "Maybe you should take a cab. It's late." He didn't want her to get mugged on the way home, but Valerie smiled.

"I'll be fine. It's nice to get some air." And it was so pretty while it snowed, until the next day when it turned into a mess.

"Thanks for coming to see me," he said, looking boyish. "I like hanging out with you," he said, as he pulled her gently toward him as he leaned on his crutches. "You're good company, Valerie," he said, and meant it.

"So are you." She smiled shyly, feeling different vibes from him than she had before, and she wasn't sure what they were. Probably nothing. They just liked each other, and were both lonely and bored. And the aftermath of the attack had shaken them both up. Valerie still got anxious every day when she went to work and walked into the building. And although Jack had gone to April's restaurant with her once, he seemed to prefer staying home in his cocoon where he felt safe, and didn't feel ready to go out again. It had affected both of them more than they'd realized at first, but they'd been warned that that could happen, and more than likely would. There was no way to survive something as traumatizing as that without aftershocks. They'd been told to expect to experience aftereffects of the trauma for as much as a year.

"Will you come back tomorrow?" he asked, still holding on to her jacket, as though trying to keep her from running away. She laughed at his question, and was touched by the look in his eyes.

"You're going to get tired of me if I come every day, silly," she teased him.

"We didn't watch the movie. We could watch it tomorrow night." He sounded needy suddenly, which seemed unlike him, and she was sure it was a result of what he'd been through, and a sign of post-traumatic stress.

"I have to go to a network dinner tomorrow night," she said with regret, and he looked startled.

"I was supposed to go to that too. I guess I can't, or shouldn't. I hate those things anyway."

"So do I, but they're command performances. And I have no excuse. I didn't get shot in the leg. You're off the hook."

"I'll call you," he said, and they kissed each other on the cheek and she left.

She was walking down Fifth Avenue in the falling snow, thinking about him, and her cell phone rang. She thought it might be April, who often called her late when she closed. But it was Jack.

"Hi," she said, as the snow fell on her head and wet her face. It felt great. "Did I forget something?"

"No. I was just thinking about you and wanted to say hello. How's the snow?"

"Gorgeous," she said, grinning. She hadn't had a call like that from a man in years, for no reason at all. "You'll be out in it again in no time." She knew how restless and bored he was.

"Valerie, I really like you," he said suddenly. "I love talking to you, and spending time with you." And then he added, "And you're a great cook." She laughed.

"So are you." They were living on takeout food, which wasn't unfamiliar to her. "I have a good time with you too," she said, as she stood at a corner, waiting for the light to change. She was halfway between his place and her own, with Central Park glistening white across the street, blanketed by the snow that had been falling that night.

"What if something happens between us?"

"Like what?" she said, looking vague as the light changed. There was no traffic on the street.

"Like boy-girl stuff. You know." He sounded cute and young as he said it, and she smiled.

"That sounds a little crazy, doesn't it? I'm old enough to be the mother of the girls you go out with." Or worse, the grandmother. She didn't say it. But the thought was like a punch in her stomach. He went out with women forty years younger than she was.

"What difference does that make? Falling in love isn't about age. It's about people. And those girls aren't appropriate for me either. They're just a hobby, or they were. Because I had nothing else to do with my time. You're the Super Bowl, baby," he said, and she burst out laughing. "They're just practice in the backyard."

"I've never been called that before." But she knew that it was a compliment coming from him. "I don't know, Jack. I thought we were friends. It would be a shame to screw that up."

"What if we didn't? What if it was right for both of us?"

"Then it would be a good thing, I guess." But it was too soon for either of them to know that yet. And she didn't want to be just a fling to him, between shifts of his young girls.

"Why don't we keep it in mind?" he said softly, and she didn't answer for a minute, not sure what to say. "How does that sound to you?" He wanted an answer from her, and she didn't know which one to give. She wasn't sure.

"It sounds interesting," she said cautiously.

"Possible?"

"Maybe." She wouldn't rule it out, but she thought that in theory he was too young, and she too old, although there was only a ten-year difference in their ages. But it seemed like a lot to her, particularly given his history and lifestyle.

"That's all I wanted to know," he said, sounding happy. And then she thought of something.

"Are you involved with anyone now?"

"No. Are you?" He was pretty sure she wasn't from all she'd said. But it never hurt to ask. Sometimes old lovers were lingering in closets, and still dropped by for sex from time to time. That was always good to know.

"No, I'm not."

"Good. Then we're both free. Let's just see where it goes." But she liked where it was. It was so comfortable being friends with him that she hated to turn it into a dating or seduction game, playing cat and mouse. She loved the friendship they were just beginning to share.

"I like being your friend," she said softly.

"Me too. That'll work for now. Where are you anyway?"

"I just got to my place," she said, slightly out of breath from the cold. "I'm outside."

"Well, go on in. Don't catch cold. I'll call you tomorrow. Sleep tight."

"You too."

They hung up and she walked into the building, thinking about him. She didn't want to do anything foolish or that she'd regret. But she liked him, a lot. And then she remembered his theory about being brave enough to open new doors. She had no idea if they'd ever open this one, or even if she wanted to. But at least it was nice to know, she reminded herself as she went up in the elevator, that the door was there, whether you opened it or not.

Chapter 13

Valerie saw Jack half a dozen times before the Super Bowl. She went to his apartment for dinner, and he took her to April's once. They went out for pizza at a restaurant for a change and a real movie in a theater, and they always had a great time. They went to an art exhibit in SoHo, of an artist Valerie knew, and a play at Lincoln Center. They talked endlessly about every subject, and the relationship between them was growing warmer but building slowly, and neither of them was rushing it. They had no idea if it would ever be more than this.

The most exciting time she saw him was at the ceremony a week before the Super Bowl, when the mayor gave him the award they'd promised him, at a highly publicized event at City Hall. The medal they bestowed on him was for bravery in the service of his fellow citizens in the face of grave danger. They gave him a certificate and a medal and the governor was there too. He had always been a big fan of Jack's.

Every news team from every channel attended, and Jack invited Valerie to be his guest. His son came down from Boston, and Valerie thought he was a very nice young man. He was tall and clean-cut and as handsome as his father, and he looked very proud of him as they gave Jack the award. Valerie had brought April with her, and the four of them spoke for a few minutes before Jack had to go for a photo op with the mayor and governor. He was using a cane by then and not crutches.

Valerie left with April after the ceremony, and Jack called her later to thank her for coming. It had been a touching event, and both April and Valerie had cried. There had been a moment of silence in honor of the lives that had been lost. All April could think about was what if her mother had died, and Valerie was shaken by it too. April had worn a big, heavy down coat, and her growing pregnancy still didn't show. She was nearly five months pregnant by then and hadn't heard from Mike in nearly a month, and was pretty sure she never would again. April kept reminding herself that she had never expected him to participate anyway, so this was no different. The only difference was that he had turned out to be so likable and appealing that now she would have liked him to be involved. The pregnancy had turned out to be more emotional than she had expected. She cried a lot, which was unheard of for her. And she felt fragile and vulnerable, which was her hormones working overtime, but it was unsettling anyway. Her doctor said it was to be expected, espe-cially in a first pregnancy where April had no frame of reference and everything was new to her.

April said something about it to her mother in the cab leav-ing City Hall after the ceremony. "I never used to cry," she said, blowing her nose.

"You've also never been pregnant, and by a guy who refuses to give you any emotional support." Valerie was seriously an-noyed with Mike about it, and she and Pat had discussed it sev-eral times, but there was nothing they could do. Pat had asked her if she thought he should call Mike, but Valerie didn't think so, and thought April would be upset if she found out. She said it was really between the two of them, but April's father was upset too. He thought disappearing was a rotten thing for Mike to do. This wasn't how they had wanted their daughter to have her first child.

April was very brave about it and didn't complain. She worked as hard as ever, and Jean-Pierre seemed to lend an extra hand wherever possible, almost too much so. He was always at her beck and call, anxious to help her. It was making her un-comfortable. April didn't want to take advantage of it and en-courage him. She had other things on her mind.

April and Valerie talked about her going to the Super Bowl in the cab. April still thought it was funny that she was going, but she had to give her mother credit for doing something new. And she and Jack had apparently become good friends, after their shared experience of the terrorist attack. April was aware that her mother was spending a lot of time with him, but April didn't think there was anything more to it. They had survived a terrifying experience, and they were just friends. And for the moment, that was how Valerie thought of it too. They saw each other frequently, but neither of them had stuck their neck out farther than that, and she was glad. She had no desire to spoil a good thing, and it might.

The buildup to the Super Bowl was tremendous. There was endless press about it. Jack was back on his feet by then, though still with a cane. The network put him back to work, and he did several pre-Bowl interviews with major players and both coaches. He was fully back on deck again, and running in a thousand directions all at once.

He stuck his head in Valerie's studio one day when she was taping. She couldn't react, and he just waved and disappeared. They never saw each other at work; neither of them had time.

Valerie's work life was going smoothly these days. Dawn had turned out to be even more efficient than Valerie had hoped. And she had dyed her blue streak purple. Valerie just smiled about it. She was growing fond of her.

It had been emotional for Jack going back to the building at first, more so than he had expected. All he could think of as he walked in was what had happened in the lobby when the hostages were freed. He had arrived in his office shaken and pale. He missed Norman, the young production assistant who had been killed. And other staff members were missing too, which they all noticed. Valerie had also lost a cameraman from her show, in addition to Marilyn. There had been a service in the lobby for the victims several weeks before. All the employees and families had attended and Dawn had come with her and cried, even though she hadn't worked there when it happened. She felt a special bond to Marilyn, through all that Valerie said about her. It was still a hard time for them all, but everyone was doing their best to put the experience behind them and move on. And no one liked talking about it at work. It was too real.

The night before they left for the Super Bowl weekend Jack reminded Valerie again of everything she needed, and all the parties they were going to. There were events every night and throughout the day. She had done a very funny broadcast on her own show, saying that after years of telling people how to do Super Bowl parties, she was actually going to the game to see for herself.

There was going to be coverage of her there too. Her attendance and Jack's, and particularly together, were major media events for the network, and they planned to take full advantage of it. Jack was actually going to interview her briefly during one of his broadcasts. And Valerie needed clothes for every appearance, every party, and the game, since she would be televised there too. She had three valises packed to take with her on the corporate plane. The head of the network and his wife were flying down with them.

"Three valises?" Jack said, sounding shocked when she told

him. "Are you kidding? I'm only taking one, and I'm on air every day."

"Yeah, but you don't need coats, shoes, and matching purses," she answered glibly.

"Christ, Valerie, the girls I usually take to the Super Bowl wear a miniskirt and a rhinestone bra."

"Yeah, I'll bet. Well, you can still take one of those. It's not too late."

"I'll go for the coats and matching bags. At least you won't throw up all over me when you get drunk on beer."

"Now, there's a plus." She chuckled. She was actually excited about going now. They were flying to Miami in the morning and staying at the Ritz-Carlton in South Beach. She hadn't been to Miami in years. And this was clearly a major event in American culture that she had never paid much attention to before. It was totally out of her realm. He had already been briefing her on football for several weeks. She knew the names of the important players, both coaches, and could identify some of the plays by the correct terms, after he explained them to her with the help of taped games and replays. She had paid attention and learned her lessons well. And Greg, his son, was coming down from Boston with three friends and meeting them there, but staying at a different hotel. As little as Jack said his son cared about sports, he still loved coming to the Super Bowl. It reminded him of when he was a little kid and watched his dad play.

Jack picked her up in a limo on Friday morning at six o'clock, and they were at Teterboro at seven to board the network's corporate jet. Bob Lattimer, the head of the network, was there, looking excited and relaxed, with his wife, Janice. She was from Texas and knew everything there was to know about football. By sheer coincidence, her father had been a college football coach, and she continued Valerie's education on the flight, while picking her brain for suggestions for their daughter's wedding in June. It was a fair trade.

Jack and Bob talked football all the way down. They talked about the team they were sure would win, the best players, the teams' weaknesses and strengths. Valerie felt as though she was taking a total immersion course as she smiled across the aisle at Jack. She had worn white slacks, white Chanel flats with gold tips, and a blue cashmere twinset, and was carrying a white cashmere coat, with diamond studs on her ears. She looked as though she had stepped off the pages of *Vogue.*

"You look gorgeous!" Jack whispered to her, as they walked off the plane, and a flock of photographers took their picture. It had all been set up in advance. The network wanted to take full advantage of their two big stars. "Thanks for being such a good sport," Jack said, as they came down the stairs from the plane. She knew what she'd been getting into, and she had agreed. It wasn't a surprise or an ambush. It was all prearranged and approved by her as to how it would happen. And Jack looked equally handsome in a blazer, open blue shirt, gray slacks, and alligator shoes without socks, since the weather was warm. He looked sexy and totally at ease, and was able to stand to his full height again, which was impressive. For the photos, he got rid of the cane. And he looked tall and powerfully built as he stood next to Valerie in the photographs. They talked to the press briefly, and he said that Valerie was their visiting dignitary, and was going to lend some class to the event, as all the reporters laughed. There was no implication that there was any kind of romance between them. No one would have thought it. They were just two major network personalities coming to the Super Bowl, and he was the star sportscaster for the game, as he always was. This was where Jack shined. Valerie loved seeing him in his element, and had new respect for him as she saw how knowledgeable and competent he was.

A limousine was waiting to take the two of them to the hotel, and Bob and Janice Lattimer went to a fully staffed house on Palm Island that had been rented for them for the weekend.

It was a half-hour ride from Signature Aviation at the airport to the hotel. And when they got to the Ritz-Carlton, there was more press. It was apparently a big deal that Valerie Wyatt was there. Other stars would show up for the weekend, but her presence was definitely making a big splash.

She knew from their schedule that they were attending a luncheon at The Restaurant, and there would be a press conference before it where Jack was expected to speak. She didn't have to do anything except be there, and he had meetings that afternoon. She was hoping to do some shopping on her own. Dawn had surprised her and said she knew Miami, and had told her where to go.

Jack had an enormous suite, and she had a similar one across the hall from him. The living room of hers was handsomely decorated, with a beautiful view of Miami and the ocean, and the bedroom was comfortable and huge too. He came across the hall to check on her and make sure she was settling in. He looked distracted and busy, but was attentive to her in spite of it.

"Everything good, Valerie? The way you want it?" he asked, looking concerned.

"It's terrific," she said, beaming at him. "I'm feeling very spoiled." He was impressed that she was so easy about things. He knew that some women as important as she was behaved like divas and nothing was ever good enough. Valerie was appreciative of everything the network did, and loved her suite. "Is there anything I can do to help you?" she offered.

"Yeah," he said, looking tired as he sat down. The leg was bothering him, although he didn't want to admit it, and he was more tired than he had expected to be. He didn't have all his strength back yet, although he looked great. "Go to these meetings for me. I'll go down to the pool and sleep." She laughed at the suggestion, and he came back half an hour later to pick her up, and by then she had changed. She was wearing a pink silk dress and high heels for the lunch. It was sexy and pretty, but in good taste. The women he usually brought with him had to be carefully monitored so they didn't embarrass him wearing see-through dresses, and a thong to the pool. It was a lot easier having Valerie along, and a whole different scene.

They arrived at the luncheon in a white limousine, and Jack was part of the press conference, as expected, talking about what the fans could look forward to and how he thought the game would play out. And they got just a brief clip of Valerie and asked her what she thought of the Super Bowl so far, and she said she thought it was just great. They didn't need more from her than that.

After lunch, her own car picked her up, a white Escalade, and she disappeared to Bal Harbour, and browsed through all her favorite shops, everything from Dolce & Gabbana to Dior and Cartier. The shopping center was terrific, and she did a fair amount of damage and bought three bathing suits, a pair of sandals, and two sweaters, and then went back to the hotel for a massage.

She didn't see Jack again until seven, when he stopped by her room, and with a loud groan lay down on the couch in her suite. He was so tall, his feet hung off the end.

"God, I'm beat, and it hasn't even started yet." He knew the next few days would be insane. They always were.

"Do you have time to take a nap?" she asked, with a look of concern. She was wearing a white terrycloth robe and looked relaxed after her massage. She'd had an easy afternoon.

"Not really," he answered. They had to leave in half an hour for a cocktail party. Some of the big football players would be there, and he had to attend. Jack had a double role here, as a retired Hall of Fame player, and as a star sportscaster, and he had to go a lot of places to wear both hats. He forced himself back off the couch a minute later, and went to his own room to get dressed. He would much rather have stayed in the suite with her,

213

ordered dinner, and watched a movie on TV. But there was no chance of that.

He came back in a black Prada suit with an impeccable white shirt, looking very stylish, and she was wearing a short black cocktail dress and towering high heels. They made a handsome couple, he noticed in a mirror they passed as they left her suite.

"We look pretty good together," he commented.

"You'd look good with anyone, Jack," she said, smiling at him, and he leaned down to kiss her cheek.

"So would you, pretty lady. I'm just happy that it's me."

"You don't miss the miniskirts and rhinestone bras?" she said, and he laughed.

"Not likely. And that dress looks pretty short to me," he said, referring to what she was wearing. It was short, but fashionably so, and showed off her legs, as did the heels.

They both drifted into the crowd and lost each other at the cocktail party, and were photographed, although separately, and an hour later they were whisked away to another dinner event at The Forge, attended by many of the major players, their wives, the owners of the teams, and just about anyone important who was in town. It was quite a scene. There was dancing afterward, but all the players left immediately after dinner. It was nearly one in the morning by the time Jack and Valerie could slip away and go back to the hotel. Jack looked drained.

"Are you okay?" she asked, looking worried about him. "How's the leg?"

"It's okay." He hadn't danced, though. He wasn't up to that

yet. "I'm just tired. It's tough being on all night like that. You look as fresh as when we left the hotel. I don't know how you do it," he said admiringly.

"I'm not working as hard as you are," she pointed out, "I'm just a tourist here." And she hadn't been shot a month before.

"Thanks for being here," he said, as the limo pulled up to their hotel.

"I'm having fun," she said, and meant it. "This is totally new to me. And you're right about opening new doors. This is really cool," she added enthusiastically, as he laughed and they both got out.

He left her at the door to her suite and kissed her chastely on the forehead. He would have liked to come in and chat with her, but he was just too tired. Getting back to work with a bang like this was wearing him out. Being shot had definitely taken a toll, more than he wanted to admit. He slept like a log that night, and was up at the crack of dawn and went to the gym to work out. He was still cautious about it, but he had exercises he had to do. And he knocked on Valerie's door on the way back to his room. She was wearing her nightgown and a robe, and said she had slept well too.

The first thing on their agenda was a brunch at eleven, hosted by the network, followed by a luncheon afterward. Then he had interviews to tape with important players. He interviewed Valerie briefly first, and she admitted that she was a neophyte and knew little about football but was having a ball being there. After that, he did longer interviews of the major players, coaches, and team owners, and Valerie went to the pool. Jack worked till dinnertime, and there was another huge party that night, hosted by one of the major sponsors of the game. She wore a short gold dress and looked spectacular, and Jack introduced her to several legendary players, including Joe Namath, who had come for the weekend too. It was one of those unforgettable weekends, when everybody came. Jack was constantly talking to someone, being photographed, or introducing Valerie, signing autographs for fans, talking to players he knew, or posing for photographs with her or other Hall of Fame players. He never stopped. She watched him in awe as he worked the room. He was great at what he did, personable with everyone, and adored by all. The network knew what they were doing when they hired him, she realized. Before she knew him, she had just assumed he was some ex–football player. Jack was an icon in the football world. There was no question in her mind now as to who was more important or more famous. She finally understood that Jack Adams was a football legend whom generations would talk about and remember. No one was going to remember her weddings or her books in fifty years, but they would surely still be talking about him. She hadn't fully realized that until today.

They went to three different parties that night, all around Miami, and wound up at a nightclub where some major movie stars and rappers were hanging out. It seemed like every famous person on the planet was in Miami for the game. They got back to the hotel at three A.M. The players didn't stay out that night, they had to go to bed early before the game the next day. The game was starting at six, and Jack had to be there at noon, to do background newscasts, and interviews all day. This time, he followed her into her suite before he went back to his own. Although it was later, he looked less exhausted than he had the night before. He felt like his old self and was on a roll.

"What an evening!" she said, as they sat down in her room. "It was awesome! I am having an absolutely fantastic time!" She beamed at him. And she had had a ball at all the parties they went to that night. "I think I'm going to tell people to forget Super Bowl parties from now on, just come down for the weekend and the game." He laughed as he looked at her. He was happy she was enjoying it so much. And she was much more fun for him than the girls he usually brought. She was beautiful, elegant, intelligent, fun to be with, she had a great sense of humor and talked to everyone, and she wasn't drunk off her ass, flirting with some linebacker while his wife threatened to kill her. It was a lot easier bringing Valerie than the girls who'd come with him before. "It really has been a fabulous weekend." She smiled at him. "Thank you for inviting me."

"I'm glad I did. It's been fun for me too." He knew she had a VIP seat in a box the next day, and he wouldn't see her until after the game. "Let's have breakfast in your suite tomorrow before I leave. I'll be gone most of the day." She was planning to relax and hang out at the pool before the game. And then he reminisced for a minute about how exciting it used to be for him before a Super Bowl game. She had learned since they'd been there that he had been Super Bowl MVP of his team twice. And she had seen his four Super Bowl rings among his trophies in his den in New York. It all had more meaning to her now since she'd actually seen what a big deal it was. Being in the thick of it with him in Miami had already taught her a lot.

"It must have been hard for you to give all this up and retire," she said sympathetically.

"I didn't have a choice," he said sadly for a minute, remembering. "My knees were shot. I was thirty-eight years old, and if I pushed it, I could have hung in for two more years, max, and maybe wound up in a wheelchair. It wasn't worth it. I had seventeen great years in the NFL. That's a lot. And they were seventeen very, very sweet years. It doesn't get better than this, if this is what you love. It's a lot of work, but I never regretted it for a minute."

"That's a nice way to feel about what you do."

She loved her work, but she realized now that this was different. This kind of stardom was very different from hers. And there was a glory and magic that went with it, which was almost unique, except in sports. Major rock stars got this kind of adulation and acclaim, but athletes and their adoring fans were a very special world.

She was glad she had come here and seen it. It had helped her to understand Jack better, and the life he had lived. Given the huge star he had been, it was amazing to her that he wasn't intolerably conceited. Instead, he was proud of what he'd done, but reasonable about it. He had achieved great things in his field that few men ever did, but he was a remarkably normal, real person, and she loved him for it. Coming to the Super Bowl had given her a whole new perspective on him, and how serious he was about his work. She truly liked him as a person. He'd been nothing but respectful of her. He seemed to appreciate everything she said and did, and they had a genuinely great time together. He was a pleasure for any woman to be with.

"I've honestly had a fantastic time here," she said, looking happy. This door had been worth opening, to a whole other world she would otherwise never have seen. "Did you see Greg today, by the way?" She knew his son had arrived in Miami for the game, but she hadn't seen him, and she wondered if Jack had.

"Just for a few minutes. He's going to come sit in the broadcasters' box with me for a while, before the game. There are a couple of players he wants to meet. I was hoping we could have dinner with him tomorrow night, but he's got to leave right after the game, and everything will still be nuts for me then. I probably won't get to see you till way after the game. I hope you don't mind."

"Of course not. This is what you do. I understand." Their plane was scheduled to take off at midnight, and she suspected he might be taping interviews till then. "Now I can't wait to see the game." Everything that had led up to it so far had been terrific. She had enjoyed all the parties and people, the outfits and the sights. It was an extraordinary combination of people involved in football, and the fans that followed everything they did, just as they had once followed him.

"I hate to go back to my room," he said finally as he got up. It was three-thirty in the morning and he had to get up early. All his pregame interviews were done, but he had to be at the stadium to organize everything. This was the high point of his year. "See you in the morning, Valerie," he said with a yawn, and as she walked him to the door of her suite, he smiled down at her, and then kissed her on the mouth, ever so gently. But it was almost a real kiss this time. Not quite. But it wasn't the same kind of friendly peck she'd had from him before. "We have to talk one of these days," he said, as he put an arm around her, "but not here. When we get back to New York." She nodded. She had a feeling she knew what he had in mind. She was glad he hadn't rushed it. She wouldn't have been ready to make any fast moves or decisions, or to fall into bed with him. She didn't want to be a groupie, a passing fancy, or a one-night stand. If she got involved with him, she wanted it to mean something to both of them, and be real.

"No hurry. I need to get a miniskirt and a rhinestone bra first," she said with a serious expression, and he laughed.

"You know, I'd like to see you in that, just once." He loved the elegant outfits she had worn during the weekend. She had stood out in every crowd. And people recognized her everywhere.

"I'll see what I can do," she promised, as he bent down and kissed her again. And this time, it was a real kiss. She knew he meant business, and she melted into his arms and kissed him back. He looked startled when they finally stepped away from each other, his eyes open wide, and they were both out of breath.

"Lady, let me tell you something, with kisses like that, you don't need a rhinestone bra!"

"Goodnight, Mr. Adams," she said demurely as she opened the door and he ambled slowly across the hall to his own suite, and looked back at her with tenderness and passion in his eyes. Something had happened to both of them during the weekend. They had been swept up in the excitement, but they had stayed grounded with each other and what they shared was beginning to seem very solid.

"Goodnight, Ms. Wyatt," he responded, and with that, she smiled at him, and gently closed the door.

Chapter 14

As promised, Jack showed up in her suite at ten o'clock the next morning, dressed for work. He had an hour to spend with her over breakfast, and told her about everything he had to do before the game. He was looking forward to it, and seemed in great shape and high spirits. He had pancakes and bacon, sausages, muffins, two glasses of orange juice, and a cup of coffee. He was a big man, and he knew he wouldn't have time to eat again for hours. She asked him questions about the game, and by the time he finished eating, he had to leave. He kissed her on the way out, and it was another kiss like the last one of the night before. Things were heating up between them, and she realized it was probably a good thing that they weren't spending another night. She didn't want to get caught up in the holiday atmosphere around them and do something they'd both regret. If they leaped into the abyss together, she wanted it to be real and well thought out, and so did he. After kissing her, he gently patted her behind as he walked out the door.

Valerie spent the rest of the day peacefully, and had lunch at the pool. She had another massage because she had nothing else to do, and packed her bags before she left for the game. She was wearing white jeans and a T-shirt, red loafers, and she had a red cashmere sweater over her arm in case it got cool that night. And she was excited when she left the room. Jack had called her on his cell phone every chance he got, whenever he had a break. He said everything was crazy at the stadium, as usual. He had done half a dozen more interviews by that afternoon, and called her again when she was in the car.

"I'm on my way," she said, sounding excited.

"I'll be able to see you, but you won't see me," he told her. "I'll meet you back at the hotel about eleven o'clock." He needed two hours to do victory interviews and wrap up after the game. There would be a victory party that night for whichever team won, but they weren't planning to go to that. Like Valerie, he had already packed his bags and left them in his suite.

She wished him luck then for his broadcast and said she knew it would be great. April had promised to watch it, so she could see him and her mother when they played her taped interview at halftime. And Valerie had TiVo'ed it at home, so she could watch him when she got back.

Valerie got to Dolphin Stadium at five-thirty, half an hour before the game. She wanted to get to the VIP box and check out the scene before the game started. Fans were already thronging into the stadium when she got there, and some had been seated for an hour. People were selling souvenirs, buying hot dogs, drinking beer by the gallon, and half-naked girls were already cheering for their teams. It was a rowdy crowd. There was an astonishing amount of security, and Valerie knew from Jack that nowadays they did everything possible to prevent terrorist attacks, which were a real fear now and never had been in his day. It took Valerie a full ten minutes to get to the box and take her seat, and by then the lavish pregame show had started. Bob and Janice Lattimer were there. They were staying in Miami till the next day, and would be going to the victory party that night. Bob introduced her to several other people in the box, and Valerie took her seat, and saw Jack begin his broadcast from the monitor in the box.

They stood for the national anthem, performed by Stevie Wonder, and two minutes later the game was off and running. There was a wild cheer from the crowd when one of the star quarterbacks made a touchdown in the first ten minutes. Janice explained the plays to Valerie, and she had no trouble understanding what was going on. The other team scored a touchdown in the second quarter. The score was even at halftime, and a blimp hung over the stadium with cameras shooting the scene and the huge halftime extravaganza, complete with dancers and sparking rockets, several acts from Cirque du Soleil, and a brief performance by Prince.

Valerie watched Jack do an interview with Joe Montana and Jerry Rice after her own interview during halftime, and then the game was back on. The action was fast and furious, and the score kept bouncing back and forth between the two teams. The crowd was going wild. There were shouts of agony or glee even from the VIP box and Jack was busy commentating for the crowd at home, as Valerie watched him on the screen as often as possible, without missing the action on the field. And finally a field goal won it, as the favored team came in with the expected victory Jack had predicted to her that morning. But it had been close. There were tears of joy on the field, and probably many of disappointment too. And Valerie was smiling as she turned to watch Jack wrap up. He was waiting for some of the players to come and talk to him, and he was killing time till then by commenting on details and surprises of the game. Valerie was one of the last to leave the VIP box as she watched him on the screen.

She rode back to her hotel, after saying goodbye to the people she had met in the VIP box, and thanked Bob Lattimer for the trip and his wife for all her explanations, and wished her well with her daughter's wedding in June. As far as Valerie was concerned, it had been a fantastic night. She got back to the hotel at nine-thirty, and flipped on the TV to watch Jack do the last of his interviews. He finally went off the air at ten, and half an hour later he was back in her suite. He was still on a high from the game as he walked into her room. He looked happy but beat. She congratulated him on his accurate prediction, and said he had done a great job commentating the game. And as always, he looked terrific on air.

He helped himself to a beer and sat down, talking about the game with her, and twenty minutes later he called the bellman to get their bags. He hadn't stopped for three days. And she noticed that he was limping slightly again. He had worked nonstop since they arrived, and she had enormous respect for what he did. She had had no idea how demanding it was, just as he hadn't understood that about her career before they met.

They were still talking about the game and the players in the limousine. At eleven-thirty they were at the airport, and the plane was waiting for them. It was going to come back to Miami the next day for Bob and Janice, but Jack wanted to get back. He was exhausted, and Valerie had to go to work.

They walked up the stairs to the plane, and Jack didn't begin to unwind until he sat down. The flight attendant had sandwiches waiting for them, and a bottle of chilled champagne. She poured them each a glass, and Valerie toasted him with a warm smile.

"To the real hero of the Super Bowl! You did a terrific job!" He was touched by her praise, and pleased with how the broadcast had gone too, and he was happy to hear that she thought his interviews were good. He always put a lot of thought into them and had been well prepared, and she said it showed. She was truly impressed by how hard he worked, and how conscientious he was about his broadcasts. For Valerie, the weekend had been perfect from beginning to end.

The plane took off ten minutes after they'd gotten on board, and Valerie remarked how much easier it was than commercial travel. Jack looked over at her, smiled, and took her hand in his own.

"Thank you for being so wonderful all weekend." She had been lively, enthusiastic, interested in everything, great to be with, loving, supportive, everything he could have wanted.

"Sorry I didn't manage to come up with a rhinestone bra. Next year," she promised, and he laughed.

"You get my vote for MVP," he said, and then leaned over and kissed her, as passionately as he had that morning and the night before. They seemed to be growing closer every day. They had been seeing each other as friends for a month, since the terrorist attack. And they'd spent a lot of time together, and were coming to know each other well. And they had fun together.

They talked for a few more minutes, and then he fell asleep until they landed. They touched down in New York at three in the morning, after taking off at midnight from Miami. There was a limousine waiting next to the runway to take them home. And an hour later, they got to her apartment, and he was about to drop her off, and then said he'd go upstairs with her, and make sure she got in safely. She laughed at the additional attention. She was in no danger in her own building, but he insisted. What he really wanted was to kiss her away from prying eyes.

The doorman set down her luggage in the front hall of her apartment and went back down in the elevator, as Valerie took her coat off, and Jack then took her in his arms. He was hungry for her, and a minute later, they were kissing passionately again. She could hardly catch her breath when they stopped.

"I have a question to ask you," he said softly, as he nuzzled her neck with his lips and held her close. "Can I spend the night?" She pulled away from him and looked into his eyes. "I won't if you're not ready . . . we have time . . ." But he wanted her more than he had any woman in his life. She was worth waiting for, but he had been burning for her all weekend, more than any twenty-two-year-old in a miniskirt and rhinestone bra.

"Is this crazy?" she whispered back between kisses. It didn't feel like it to her, it felt right, but she wanted to be sure it did to him too.

"This makes more sense than anything I've ever done," he said, and she nodded. She thought so too.

"Yes," she said simply in answer to his spending the night, and he called the driver of the limo and told him to send up his bag and then he could go home. It arrived five minutes later, and Jack carried it to her room and set it down. She was sitting on her bed, smiling at him. The room looked immaculately neat, and hadn't seen a man in years. There was one lamp lit on the bed table, and the light in the room was soft. He gently took her clothes off and lay down with her, as they looked at each other in her enormous bed. She felt like she had been waiting just for him, for a long time.

"I don't want to hurt you," she said gently. "Is your leg okay?" He nodded and then laughed.

"I've got a bullet wound in my leg, a bad back, football injuries to my knees. Baby, you are getting yourself one very banged-up old man." But he looked and felt like a boy in her arms, and then she turned off the light. She had worked hard with her trainer, and looked great for her age. But she didn't want him comparing her body to a twenty-two-year-old's. He kissed her, and all the passion that had been waiting in both of them exploded. They both forgot about his leg and his back, they were so hungry for each other that they couldn't get enough of each other, and made love for hours. He'd never had a night like that before, and the difference, he realized, as he drifted off to sleep holding her, was that this time, for the first time, he was in love, and so was she.

Chapter 15

April called her mother the next morning as Valerie stood
naked in the kitchen, making scrambled eggs for Jack. She
had burned the first batch, and was now diligently scrambling
the second, while he read the sports page of the paper. He had
made her so comfortable and happy that she didn't mind standing there nude with him.

"How was it?" April asked her.

"Incredible," Valerie said dreamily, no longer thinking of the
game, and then rapidly rescued the eggs before she burned
them again, and told April she'd have to call her back. She said
she was on the other line.

Jack kissed her as she set the eggs down in front of him, and
he ran a hand slowly down her body. He was an extraordinary
lover, and had been exquisitely happy with her too, and he insisted that neither his leg nor his back had gotten hurt. He had

been afraid to have sex for months, and suddenly it seemed as though he could do anything he wanted. But their lovemaking hadn't been acrobatic, it had been tender and so powerful it was overwhelming. He had never felt that way before.

He looked happy as he ate the eggs.

"I'm better with French toast," Valerie apologized, and he laughed.

"Yeah, I'll bet. I'm just teasing you. The eggs are great, and so are you. What are you doing today?" He had taken the day off, to bask in the glory of the Super Bowl. He didn't have to be on air again for two days, so he decided to give himself a well-deserved break. He had left a message on his assistant's voicemail before breakfast.

"I have to work." And Dawn was expecting her.

"I think you should call in sick," he suggested, and she laughed.

"I never do that. What if I lose my job?" She knew that wouldn't happen. And she had no tapings until Thursday, but she had a lot of work to do. She had taken Friday off to go to the game, which was something she never did.

"If you get fired, I'll support you. Maybe I'll quit mine." He was kidding. They both laughed. After their night of passion, neither of them was in the mood for work. This had never happened to Valerie before.

"Great. We've been lovers for . . ."—she looked at the kitchen clock—"five hours, and we're already both headed for unemployment."

231

"Sounds good to me," he said happily. "We can stay in bed all day and make love." She had to admit it sounded appealing to her too.

"Maybe I could," she said dreamily. "I haven't taken a sick day in a year, come to think of it, maybe two."

"I think it's an excellent idea," he said, putting his arms around her, and getting instantly aroused.

She reached for her cell phone on the table, between kisses, and left a voicemail for Dawn, telling her she had come back from Miami with a terrible sore throat and was taking the day off to stay in bed. It was half true anyway, about staying in bed, as he took her by the hand and led her back to her bedroom. They were passionately making love again five minutes later, and lay spent in each other's arms when it was over.

"You're too young for me," she panted, totally out of breath. "You're going to kill me."

He was just as breathless as she was. "You make me feel like a kid again," he said, holding her close, and stroking her hair, and a few minutes later, they fell asleep in each other's arms and woke up again at noon.

They got into the shower together and wound up making love again, and after that they went back to the kitchen and Jack made lunch. He made them both club sandwiches, while Valerie commented that she was relieved that the woman who did her cleaning didn't come in on Mondays. And exceptionally, she had taken the following day off too. The coast was clear for their wild, abandoned lovemaking. And after lunch they went back and watched old movies in bed. Valerie had never spent a day like this in her life. She felt totally self-indulgent and lazy, and in love, as she nestled in his arms.

April called her late that afternoon and sounded worried when her mother answered. "Are you okay? I called you at the office, and they said you were sick. You didn't sound sick this morning. What's wrong? And you never called me back."

"I'm sorry, darling. I have a terrible sore throat. I think it might be strep."

"Did you see the doctor?"

"No, not yet," she said guiltily, smiling at Jack, as he ran a lazy finger around her breast, and she responded instantly to his touch. "I will. I promise."

"If it's strep, you need antibiotics," April said firmly.

"I'll call immediately. I just stayed in bed all day."

"That's good. Stay warm," she advised her. "I'll call you later and see how you feel."

"Don't worry if I don't answer. I'll just be asleep," Valerie said, not wanting to be interrupted if they were making love.

"How was the Super Bowl, by the way? You said this morning it was incredible."

"It was." She had been referring to Jack, not the game, as she burned the eggs. But the game had been great too.

"I watched the game in the kitchen. I thought Jack's commentating was very good, and his interviews. Was he nice to you?"

"Very," her mother assured her, smiling at him as he lay in bed next to her. "How are you feeling?"

"Fine. Fat. I think it's going to show pretty soon. I hate having to explain it to everyone. I'd like to keep it under wraps as long as I can." She was a week shy of five months pregnant, and she felt huge, after being thin all her life.

"I don't think you can do that for much longer," Valerie said. "It's no one's business. You don't have to explain anything."

"I think some of my staff have already figured it out." Jean-Pierre certainly had, and he was being exceptionally attentive and helpful, and carrying anything heavy for her. She appreciated his help, but his obvious attentions were making her increasingly uncomfortable. No matter how cool and professional she was with him, he refused to back off.

"I'll call you tomorrow, sweetheart," Valerie said in a gentle tone.

"Take care of your throat. Tea and honey. And call the doctor."

"I will. Thanks for calling back."

Valerie hung up and turned to Jack. And he kissed her again. He spent the night with her again that night, and totally out of character, she took the day off the next day, and told her office she had strep.

"I can't keep doing this," she said, looking embarrassed, as they ate dinner out of her fridge. "I have to go to work tomorrow. I have a mountain of stuff on my desk."

"I think we should both quit," he teased, but he had to go to work the next day too. It had been nice to take two days off and spend them with each other, talking, sleeping, making love, and watching TV. It was a first for Valerie, and she hadn't looked or felt this relaxed in years, or as happy. She hoped it wasn't just a passing fancy for him, but it didn't feel that way. This felt serious to both of them. "Why don't we go to my place tonight?" he suggested. "My maid doesn't come in on Wednesdays." They were trying to keep this quiet for as long as they could. Valerie didn't want to tell April yet, or anyone. This was their secret for now, and she was still somewhat uncomfortable about the difference in their ages. And he had been such a womanizer that whoever he went out with was bound to cause comment, particularly if it was she. But she didn't feel any older than he. She felt protected by him, and safe in his arms. And the years between them vanished in bed.

Around ten o'clock that night she packed a small bag to go to his apartment, and put her clothes for the office on a hanger, and they took a cab to his place. He had his suitcase from Miami with them. Hers were still unpacked in her bedroom. All she had taken from them were her makeup and her toothbrush. She set them down in his bathroom and hung her clothes in the closet. She felt very much at home. And they took a bath in his enormous marble tub.

"What are we going to tell people?" Valerie asked, looking pensive, as they ate ice cream in his kitchen after their bath. "Or should we just lie low for a while until we figure this out?"

"I already have figured it out," he said calmly, as he smiled at her. "I'm in love with you. Do you think sky-writing over Manhattan would be too showy? Maybe just an announcement to Page Six," he said, referring to the gossip column in the *New York Post.*

"Don't worry. They'll guess soon enough," Valerie assured him. "I've always liked the old expression 'Discretion is the better part of valor.' But I'm not sure how discreet it's going to be when people figure this out. We're both pretty visible people."

"I suggest we just suck it up and enjoy it. We don't have anything to hide. We're both single. Do you think April will mind?"

"I don't think so," Valerie said thoughtfully. "I don't see why she would, and she likes you. What about Greg?" Jack's son was younger and might be upset, Valerie thought.

"He said he liked you when he met you," Jack said simply. "So we're covered. Our kids are the only ones who matter. To hell with everyone else." He meant it. Other than that, all he cared about was her. It all seemed very simple. So much simpler than she had ever hoped for. She thought of Alan Starr then and his prediction on her birthday. He had finally been right.

They went to bed then, and got up early the next morning. Jack made breakfast. He made eggs and bacon worthy of April's restaurant. They were delicious, and after debating about it for a minute, they decided to share a cab to work. They walked into the building together, and no one seemed to notice or care. The building was teeming with people as always, and he kissed her lightly when he got off the elevator. No one fainted or screamed or pointed. He smiled at her and said, "Call you later," and got off.

When she got to her office, Dawn looked concerned. "How's

your throat?" Although she was young, she was very maternal with Valerie at times. She liked her a lot, and loved her job. And Valerie was equally happy with her.

"Fine. Why?" Valerie looked blank. She had completely forgotten her excuse for not coming to work. "Oh, that. Much better. Strep. I'm taking antibiotics." She walked straight into her office and got to work. She was taping her big Valentine show the next day. It seemed well suited to the mood she was in.

Jack came down and visited her at lunchtime. He was in great spirits. They had won the ratings hands down for Sunday. Everyone was pleased, and she was proud of him.

She had to work late that night, and she promised to stop at his apartment on her way home. She got there at eight-thirty, and never left. She had to go to her place to dress for work the next day. The maid was there and said she thought Valerie was out of town. That was the only possible reason for her not sleeping in her bed. Valerie realized that everyone would know soon. It was too complicated to lie. She just smiled and didn't say anything. She put on a red Chanel suit for the Valentine show. Jack came by half an hour later to take her to work. They were suddenly inseparable, but Valerie liked it. She loved being part of a couple with him. She told him about the show she was doing that day, on their way to work.

"What are we doing for Valentine's Day, by the way? Why don't we go to April's?" he suggested, and Valerie nodded, thinking that she should say something to her before that, but she wasn't sure when.

As it turned out, Valerie stopped in to see April on Saturday for lunch on the way to the hairdresser. The opportunity presented itself easily, when April questioned her about him.

"You're seeing an awful lot of him, aren't you, Mom? He's a very busy guy. I don't want you to fall for him and get hurt. He's in here with young models all the time." Valerie nodded thoughtfully and looked at her. She had never lied to her daughter and didn't want to start now, more than she already had.

"To tell you the truth, I already have fallen for him. And maybe I will get hurt, I don't know. He's ten years younger than I am, but it doesn't seem to matter. He's fallen for me too." April was quiet for a long moment and looked at her mother, not sure what to say.

"Does he treat you well?" she asked quietly.

"Very. He's wonderful to me. Kind, respectful, smart, fun to be with. It seems to work. Maybe it won't last forever, nothing does, I guess. But it sure is nice for now," she said, feeling guilty that this was happening to her and not to April, who had a right to it too, and needed it a lot more. Life just wasn't fair. She was sixty years old and madly in love, and April was five months pregnant by a man who wanted nothing to do with her or the baby, and she was alone. "I'm sorry, sweetheart. I feel kind of greedy having this right now. I'd much rather you have a good man to take care of you."

"I'm doing okay," April insisted, but she looked tired. She had been sad ever since the last time she'd seen Mike and his visit to the doctor had blown up in her face. "And I'm happy for you, Mom," she said sincerely. "You deserve it. I don't see why you should be alone. He's lucky to have you, and you're still young. I've always wanted you to have someone who is good to you. Dad is happy with Maddie. Why shouldn't you have someone too? And maybe Jack figured out that all those young girls weren't what he was looking for." She hoped so, for her mother's sake.

"Apparently. I still get nervous about it, though. Sixty is sixty, no matter how much I lie about it. And twenty-two is twenty-two."

"He was probably bored with them," April said sensibly. She hadn't expected it, but she was pleased about Jack and her mother. Valerie told her that she and Jack wanted to have dinner at the restaurant on Valentine's Day, and April was delighted. "I'll make you two a special dinner," she promised, and she hugged her mother when she left and told her again how happy she was for her.

"What did she say?" Jack asked Valerie when she got back to his apartment. They had spent every night together, at his place or hers, since they got back from Miami. And he had been a little nervous about April's reaction. You never knew with kids, at whatever age. He had mentioned to Greg on the phone that week that he and Valerie were dating, and Greg thought it was fine. It was not an issue. But girls were different, and he knew that Valerie and her daughter were very close.

"She was great," Valerie reassured him, and then kissed him. "She's going to make us a special dinner for Valentine's Day; I told her you wanted to eat there."

"Not with arsenic in it, hopefully," he said, still looking nervous, and Valerie laughed at him.

"I told you, she's fine. She has her own problems these days."

"What kind of problems?" he asked, looking concerned. "Is the restaurant doing okay?"

"The restaurant is terrific," she said, and didn't explain. But he was relieved to know that April was fine with their romance too. Green light. Go. Full steam ahead. All aboard. It made him feel better to know it. And so far, no one else had caught on, even though they'd been friendly and seen a lot of each other at work. People just assumed they were friends, since it had started that way. It was going to take them a while to understand, which was fine with them, although Valerie had the feeling that Dawn suspected but hadn't said anything. As he had said earlier, their kids' approval was all that mattered to them, and they had it.

Valerie and Jack went to dinner at April's restaurant on Valentine's Day, and she prepared a superb dinner for them, and sat down with them afterward. She was still at the table when one of the models Jack used to go out with walked in with a very good-looking young male model. She stopped at their table, and reminded Jack to call her sometime, and dismissed Valerie with a glance. It was obvious to her that he was having dinner with friends, particularly with April sitting at the table.

"I've missed you," she cooed at him, pouting, and giving him a look that left nothing to the imagination. And a minute later, April had to take care of a problem in the kitchen. Valerie was unusually quiet when she left, and Jack could see that she was upset.

"Don't let that idiot girl get to you," he said bluntly to Valerie. "I only went out with her once. She's a nutcase. She stole a hundred dollars out of my wallet. I guess she likes getting paid." He had gone out with nice ones too, but this girl had been one of the worst. He considered it bad luck that she had shown up at April's that night. And Valerie looked visibly shaken by it.

"You obviously slept with her, from the look she gave you," Valerie said, looking tense and hurt. And Jack sighed as he took her hand in his own.

"Sweetheart, I was stupid enough to sleep with half the models in New York at one point, but that doesn't mean I want them now, or ever will again. I love *you*. I feel stupid as hell for the life I lived before, and every now and then one of them is going to pop up like tonight, and make an ass of me, which I deserve and you don't. But don't let it ruin things for us, or upset you. I never cared about any of them, I was just having fun. This is a whole different world with us. I couldn't care less about them. You're beautiful and wonderful, and I love you," he said, looking at her soberly, and she felt better, and somewhat embarrassed for making a fuss about it, as April came back to the table and sat down with them again.

"Sorry, one of the damn dishwashers keeps breaking. I may have to get a new one," she said, and then noticed the look on her mother's face and knew she was upset. Probably about the model who had stopped to talk to Jack, but she could see how in love he was with her mother. She was genuinely happy for them, and Jack told her it had been a wonderful dinner, and thanked her.

They left a little while later, and April came out to say good-bye. Her mother looked better, but still somewhat bothered. And April kissed them both and told them to come back soon. And as she kissed Jack on the cheek, he suddenly looked at her, surprised. Her stomach had bumped into him while she kissed him. He looked down and could see that she was pregnant, and had a good-sized belly hiding under her apron. He looked back into April's eyes with a question in his gaze.

"Mom will explain it to you," she said shyly. "Or has she already told you?" It wouldn't have bothered her if she did. He was family now, by association with her mother.

"No, she hasn't," he said quietly. "Is that good news or bad news for you?" he asked, pointing at her belly, and she shrugged.

"A little bit of both. It's one of those things, a blessing in disguise maybe. I haven't figured that out yet." The cab was waiting for them and it was cold outside and April didn't have a coat on, so she hurried back into the restaurant and they got into the cab, and Jack was quiet after giving the driver Valerie's address. They were staying at her place that night, and still going back and forth every few days between his apartment and hers.

"Why didn't you tell me?" he asked Valerie, looking hurt.

"About what?"

"April's baby. She's pregnant. Who's the guy? I didn't know she had a boyfriend."

"She doesn't." Valerie sighed. "It was an accident. I met him once. He seems nice enough, he's a food critic. But he doesn't want her or the baby. Apparently, they only got together once, and poor April was very unlucky. She says they got drunk, which is unfortunate. And the antibiotic she was taking rendered her birth control pill ineffective." He felt sorry for her. It was a heavy burden for her to carry alone, with the restaurant. And it was bad luck that the father didn't want her or the baby.

"How terrible for her. Valerie, why didn't you tell me?" For the first time, there was reproach in his voice, and he wondered if she'd been too embarrassed, or was protecting April. That at least would explain it. But he thought they'd been totally open with each other, and this was a big piece of information to leave out, which must have been a worry to her. He wanted to be at the hub of her life, and useful to her, not on the sidelines. He was hurt that she hadn't told him.

There were tears in her eyes when she answered him. "Did you see that girl tonight? The one who said hello to you? How old is she, Jack? Twenty-one? Twenty-two? Twenty-three at most? That makes me thirty-seven years older than she is. That's who you used to go out with. And I'm ten years older than you are. I'm sixty and single, with a man who used to go out with twenty-year-olds, and on top of it, you expected me to tell you that I'm about to be a grandmother? I could be that model's grand-mother." She winced as she said it. "Just how bad does it get, and how old do you want me to look?" The tears were bright in her eyes. "I know it's vain and stupid, but I thought you wouldn't want me if I told you. I haven't gotten used to the idea myself, and I sure as hell didn't want to tell you at first. And besides, it's a miserable situation for April. But that's not why I didn't tell you. I just don't want to be the grandmother you sleep with." She looked so pathetic and vulnerable when she said it that he smiled at her, and had to keep himself from laughing. In a way, it was funny, here he had been sleeping with ridiculous young girls, with great bodies and no brains, and now he was sleeping with a woman ten years older than he was, and grandmother or not, he was head over heels in love with her. He put his arms around her and kissed her.

"I don't give a damn about any of those girls. I never did. And I'm going to love you, even when you're a great-grandmother. I love *you,* no matter how old you are, or how old you get, or how many grandchildren you have. Shit, Valerie, I'm no kid either, even though you make me feel like one. Half the time I look and feel older than you do." She smiled through her tears as he said it. He started to laugh then and couldn't resist teasing her a little. "And I promise never to call you 'Granny'!"

"Oh, *you!*" she said, and playfully swiped at him, and hit his arm. "Don't you *ever* call me that! If that child ever calls me that, I'll refuse to see it." But she cuddled closer to him and felt better. "I feel terrible for April. It's an awful situation," she said seriously. "I don't know how she's going to manage."

"She will," he said quietly, "and we'll help her. We can baby-sit for her, if we have to." He smiled at Valerie again then. "It can call us Jack and Valerie, no Grandma and Grampa, although I kind of like the idea of grandchildren, not right away of course, but one day."

"That's how I felt about it," she confessed. "Like at eighty. I wanted to tell you, Jack. I really did. And I almost did a couple of times, but I just couldn't get the words out. 'Oh, by the way, I'm going to be a grandmother in June.' Shit, that sounds so awful when you're trying to be young and sexy."

"You *are* young and sexy!" he reassured her.

"Not like the girl tonight," Valerie said sadly. "That's what young and sexy looks like." Valerie felt ancient when she saw her.

"No," he corrected her. "That's what crazy looks like. She was a lunatic. She's probably on drugs. She was as high as a kite when I went out with her, and I couldn't wait to get rid of her and never see her again. That's exactly what I *don't* want, and everything I wanted to get away from. Now I have, and I thank my lucky stars every day that I'm with you and not girls like that anymore. I felt stupid and I was bored, and I had nothing better to do. It was all about my ego. Everything I feel for you is about my heart, and the rest of me," he said with a mischievous grin. And as soon as they walked into her apartment, he proved it to her. He scooped her up in his arms and walked into her bedroom.

"Put me down, you'll hurt your back! That's not good for your leg!" she kept insisting, and he only laughed at her.

"To hell with my leg and my back! Are you telling me I'm old?"

"No," she said as he dumped her on the bed and fell on top of her. "I'm telling you that I love you."

"Good, because I love you too. Now enough about this crap about how old we are. It's Valentine's Day and I want to make love to you. Take your clothes off," he said, as he tugged them off her. She was laughing, and it all seemed silly suddenly, her reaction to telling him about April's baby, and the girl in the restaurant. None of it mattered. Only they did. And with that he made love to her as though they were both eighteen years old. They had been brave enough to open the right door, and lucky enough to find each other.

Chapter 16

Two weeks after Valentine's Day, April was standing on the sidewalk outside the restaurant, signing for the delivery of the new dishwasher she'd had to buy. She had her apron off and there was no hiding it anymore. Everybody knew she was pregnant. She hadn't told anyone who the father was except Ellen and her parents. And it was clear to her entire staff that she was facing it alone. They were being very nice to her, and helping her whenever possible. Two of her older waitresses in particular were being very motherly to her and said they wanted to give her a shower for the baby. Others were offering to lend her equipment she would need, and Jean-Pierre brought tears to her eyes when he gave her an antique cradle for the baby that he had found at a garage sale. It still didn't seem real to her, although the baby kicked her constantly. But she couldn't imagine what it would be like to have a child of her own once it was born. Most of the time, she tried not to think about it, and just went on about her work and running her business. She was exactly six months pregnant.

She was walking back into the restaurant, with her head down, following the men carrying the dishwasher, when some-one behind her touched her shoulder, and she turned around and found herself looking up at Mike. He looked very serious and very somber as he tried not to look at her stomach, but he had been shocked by its size when he saw her. She looked to him as though she were about to have the baby, which he knew she wasn't. But her belly was huge now. It had popped out in the last month, and all pretense of hiding it was over. She was a very ob-viously pregnant woman.

She looked at Mike uncomfortably and had no idea what he was doing there, and he seemed as though he didn't know either.

"Hi" was all he said for the first minute. And then "How are you?"

"I'm okay," she said noncommittally. "How are you?" She hadn't seen him in more than two months, since the fatal day at the doctor's when he had walked out and told her he just couldn't do it. She hadn't heard a word from him since, and hadn't called him. She respected his right not to participate if that was how he felt about it. She had given him that option right from the beginning, when she told him.

"I've been all right. I've been thinking about you. Could we take a walk for a minute?" She nodded, and knew the others would deal with the dishwasher. Jean-Pierre was in the kitchen, and he had become more than just a sommelier. He did a lot of extra odd jobs to help her, and he scowled the moment he saw Mike and didn't say hello. She and Mike started walking around the block together. She didn't want the others to see her with him or listen to them talking. No men ever came to see her, and she didn't want anyone to guess that he was the father of the baby, although Jean-Pierre had already guessed. But no one else had.

"I'm sorry I was such an asshole at the doctor's," Mike said simply. She nodded and didn't look up at him. She didn't really want to see him. But her heart was beating faster as she walked along beside him. And the baby was kicking like crazy. She had noticed that it did that whenever she got upset or excited about something, good or bad.

"It's all right," she said quietly. "I shouldn't have asked you to come. You took me to dinner once, and all of a sudden, I wanted you to see our . . . the baby." She didn't want to offend him by calling the child theirs. It wasn't. It was only hers now. She wanted it. He didn't. Or she had accepted the baby, and she knew he never would. He had made that clear at the doctor's and in his text message after, and his disappearance and silence since.

"I wanted to see it. That's why I went," he said as they stopped walking and sat down on a stoop. She looked him in the eye then for the first time, and it nearly tore her heart out. "And it was so real when I saw the sonogram, that it scared the hell out of me," he continued. "It just seemed like more than I could handle."

"I know," she said quietly. "I'm sorry."

"No, *I'm* sorry," he said, suddenly looking agitated. "That's what I came here today to say. I've been thinking about it for two months, and I know we didn't want this, either of us, but it happened. Maybe it was meant to be. Maybe it's destiny. I thought you were terrific the night I met you, even as drunk as I was. That's why I went to bed with you. And I think I was starting to fall in love with you when I got to know you better and met your family. And that scared the hell out of me too. You're everything I've avoided all my life. I spent five years with a woman and never really loved her, even though I said I did. That's why I wouldn't marry her and have kids with her. And you haven't asked me for a goddamn thing. Nothing. When I walked out on you, which was rotten of me, you didn't call, you didn't plead, or beg or whine. You didn't send me nasty emails and tell me what a jerk I am. You just went on with your life, dealing with this all alone. That's pretty goddamn brave. You have more decency and integrity than anyone I know. I've thought of you constantly for the last two months, and our baby. And yes, it is *our* baby. It's as much mine as yours, even if I ran away and was a coward. I was so goddamn scared we'd turn into my parents one day. And it took me two months to figure out that that's never going to happen. You're not my mother, you're nothing like her. You're everything she wasn't and couldn't be. And thank God, I'm not my father. And this baby isn't going to be like my brother, dead at fifteen, because nobody ever took care of him or loved him. This is a whole different ballgame. April, you're a wonderful woman.

And I don't know if I'm worthy of you, but I'd like to try to be. I'd like to see if we can make this relationship work. It's a little bit ass-backward starting out with a baby, and then trying to figure out if we like each other. But if we do, maybe we can be a family one day. And even if we can't, whatever happens, I'm this baby's father. And who knows, maybe it'll turn out to be the best thing that ever happened. I'm sorry it took me so long to get here, but if I promise not to be a shit and run out on you again, would you be willing to see me and see how this works for a while, and maybe we can figure out what we're doing?"

"You don't have to do that," she said softly. "You don't owe me anything. We were both stupid that night in September."

"You were less stupid than I was. You thought you had the pregnancy thing covered."

"I still forgot a pill or two, even without the effect of the antibiotic."

"Then we were both stupid." He smiled at her. "And even if I don't have to do this, I want to. I want to get to know you, and the baby." He looked nervous then, and she looked unsure about what he was saying. She had given up on him by then, and he could see it in her eyes. "Will you let me? I don't deserve another shot at it, but I'd like to try. And if it scares the shit out of me and I can't handle it, I'll tell you. I won't just run out on you like I did last time. I've been seeing a therapist, and I think that might make a difference." She was impressed by the lengths he had gone to, to try to face this with her. His going to the therapist seemed like a major step to her and almost made her want to try,

251

but she wasn't sure. She wondered if he was capable of making a real commitment and staying involved.

"Did you come to see me because your therapist told you to, or because you wanted to?" She looked up at him with big wounded green eyes that ripped his heart out.

"He doesn't know I'm here. I made the decision by myself last night." She nodded, and then she looked at him again. She was happy to see him, but didn't want to be too much so. She knew that if she hadn't been pregnant, she probably wouldn't have given him another chance. But she was pregnant, and in spite of her concerns and reservations about Mike, she loved him. The baby was a tremendous bond.

"Why don't we just see what happens?" she said hesitantly, not wanting to trust this too quickly. It was all she could offer him. She wasn't sure if she could trust him, or if she even wanted to. But she didn't want to lose him again either. Neither for the baby, nor herself. She wanted this to work. She had a huge investment in their relationship, in her womb.

"Will you let me take you to dinner? Or visit you at the restaurant?" She nodded, and he looked enormously relieved as she stood up. He knew that her willingness to try again was more than he deserved. She looked as though she were hiding a basketball under her shirt, and he smiled. Without thinking, he reached a hand out and touched her belly from where he sat on the stoop, and was stunned when it kicked him, hard. "Does that mean he likes me or he's mad at me?" he teased her. It touched his heart now that he had felt the baby kick.

"Maybe both," she answered, smiling slowly. She was happy he was back, even if she was afraid he'd run away again. "And what makes you so sure it's a boy?"

"A girl would be okay too. Is that what you want?" She nodded.

"That would be easier if I'm alone." He nodded too. He understood. He wasn't making any promises yet, just opening a door for both of them. It was a door he had been terrified to touch before, and now he was finally prying it slowly open. The hinges on it had rusted years before.

They walked slowly back to the restaurant, and he stood in front of it with her. "I'll call you. Could you do dinner tomorrow night?" She nodded.

"Thank you for coming, Mike. That was brave of you. Very brave." She knew how hard it must have been for him, and he had come anyway. Whatever happened, he had done the right thing, or was trying to, and so was she, by giving him a chance.

"I'll see you tomorrow," he said softly, and then awkwardly, he bent to kiss her cheek, touched her shoulder, and walked away. And as April walked back into the restaurant, she was smiling, and wiped away the tears rolling down her cheeks.

As he said he would, Mike called her the next day. He asked her what kind of food she liked to eat these days, and she requested something bland. She had heartburn now most of the time. He suggested an Italian restaurant they both knew and liked. He said he'd pick her up at eight. And he was there promptly. She was waiting in her restaurant, and went outside when she saw him arrive.

The restaurant they were going to was nearby, and they walked there easily. He asked about her restaurant, and she inquired about his work. They had lost the ease they had previously had with each other. But by the end of dinner, with a glass of Chianti for him, they both started to relax. He told her some funny stories about restaurants he'd reviewed, and one where he swore they'd poisoned him. They talked about her family, and she told him about Jack and her mother. And eventually, they strolled back to her place. They were both surprised by how long they had sat and talked. It was almost midnight. But they had a lot of ground to cover in a short time. He invited her to go to a play with him the following weekend. The theater critic at the paper had given him the tickets, and he thought it was something she'd enjoy. It was a musical comedy that was a current smash hit. She hadn't been to the theater in years.

The week after that, he took her to the movies, and for a hamburger afterward. They met at Central Park one afternoon and took a walk. And she invited him to dinner at the restaurant one Sunday night. He ordered pancakes again, and they both laughed. After three weeks of seeing a lot of each other, they were enjoying each other as they had before, even if only briefly. The stiffness had disappeared, and he had put his hand on her belly several times, and loved to feel the baby kick. She told him that if he spoke to it, it could hear him talk and would recognize his voice when it was born. He found that hard to believe, but lowered his face near her belly, and talked to it and said it better be nice to its mother, and that he was lucky to have her as his mother and that she was a fabulous chef. He was still convinced it was a boy. And one afternoon, they started talking about names. He liked Owen for some reason, and she Zoe. And then they decided they both liked Sam if it was a boy.

"Sam Wyatt has a nice sound to it." She smiled up at him. They had had another nice evening together, and were coming back to her place late, after they had seen a movie. The restaurant was already closed, and everyone had gone home.

"I was actually thinking of Sam Steinman," Mike said.

"It goes well with both," she said diplomatically, not wanting to count on anything, but their time together was going well. They held hands now in the movies or when they walked, and even at the dinner table, but he hadn't dared to kiss her yet.

"Do you want to come in for a glass of wine?" she offered when they got to the restaurant. "Or a cup of tea?" It was a balmy March evening, with unseasonably warm weather. It felt like spring. The following week she would be seven months pregnant, and she felt like she was getting bigger every day. The doctor said the baby was big.

"A cup of tea would be nice. I love the French decaf vanilla tea you have."

"So do I," she said with a smile, and unlocked the door. They turned on the lights in the kitchen, and she made them both a cup of the vanilla tea, and they sat on stools at the kitchen counter and drank it. They talked about the movie they'd seen, and disagreed amicably about the director's message. It had been a Polish film and had a very dramatic ending. She squirmed as they sat on the stool. It was harder for her to perch there now, with what felt like a beachball on her lap.

"You look uncomfortable," he said with a look of concern. But she didn't want to mess up any of the freshly set tables in the dining room.

"Do you want to come upstairs?" she suggested. She had bought two ancient overstuffed chairs at Goodwill while he was gone. Her mother had a fit when she saw them and told her to throw them away and that she'd buy her new ones, but April liked them, as she did the rest of her decrepit furniture. She said she didn't need anything better.

Feeling somewhat hesitant, Mike followed her up the stairs, and they each sat in one of the big easy chairs and drank their tea. He had enjoyed the evening with her. And then without even knowing he would or if they were ready, he leaned over and kissed her. He had wanted to for weeks, but hadn't dared. He got on his knees next to her and held her.

"April, I'm so sorry, I've been such a fool," he whispered. He wanted to make it up to her in every way he could. He kissed her again, and she reached up to him with every ounce of her being.

"Will you sleep with me?" she asked him, and he was stunned.

"Do you want me to?" She nodded. She wanted to lie with him and feel their baby between them. She wanted him to hold her. She didn't need anything else from him.

He kissed her again, and they slowly took their clothes off and got into her big comfortable bed. He had only been there once before, and it had changed their lives forever.

Her body looked beautiful to him when he saw it. She was as lithe and thin as she had ever been, and in the center of her was the enormous roundness of their baby. He ran his hands over her belly, and felt it kicking him again, and then he pulled her close to him, and lay with her, and in a few minutes, he was horrified to realize that he was aroused, and wanted her very badly. This time it wasn't drink or just raw sexual desire, it was much more than that. It was love.

"I'm sorry," he whispered into her long dark hair, which she had loosened from its braid so it fell over her shoulders.

"It's okay," she said, guiding him, and he moved away from her, terrified to hurt her. She turned and smiled at him and touched his face. "It's okay," she said again.

"We won't hurt the baby?" She shook her head and smiled.

"It's allowed."

He was very cautious with her, but he wanted her desperately. All the love and feelings he had held back for years came pouring out of him and into her, and their lovemaking was gentle and exquisitely sensual and erotic, and in the end, they both forgot the baby and plunged into the depths of passion for each other with total abandon, and then he lay peacefully and held her.

And then suddenly in the darkness of her room, he laughed. "April, I love you, but I think we must both be crazy. We've made love twice in our lives. Once drunk off our asses, and the second time with you seven months pregnant. Maybe one day we'll do it like normal people." He was a little shocked by what they'd done, but he had loved it.

"That felt pretty normal to me," she said, and giggled like a kid. It sounded like silver bells to him in the darkness.

"I'm not doing it again tonight," he warned her, "or the baby will come out and hit me." In fact, the baby hadn't moved while they were making love, and she had the feeling it was sleeping. And as Mike caressed her again, and the same urge rose in him, she made a liar of him a few minutes later.

Chapter 17

Much to their amazement, life became almost normal between Mike and April in the next few weeks. At the end of April, he moved in with her, although he had been there every night before. He went to work in the morning, and hung out in the restaurant. He helped out in the kitchen when they needed a hand. April looked blissful every time she looked at him. And everyone was relieved to see her so happy. The only one who wasn't was Jean-Pierre, and he made it obvious to April. It made his heart ache every time he saw them. He looked like a scorned lover, which she found irritating since he wasn't. He was only an employee with a crush on her and nothing more. She tried to ignore him. She had been honest with him and had never led him on. Her heart clearly belonged to Mike. And Mike thought the baby looked the size of twins. She got bigger every day.

She told her mother he was back. And Valerie told Pat. Jack

was relieved for her. He just hoped the guy was reliable and stuck around. Jack and Valerie came to have dinner with them one Sunday night. Although Jack had been leery of him, he admitted to Valerie afterward that he liked him.

"He seems like a bright guy. I just hope he treats her right and doesn't run out on her again."

"So do I," Valerie said, looking concerned. She had just bought a whole set of baby furniture for her grandchild, and Jack had teased her about it. But she was getting used to the idea.

She and Jack had planned a trip to Europe for early May, and they were leaving in a few days. They were going to travel for several weeks. London and Paris were on their itinerary, and a weekend in Venice. Jack called it their honeymoon. It was the perfect time of year for both of them to get away, since she was on hiatus and he had time off. They were still bouncing back and forth between their apartments, and couldn't decide where they wanted to live. So they stayed in both places, and decided where to spend the night, depending on their mood and schedules the next day. It seemed to work for now.

Valerie had hesitated about the trip at first with April so pregnant. But April had insisted her mother go, and now that Mike was living with her, Valerie was less concerned. And April said that if she started having any early warning signs, she'd call her mother and she could come home. Valerie had finally agreed.

The night before they left, they had dinner with Mike and April again. Valerie told April about the furniture she'd ordered for her, and April was touched. And Valerie warned her not to have the baby before she got back. She was still nervous about going.

April and Mike had discussed his being at the birth, but he wasn't sure. He was afraid it might be too much for him, and April wasn't pushing, but said she hoped he'd be there. If he wouldn't, Ellen had volunteered to go as April's coach.

Valerie called April on the way to the airport, and told her again to take care of herself and call immediately if there was any problem. She looked so vulnerable and so pregnant now. And her due date was only five weeks away. Suddenly it was all going very fast. Valerie planned to be back two weeks before the baby was due to come.

That afternoon April saw her doctor, who said everything was fine. April had told her that Mike was back the month before, and the doctor was pleased for her. She said the baby was a good size, and it was in the right position. April had had another sonogram but the baby's back had been turned and they couldn't see its sex, and April had decided not to check again and be surprised instead. It didn't matter either way, as long as it was healthy. She was still hoping for a girl, and Mike was just as hopeful for a boy named Sam. April kept insisting it was a baby girl named Zoe.

On the way home late that afternoon, she stopped for a cup of tea with Ellen, who was between patients and happy to see her. They talked about pressure points and things she could do to bring on labor, if she was overdue. April felt like she was ready to deliver now, and was already starting to have contractions if she worked too long, or was on her feet all day and night in the kitchen, which the doctor said was normal and didn't mean early labor or anything wrong. April was worried about who would cook in her absence when she went to the hospital. She didn't totally trust the sous-chefs to do it right without her.

"I have this vision of you having that baby in the kitchen, trying to fill your orders at the same time." Ellen laughed.

"It could happen. Maybe I could have it at night after we close, and be back in time for lunch," April said, smiling.

"You'd be just the one to do that," Ellen told her as she left. And April went back to the restaurant to start dinner. She had already done most of the prep work before she saw the doctor.

April smiled to herself as she started work, knowing that by then Jack and her mother were in Paris. He had been a wonderful addition to her mother's life. Her mother said she didn't want to marry him, she didn't need to. They had agreed that they were comfortable with the status quo, and neither of them had any desire to get married. In their hearts, they already were. They had been inseparable since December. Jack said it was the longest relationship he'd had since his marriage, and it was for Valerie too. And by far the best one.

They had a particularly busy night at the restaurant. Mike was out, having a long, elaborate dinner, for a review: She liked going with him sometimes, but they had too many reservations for her to join him. The restaurant was doing better than ever, and their reservations were a month out now. At this rate, she would pay her mother back earlier than she'd hoped.

Everyone in the kitchen was working hard that night, the dining room was full, and one of the sous-chefs was working the pans. April had her back turned when she heard a scream, and turned around to see a wall of flame on the stove. One of the pans had caught fire, and it had already leaped to a stack of towels that were in flames, as one of the sous-chefs threw them to the floor and stomped on them. While he did, the fire on the stove got even more out of control. One of the waiters was in the kitchen, and grabbed the fire extinguisher and pointed it at the stove, and in her panic, April took it from him and aimed it at the stove herself. But the fire wouldn't abate, and was getting worse. People were screaming, and Jean-Pierre ran in, and tried to pull April away. She pushed him off, and was aiming the fire extinguisher steadily, but the whole kitchen was in flames by then, and people were running out of the restaurant.

April could hear fire engines in the distance, but they weren't coming fast enough. Jean-Pierre and the others were screaming at her to leave, but she wouldn't. The restaurant that was her baby and first love was going up in flames, and she wouldn't leave it. The fire had leaped into the dining room through the open door, and the sirens kept getting louder. She felt her arms and the back of her hands burning, and suddenly there were men in the kitchen, finally, with hoses and water everywhere. The kitchen was thick with smoke, and a man in a black coat was carrying her out. Her head was swimming, and people were staring at her when they set her down on the sidewalk and put an oxygen mask on her. She kept fighting to get up, she could still see the flames inside the restaurant, and they were shooting water everywhere. The restaurant was going to be destroyed and she was sobbing, as two of the waiters knelt beside her and wouldn't let her stand up.

She heard the firemen call for an ambulance then, and shouting to someone that she was pregnant. All she wanted was to get up and go back inside. She was crying so hard she couldn't stop. The ambulance was there minutes later, and just as she was fighting them not to take her, April fainted. One of the waiters had called Mike on his cell phone by then. They said the restaurant was on fire, and looked like it would be destroyed, and April had just been taken away by ambulance, but they didn't know to which hospital.

Mike called 911 frantically and they told him to go to the Weill-Cornell burn center. All he could think about was April and their baby. The waiter had told him that she had fought the fire herself and wouldn't leave until the firemen carried her out.

Mike literally bolted out the door of the restaurant he was reviewing, and ran out into the street. He hailed a cab and was at the hospital in less than ten minutes. April was in the trauma unit, and he told the woman at the desk that she was eight months pregnant.

"Yes, we know," she said calmly. "There's an obstetrician with her now."

"Is she in labor?" He looked panicked. What if the baby died? Or April did? He didn't even know how badly hurt she was.

"Not that I know," the nurse at the desk answered.

"I want to see her!" he said, looking desperate.

"She's in cubicle 19C." She pointed to the double doors and he flew through them, and found himself amid a sea of people with gunshot wounds, heart attacks, head injuries, and the people with them and ER personnel, and then he saw her. She was unconscious, with an oxygen mask on, her hair still in a braid, her enormous belly sticking up, and they were treating the burns on her hands and arms. She had an IV in, and two doctors and a nurse were with her.

"I'm her husband," he said, without even thinking, and he meant it. "How is she?" April was deathly pale, and they were monitoring the baby. The heartbeat sounded strong.

"She took in a lot of smoke. Second-degree burns on her arms. How pregnant is she?" the obstetrician asked with a look of concern.

"Thirty-five weeks."

"She may go into labor. The baby is fine for now. Your wife's having some respiratory trouble. The baby may decide to bail if your wife is too distressed." Mike didn't know whether to scream or cry. He wanted to shake her for trying to fight the fire herself. How could she be so stupid? But she looked so sick and so frail as she lay there that he couldn't be angry at her. He just stood there and cried as he watched her helplessly. They worked on her for over an hour, and she finally came around, but she was coughing and throwing up and having trouble breathing. And the obstetrician reported regular contractions ten minutes apart. Her water hadn't broken, but they weren't happy with the way things were going. The only good news was that the baby's heartbeat was staying strong.

They kept her in the trauma unit all night, and Mike sat with her. She was too out of it to talk to him, and she had an oxygen mask on her face, but she knew he was there. They gave her something to try to stop the contractions, and by morning it had worked and they had stopped. April looked absolutely awful, and the stench of smoke was everywhere in the room they put her in to treat her. They kept the oxygen mask on her until that night, and said it was as much for the baby as for her.

Mike had called April's father, to let him know what had happened. He and Maddie came to see her that afternoon. They had gone by the restaurant and told Mike in a whisper that it looked terrible. But so did April. And that evening Mike called her mother at the Ritz in Paris. April hadn't wanted him to call her before. She didn't want to spoil her trip. It was midnight in Paris when he called. He told Valerie what had happened and that April was out of danger. The restaurant was a shambles, but her daughter was going to be okay, and so was the baby. They thought she'd probably have to take it easy for the next few weeks so she'd get to full term.

"Oh my God, how did it happen?" Valerie sounded shocked, and he could hear Jack in the background asking questions. She was upset he hadn't called right away, but she knew her daughter and how stubborn she was about not upsetting her mother, and correctly suspected April hadn't let him call.

"I don't know. I wasn't there," Mike said, sounding exhausted. "A pan fire, I think." Several of the people from the restaurant had come to see her that day. And they said the damage to the restaurant was almost total, as much from the water from the hoses as from the fire. April had done all she could to stop it, including risk her life, but she couldn't. They had insurance, but it was going to be a huge job to rebuild the restaurant, and he knew April would be heartsick over it. But the most important thing was that she hadn't lost the baby. All night Mike had feared this would be their punishment for not wanting it, and maybe now they'd lose it, but they hadn't. He was so grateful that both April and the baby were alive, he didn't care about the rest.

"I'm coming home," Valerie said firmly. "I'll take the first flight out in the morning," she said, as Jack nodded approval. Mike assured her that April was all right, just slightly burned and very shaken, but he readily understood that Valerie wanted to come home. She asked to speak to April, who took his cell phone from him. They had just taken her oxygen mask off. She barely managed to squeak out a hoarse croak but told her mother she was okay, and didn't want Valerie to return. She insisted she was fine and promised that Mike would keep them informed. She said they would stay at his place now, and gave Valerie the number. April insisted she didn't want them to curtail their trip, and said there was no need.

Valerie turned to Jack as soon as she got off the phone and burst into tears. It took her a few minutes to calm down, overwhelmed with terror and relief.

"What happened?" Jack asked her as he held her. From what he'd heard of her end of the conversation, it didn't sound good. But April was alive.

"The restaurant burned down," Valerie said as he held her. "April tried to fight the fire herself, and burned herself, and almost had the baby."

"I'll call the concierge and get a flight back right away!" Jack said, looking as worried as she did.

"April doesn't want us to," Valerie said, still in his arms. "Mike said she's okay, and he'll keep us posted. She sounds awful, but she's not in danger, and the baby is okay too. Maybe we should wait and see how she is tomorrow. It may upset her more if we go home." She knew her daughter. And she had to admit that it didn't sound like they needed to leave, but it was certainly upsetting. And she knew April would be devastated about the restaurant. She'd just have to be patient while they rebuilt it.

"I'll do whatever you want," Jack reassured her. "Stay or go back." He kissed her and Valerie nodded gratefully. In the end, they agreed to wait and see how April did in the next day or two before they made the decision.

Mike stood looking down at April once the oxygen mask was off. He didn't know whether to strangle her or kiss her, he was so relieved that she and the baby were okay.

"How could you try to fight the fire yourself?" He had tears in his eyes when he asked her.

"I'm sorry, Mike . . . I thought I could stop it, but it went too fast and it was too hot. They were caramelizing something, and it got out of control."

"You almost had the baby last night." Her hand went instinctively to her belly as he said it. "You were having contractions every ten minutes. They stopped it," he reassured her, but he wasn't letting her out of his sight again until she had the baby. "I told them a lie last night," he said then, "and I want you to make an honest man of me."

"What did you tell them?" She still looked woozy, but a lot better than she had the night before. She had color in her face again, and she said her arms and hands weren't too painful. The burns weren't as bad as they'd feared when she came in. She'd been very lucky, and so had he. He could have lost her.

"I told them I was your husband. I want us to make that true," he said gently, and then kissed her. Her hair reeked of smoke, but he didn't care. "Will you marry me, April? Let's do it before the baby's born. It would be a nice thing to do for him."

"Her," she corrected him with a grin, and then grew serious as she looked at him. "You don't have to marry me because I'm pregnant."

"I want to marry you because you're a menace and I want to keep an eye on you. The next time you try to put out a kitchen fire yourself, I'm going to kick your ass, April Wyatt. So will you do it?"

"What?" She was smiling at him. He was right. They were both crazy. But they always had been, right from the very first night. "Yeah actually, that sounds nice. Can I wait till I'm skinny so I can wear a pretty dress? I only plan to do this once."

"Me too. But I don't care if you wear your bedspread. Let's do it before your due date, if that's okay with you."

"I've always wanted to be a June bride." She was smiling broadly and still couldn't believe he had asked her. It felt like a dream.

"You're a nutcase. Maybe that's why I love you. But I'll say one thing, you've got more balls than a Christmas tree," Mike commented about her attempt to fight the fire. A part of him admired her for what she did, and another part of him wanted to yell at her for doing it.

"Can I call my mom?" she asked in the same hoarse croak, but she was beaming. He dialed the number at the Ritz again and handed her his cell phone. He was relieved that she looked so happy. The night before she had looked half dead. And their baby could have died too.

April asked for her mother's room, and Valerie answered the phone immediately, afraid of more bad news. She was relieved to hear April's voice.

"Hi, Mom," she said hoarsely. "I'm engaged."

"Are you on drugs, for heaven's sake?" Valerie asked her, still deeply upset by the news of the fire, only moments before.

"I don't know," April said honestly. No one had told her what was in the IV, and she felt giddy. "We're getting married."

"When?"

"In June, before the baby." She was holding Mike's hand as she said it, and he smiled.

"Could you please calm down until we get home?" Valerie said, her nerves frayed. "First you try to put out a fire, then you get engaged. Just sit tight and don't do anything till we get home. Sleep or something." She smiled then. At least it was good news this time. And she thought it was the right decision. She liked Mike, even if he had gotten off to a bad start. But she had always hoped he'd pull through, and he had. "Can I give the wedding?" her mother asked her, and April laughed.

"Of course."

Jack was gesticulating as she asked April about the wedding, and Valerie nodded at him. "Jack says we can give it at his apartment, it's bigger," her mother told her, beaming.

"Whatever," April said vaguely, it was hard to talk. "We only want a few people. We can do something bigger later, after the baby. When I can wear a decent dress." And then she wiped tears from her eyes. What had happened had been so scary, and she was worried about the baby too. "I love you, Mommy. I'm sorry I did something so stupid. I won't do it again." She sounded like a little girl as she said it, and looked up at Mike from her bed.

"I know you won't, sweetheart," her mother said kindly, with tears in her eyes too as Jack held her hand. "I hope nothing like that ever happens again." She knew how distraught April was going to be when she realized the condition the restaurant was in. She was still pretty dazed. It had been an enormous shock for her. "Just be a good girl now and take it easy. You have a wedding to get ready for, and a baby. Get some rest."

"I will," she said, and hung up, and handed Mike his phone back. And after he kissed her again, she smiled and went to sleep.

Chapter 18

They let April go home the next day. The baby was fine, and she wasn't having any contractions. And her oxygenation was back up to normal levels. She was still hoarse from the smoke, but other than the bandages on her arms, she was fine. Everyone kept telling her how lucky she was, and she knew it too, except for the restaurant.

They went to Mike's apartment, and he wouldn't let her go to view the damage on the way. But two days later he couldn't keep her from it. She stood and sobbed as she surveyed the debris. There was broken glass and water everywhere. They had knocked the plate-glass windows out to get in the hoses. The water had done far more damage than the fire. She didn't even know where to start fixing the place up. But Ellen's husband, Larry, came over and met with her. He assessed the damage and promised to line up subcontractors for her. He offered to do the job, and said he was sure they could complete it in three or four months. That meant August 1, or Labor Day, worst case. She said she could live with that, and the insurance money would pay for it. It had been an honest kitchen fire, there was no question of arson. Now she just had to sit it out for the next three months, or four at worst.

She was depressed when she went back to Mike's apartment, but he kept reminding her that it could have been a lot worse. And with Larry taking care of everything, she knew her restaurant was in good hands. She didn't know what to do with the employees, but offered to keep them all on. The only one who decided to go back to his old job was Jean-Pierre, but she thought it was the right decision and accepted his resignation with relief. His feelings for her made it too difficult for him, and for her. She was in love with Mike, not Jean-Pierre, no matter what his hopes had been about her. He was a great sommelier, and she was sad to see him go, but it was better that way. She had felt him watching her all the time with longing, and hostility whenever Mike was around.

Mike stayed home with her as much as possible. Her obstetrician had told her to take it easy for a week, so the contractions didn't start again. And she had nothing to do now anyway. She knew that Larry was meeting with subcontractors for her. And the restaurant had to be cleared of the debris. They weren't sure yet, but it looked like nothing could be saved.

She was lying in bed, thinking about it one afternoon, aware that Larry was seeing an electrician at the restaurant at three.

Mike was at the paper, and she was feeling fine. It seemed stupid to just lie around. She put on jeans and a T-shirt, braided her hair, and left Mike's apartment. He called her on her cell phone, and she told him she was in bed. She stopped on Third Avenue at a Walgreens to buy some gardening boots, and ten minutes later she got to the restaurant just as Larry and the electrician drove up. She was standing outside, looking mournful. She had brought her keys and unlocked the door. She'd given Larry a second set and he was surprised to see her there. He knew she was supposed to be resting.

"I thought you were home in bed," he said suspiciously, and then introduced her to the electrician. The three of them walked inside together, and the acrid smell was enough to make all three of them choke. They were standing in eight inches of water. "We've got to get this place dried up," Larry said. The basement, with all her wines, was flooded too. None of the bottles were actually on the ground, but in racks, so presumably they were okay. April made her way down the basement stairs to check, while Larry showed the electrician around. She let out a sigh of relief when she saw that the wines were safe, and lumbered back up the stairs.

They were standing in the kitchen when her cell phone rang again. It was Mike.

"What are you doing?" he asked casually.

"Nothing," she said innocently. And just as she said it, there was a tremendous crash in the kitchen, as the electrician pulled some boards away.

"What was that?" Mike asked, sounding worried.

"The TV," she answered rapidly, as she walked away from the others, so he couldn't hear their voices.

"There's something I've got to do. I'll be home a little late," he said mysteriously.

"That's fine. I'm just taking it easy here," she said, climbing over a pile of debris.

"Why do I have the impression that you're lying to me?" he said, as another board came down. This one made only slightly less noise than the first one. She almost told him the truth about where she was, but didn't dare.

"Don't worry so much. Honest, Mike, I'm fine."

"I don't trust you," he said, and she laughed. He was right.

"I love you. See you tonight" was all she answered. He had been wonderful to her since the fire, but he couldn't be with her all the time. He had to go to work, and he said he had a review to write that night. He still had to go back to the restaurant from where he'd bolted the night of the fire, but he hadn't had time to set it up yet, and he hated leaving her alone at night.

"See you later. Take it easy. Is there anything you want?" He was trying to be helpful, and had been really sweet to her. Now that he had decided to get on board, he was fussing over her all the time. The fire had scared him to death. He knew in an instant how much she, and the baby, meant to him. Every minute with her seemed like a precious gift to him now.

"Yeah, I want my restaurant up and running again," she said glumly, as she looked around.

"It'll happen. You heard what Larry said. Worst case by Labor Day. With luck, maybe three months." He knew how impatient she was, and how devastated she was by what had happened. But it could have been a lot worse. She and the baby could be dead.

"It looks a much bigger mess than that," she said.

"How do you know?" Mike asked, suspicious again, and she caught herself quickly.

"Uh . . . that's what Larry said. He and the electrician just called." He didn't believe her, and he had a sudden instinct about where she was. She was incapable of sitting still for five minutes, or staying away from the restaurant she loved so much.

"So did they change the reopening date?" he asked, sounding worried.

"No. I just don't see how they can do it in three months. He still thinks they can, or in four. But he promised we'd be open again by Labor Day." She sighed. It seemed an eternity to her. Four endless months.

"Why don't you try thinking about it as maternity leave? That'll give you two or three months with the baby while they put Humpty Dumpty back together. It'll be over before you know it. And summer is always a little slow."

"No, it's not." She sounded insulted. "We get all the people who don't go away for weekends. And even our regulars come in during the week."

"Sorry. Well, you're just going to have to take the summer off this year, or the better part of it. The baby will keep you busy. Maybe we can go to Long Island for a couple of weeks in July." He was trying to make suggestions to comfort her, but she would have none of it. She wanted April in New York open again, as fast as it humanly could be done.

"I don't think so," she said cautiously, not wanting to hurt his feelings, but she was a woman of determination, with a plan. "I should be here to oversee the work."

"I'll bet you will." He laughed. "Just try not to overdo it for now. You can watch, but don't lift anything. I don't want you to get hurt, April." They both knew she was in the home stretch, so to speak. The baby's due date was in just over four weeks. Now that they were together, time was moving fast. It had been two months, and he couldn't have been more loving to her if the baby had been planned. He was still nervous about it, but much less so than he had been before. The therapist he was still seeing had helped. Mike was totally on board. He talked to his friend Jim about it frequently, and he said he was proud of Mike. "See you tonight," he said, and signed off.

Mike had called his parents about the baby too. It was the first time he had called in years and predictably, it was a disaster. His mother was drunk when he called, didn't recognize his voice, and didn't care about the baby. She didn't even ask if he was married. His father was out, and he left his cell phone number, and they never called him back. Mike talked to his therapist about it and decided to close the door on that part of his life forever. They hadn't changed, and he had April and the baby now, and the opportunity for a happy life with them.

April went back to Larry and the electrician, who said he

could give her a better electrical setup than the one she'd had before. He told her where and how. It would be slightly more expensive, but she thought that it was worth it. He wanted to give her more built-in safety features, and greater electrical capacity than her old system had allowed. He said it would take two months to do the work, and he could start in two weeks, after he finished a job he was working on right now. Larry had put pressure on him to help her out. He had made a point of saying that she was unmarried, pregnant, and the restaurant was her only means of support. He was willing to play the violin if he had to, to help her get the job done, and she thanked him warmly after the electrician left.

"What do you think?" she asked him honestly. "You think we'll really get it up and running again?" He didn't doubt it for a minute, knowing her. She was a woman who, when she set her mind to something, would stop at nothing and overcome every possible obstacle in her path.

"It'll be even better than before," he promised, and he assured her again that it could be done in the time that he'd allowed. "I know you," he teased her, "you'll have the baby, put the restaurant back together, run for mayor, and open in the Hamptons in July. Maybe this would be a good time to look into that second restaurant you want, April. You can check out locations and see what's around."

"I just want to get this one going again," she said, looking anxious. Her mother called on her cell phone while she was talking to him, and she told her where she was.

"Aren't you supposed to be home in bed?" She was upset to hear what April was doing.

"Yeah. Sort of," she admitted, "but it's driving me crazy. We've got so much work to do, and I wanted to hear what the electrician said. He says it's going to be okay."

"Yes, but you and the baby won't be if you don't stay home and rest." She sounded like Mike, and April knew they were right. But it was too much to ask of her to stay away, with all of this going on.

"I won't do anything stupid, Mom. I promise. And I feel fine." She was still a little hoarse from the smoke inhalation, but otherwise she was okay, and she felt strong. And the baby was kicking her mightily again. In spite of the trauma she'd been through, her belly had grown again. She really did look now like she had a basketball under her shirt. The rest of her looked no different than before. Her constant moving around and hard work at the restaurant had kept her in shape.

When April asked, Valerie said she was having fun in Europe with Jack, and a few minutes later, April went to find Larry, who was studying the damage in the kitchen. None of their equipment could be saved. The hoses had finished off whatever the fire hadn't.

"I'm going to get the place cleared out by next week," he told her. He had looked at everything and already had a plan. "Then we've got to get it dry. You'd better start looking at new equipment. It's going to take time to find everything you want." She nodded. She had already been through it when she set April in

New York up the first time. This time would be harder, because they had so much damage to undo first. But Larry promised her they would be fast. He was meeting several more contractors there the next day. April promised to come in. He hadn't let her move anything heavy, but just being there in the heavy smell of smoke in the aftermath had made her feel a little sick.

She thanked Larry, they locked up, and she took a cab back to Mike's apartment. She was lying innocently on the bed when he got home at eight o'clock that night. She had washed her hair and scrubbed herself to get the smell of smoke off her, and added a dash of his aftershave. She had almost nothing at his apartment, everything she owned was still in the apartment above the restaurant, and most of that was going to have to be thrown away too. It reeked of smoke. She knew her mother would be thrilled to see the Goodwill furniture go.

Mike smiled at her as he walked into the bedroom, and bent down to give her a kiss. He instantly made a face. "You stink!"

"I beg your pardon?" she said, looking insulted. "That's your aftershave I'm wearing."

"You smell like Smokey the Bear. Don't tell me you've been in bed all day," he said, scolding her. But he had guessed it anyway. He would have had to tie her down to keep her away from the restaurant.

"I'm sorry." She looked at him apologetically. "I just can't not be there, Mike. There are so many decisions to make."

"So what did Larry say?" he asked, as he sat down in a chair next to the bed.

"He still thinks we're on track for Labor Day, and we met with the electrician. He's going to give me all new panels in a different location that'll work better for us, and give us more voltage. He says it's safer." It hadn't been an electrical fire, but it could have been, and that would have been worse. April brought him up-to-date on everything that had happened, and told him she had checked her wines and they were safe. And when she finished, he tossed some papers at her. She caught them in midair. "What's that?"

"Read it. See what you think. It's for Sunday's paper." She knew that was the most important day to run the restaurant reviews he wrote. There were three pages printed out from his computer, which she knew was a column that would run the full length of the page. Sometimes he used his column to cover two restaurants, but when he loved it or thought it warranted the space, he would write about only one. "I made full disclosure to my editor about our relationship. He got clearance from the editor in chief. It's all aboveboard."

"The following is a news item as well as a review," the column began.

For those of you who are not aware of it, there was a kitchen fire at April in New York this week. No one was injured, although the premises were damaged. The restaurant is already under repair and will be open for business again hopefully in August, and no later than Labor Day weekend. For those of you addicted to the food that master chef and owner April Wyatt serves there, even a three-month hiatus will be upsetting news.

Last September, I wrote a review of April in New York, which was less than complimentary. Knowing the credentials of Ms. Wyatt, I was irked by what I considered the plebeian fare she offered. Everything from melt-in-your-mouth mashed potatoes to traditional mac and cheese, meat loaf the way Hall of Fame Super Bowl stars like Jack Adams like to eat it, and pancakes for both adults and kids. I smirked at the root beer float on the menu, and had been told that the burgers and fries were good. If I remember correctly, I think I commented (in fact I know I did) that it was like Alain Ducasse, where she trained for two years and became his main sous-chef in Paris, cooking for McDonald's. What kind of restaurant was this? Pizza? Banana splits? Matzoh-ball soup? Okay, also steak tartare and gigot and escargots the way you only get them in Paris. This reviewer stands corrected. As those of you who practically live there know, I missed the point. April in New York is not only a place to find an exquisite dinner—perfect lobster, the finest sole meunière, osso bucco the way only an Italian can make it (she trained in Italy too, a total of six years in Europe before she brought her skills back to the States)—but it's also a home away from home, where lucky diners can find the best of the foods they love and grew up with, and real comfort food on a bad day, the kind your mother should have made and didn't, or at least mine never did. It's where your palate can be challenged, tempted, teased, and thrilled, and your soul comforted, depending on your needs of the day. The fish is not only fresh but exquisitely prepared. It's *perfect.* Chicken, roasted or Southern fried, melts in your mouth, and the mashed potatoes that go with it do the same. White truffle pasta or risotto in season were the only ones I've tasted that good in the States. Her wine list is the best collection of moderate-priced unusual wines I've ever seen, and are from Chile, Australia, California, and Europe. What April Wyatt has done is create a magic kingdom where the palate reigns supreme. But more than that, she offers a kind of atmosphere and comfort that meets other needs as well. Adults wait a month for reservations, and your kids will beg to go there. And don't miss the Grand Marnier soufflé. I am totally willing to admit that I missed the boat on this one. And I've been there often since, and realized how big a mistake I made. While others feasted on goose, pheasant, venison, lobster, turkey, and roast beef and Yorkshire pudding on Christmas, followed up by Yule logs and plum pudding or chocolate soufflé, what did I eat? Two stacks of the best buttermilk pancakes I'd ever had, with maple syrup. Why? Because I'd missed breakfast? No, because I *hate* the holidays, and Ms. Wyatt made them bearable for me with the comfort food I needed, and followed it up with a hot fudge sundae, sugar cookies, and homemade truffles Ducasse taught her to make himself. Don't miss this one! You'll have to wait until the end of summer, and for those of you already suffering from serious withdrawal, take heart, April in New York will be up and running again by Labor Day!

There were tears running down April's cheeks as she finished reading it and handed it back to him. She didn't know what to say. He had not only reversed his earlier damning position, but he had written the most incredible review she'd ever seen. But he believed every word of it, and they both knew it was true. And now everyone who read about the restaurant would know it too. When he wrote it he had had a moment of concern about what his editor would ultimately think when he found out that Mike was engaged to April, so he told them, and they still liked the piece. Mike stood behind every word he had written. He truly believed that her restaurant was one of the best in the city, for all the reasons he had stated. Her skills hadn't been underused there, she had used them in the most sophisticated, unpretentious way, to serve elegant meals to those who wanted them, and simple wholesome meals to those who didn't. Where else could you find athletes, movie stars, food buffs, and even six-year-olds thoroughly loving their meal and all under one roof? Only at April in New York. And even if he didn't love her, he thought her food was terrific, and admired the sheer guts of what she did, even in the face of tough critics and food snobs like him.

"Thank you, thank you!" she whispered, and threw her arms around his neck. He had done exactly what she had hoped he would do in the beginning. But this was even better. It wasn't just an objective review of her menu and wine list, it was also written from the heart and explained the philosophy behind it, and he had even let people know when she was planning to reopen. It was the best of all possible worlds. And then she suddenly worried about something as she hugged him and pulled away to look at him. "You didn't get in trouble for this, when you told them about us, I mean?" Mike shook his head, smiling at her, ecstatic that she was so pleased with it. He had hoped she would be. He owed her that. His earlier review had been unnecessarily bitchy, but the menu had annoyed him, even if he did think she was the sexiest woman who had ever lived. He thought she had taken the easy way out. But she hadn't. April always took the high road—in everything. She was that kind of woman. Instead of just easy food or hard food, she served people both kinds and wasn't afraid to do it. He believed every word in his review.

"It's all true," he said simply. "Truth is the best defense for anything. April, people all over New York talk about your restaurant. It's really something to be proud of, and when you open again, it will be even better. This will give you a little time to try new dishes, add some new things to the menu. Consider it maternity leave. Other women take three months off to have a baby, or even six. Enjoy it, play with your menu, watch your dream be reborn again. You have nothing to worry about. And I had noth-

ing to apologize to my editor for, except my first stupid, igno-
rant, utterly pretentious review. I owed this one to you." She sat
cross-legged on his bed, beaming at him.

"This is the best gift you could have given me," she said,
deeply moved by his generosity and the eloquence of his review.

"No, that is," he said, pointing at her belly, "and it's the best
one you could have given me, even though I was stupid about
that too. When are we getting married, by the way?" he asked
with interest.

"What about Memorial Day weekend? That gives my mother
two weeks to do it when she gets back. Although knowing her,
she could throw it together in five minutes. And it's a week before my due date." It was a little tight, but it made sense to her.

"What if the baby comes early?" he asked, looking worried.
He really wanted to marry her before the baby came. He thought
it was important to do that.

"We'll bring it to the wedding," April said simply, and he
laughed at her. She was quite a woman. He had realized it when
he met her, but then dropped the ball along the way. Fortunately, she hadn't. April never dropped the ball. She grabbed it
and ran with it, in everything she did. Even now after the fire.
"How many people do you want at the wedding?" She had forgotten to ask him before, and her mother had emailed her to ask.

"Just me and you. I don't want my parents, I haven't seen
them in ten years and they're too drunk to care." He had never
heard from them again since his call. He was ready to let them
go forever and his therapist agreed with him, they were a lost

cause. He wanted to look forward, not backward, to the life he was going to share with April. "I'd like my friend Jim and his wife. He was a fan of this relationship and the baby even before I was." They had been to the restaurant twice before the fire and April liked them both very much.

"Can we go on a honeymoon?" she asked, looking like a young girl, and he laughed at her.

"Yeah, at the hospital. You can't go away now, silly. Why don't we stay at a hotel for the weekend, and pretend we're not in New York? Or pretend we are and enjoy it."

"I'd really like to go to Italy with you," she said, looking disappointed. They could go to all the restaurants they both knew and loved and talked about.

"Why don't we go in August, before you reopen?"

"What'll we do with the baby?" She was planning to nurse, and since she could have it with her at the restaurant for the first months, it wasn't a problem.

"Take it with us. We can get him used to great food right from the beginning," he teased her. "Sounds like a plan to me. Now all we have to do is get married, have the baby, and reopen the restaurant." He made it sound like a snap of the fingers and one, two, three, and April laughed at him.

"I have a feeling none of it will be that easy," she said, looking worried. "The wedding maybe, thanks to my mother. Getting the restaurant open again is a project, and I'm feeling nervous about getting this thing out of me," she said, pointing to the basketball on her lap, and he nodded. It looked huge to both of them. She was a tall woman but narrow-framed, and it seemed impossible to believe that anything that enormous could emerge with ease. "Are you still planning to be there?" she asked, sounding anxious. He said he would, but she knew he was scared. If he was not there, she knew Ellen would be.

Mike nodded, looking pensive. "I think so. I want to be," although it seemed scary to him too, and watching April in agony would be upsetting. She didn't talk about it, but he knew that as the time grew closer, she was as worried as he was. The logistics of it looked damn near impossible to him, and to her too.

They talked about their trip to Italy as April cooked him dinner. She whipped up a primavera pasta from things he had in his refrigerator and a frisée salad with bacon and poached eggs. By the time they went to bed that night, they had agreed on Florence, Siena, Venice, Rome, Bologna, and Arezzo, where April knew a restaurant she insisted they couldn't miss. They agreed to put off Paris for another trip, since everything was closed in August. And as they piled into bed, after she took another shower to get the smell of smoke off her, she put her arms around him and thanked him again for the great review. He was relieved that he had done it. He had wanted to for a long time, as a gift to her. And this seemed like the right time.

"Larry thinks I should look into opening a second restaurant now," she said as he turned off the light and she yawned, and Mike looked at her with horror.

"One woman, one restaurant, and one baby are all I can handle right now," he said honestly, and that was already a lot for him. He had come a long way in the past four months, farther than he ever thought he could. "Could we settle for that for the moment?" She nodded, smiling at him, grateful for all they had. And she wasn't ready to open a second restaurant either. She had enough to do rebuilding the one she had.

"Do you think we'll ever have more children?" she asked, as she lay in bed next to him. She couldn't imagine how Ellen managed three, and she had been an only child, but she liked the relationship between her two half-sisters, and sometimes envied them that.

"I don't know," he said honestly. "Let's get this one out first." It seemed like a big project to him. He put an arm around her shoulders and pulled her close to him. She was a woman who climbed mountains and was willing to conquer the world. Mike was a lot more easily daunted, but he was following her example and learning a lot from her. As he held her, he could feel the baby kick him, hard. It was difficult to believe that a month from now, they'd be parents. He was excited by the prospect, but if he thought about it too much, it still scared him to death. April was a lot calmer about it. And as he held her in his arms, thinking of all that lay ahead for them, he drifted off to sleep, and April looked at him and smiled. As it turned out, their crazy one-night stand had turned out to be a very good thing.

Chapter 19

A fter the initial shock of the fire at April's restaurant, and being reassured that they weren't needed at home, Jack and Valerie had a fantastic time in Paris. They both loved staying at the Ritz and had stayed there before. They enjoyed the same restaurants, although Valerie introduced him to some new ones, and April told them about others that were intimate and unknown. Paparazzi took their photographs occasionally as they went in and out of the hotel. Neither of them was major news in Europe, but they were both well-known. And they loved being with each other.

Jack was astonishingly generous with her, and bought her a gold bracelet, and a fur jacket she saw and fell in love with. He surprised her with it at the hotel, after saying he had to go out and get some air. Life with him was a constant series of thoughtful, loving gestures, and Valerie was discovering a side of herself she had never known existed. For once in her life, she wasn't thinking about work, but only her man.

They played "what if" games that Jack invented sometimes at dinner. If the network asked her to choose between him and her job, just how much did she love him, and what would she do?

"That's easy," she teased him. "I'd keep my show, and meet you on the sly in cheap motels in New Jersey." And what if he had to give up sportscasting for her, or his place in the Hall of Fame, would he do it?

"Sportscasting, yes. Hall of Fame, not so easy. I worked my ass off to be in it in the first place," he said sensibly. And there were times when they both talked seriously about what they wanted to do about their jobs as they got older. They were in an industry that prized youth.

"Barbara Walters has always been my role model," Valerie said to him. "She has stayed on top for her entire career, and never slipped for a minute. She had to compete with men, her peers, younger women, and she's still the best and the biggest in the business, and what's more I really like her."

"Is that what you want? To stay in the business forever? It's a hell of a fight to stay on top the way she has, and I'm not so sure it's worth it," Jack said, as they finished dinner in a cozy restaurant on the Left Bank that April had recommended. Their joint favorite was still the Voltaire, on the quais along the Seine, but that night they hadn't been able to get a table. Everyone in Paris wanted to go there, and only the cream of "le tout Paris" got in.

"I used to think so," Valerie said in answer to his question about staying in the business. "What else is there?" And then she corrected herself, "Or what else was there before you? April is all grown up and has her own life, now more so than ever, with a restaurant, a husband, and a baby. What am I supposed to do with the next thirty years, if I'm that lucky? Or even the next ten? I always thought work was the answer. But I thought that when I was thirty too. I guess I'm just a workhorse. But I have to admit, sometimes now I'm not so sure." She was happy with him, happier than she ever had been, but she also couldn't give up a career for him, nor would she want to. What if either of them decided to move on, or things didn't work out for them? It could always happen. Sometimes things changed, even in the best of relationships, and this was just the beginning. She wasn't willing to put her career on the line for him, and he knew it. She had worked too hard to get there to risk it for any man, and she didn't think she should. But she was willing to accommodate him to the best of her ability, within the framework of how she worked and lived.

He asked her a surprise question then. It had crossed her mind once or twice, but she didn't have the answer to that either. "Do you suppose we should think about getting married eventually?" They were both old enough to know what they wanted, and who. She had always thought she wanted to get married again, but now she wasn't as sure. She loved him, without question, but did they need the papers to go with it? They weren't going to have children. They both had interesting careers. They loved each other. But just how much did they need to prove? And to whom?

"I don't know. What do you think?" she said, smiling shyly at him. It was a big subject, and there was still the factor, and always would be, that she was older than he. What if he fell in love with a younger woman one day? She didn't want the heartbreak of divorce again, especially at her age. Losing him would have devastated her. "I'm of two minds about it. Basically, I believe in the institution and what it stands for. I always did. But at this point in our lives, sometimes I think it's more trouble than it's worth. Do we really need the paperwork to tell others what we feel? And it's like any other contract, the day one of you wants to get out of it, there's nothing you can do to keep them there. People who want to get out, do, and then it's a giant mess." He didn't disagree.

"I'd get married if it was important to you," he said generously, and maybe one day it would be, but it wasn't yet, and she made that clear. "I'm open to it. But I don't need it myself. And I agree with you about divorce. Mine was pretty nasty. But we're good friends now. At the time it was a huge battle, over visitation with Greg, the property we had to split up since I had already hit the big time and was making a lot of money by then, and I was really pissed that she wanted out to marry someone else, and had cheated on me with the team doctor. And she was pissed about all the girls I'd cheated on her with. It was a pretty ugly time, and I'm surprised we wound up friends."

"It was easier for me and Pat," Valerie admitted. "Neither of us had any money, we were more than willing to share April, and he hadn't met Maddie yet. He was pretty devastated. He wanted to stay married, mostly because he didn't want to admit that our marriage was a failure, and I wanted out. I knew it was the wrong situation for me. His academic life and everything that went with it bored me to death. What made sense eight years before that, or we thought so anyway, no longer did. I grew into someone entirely different from the woman he had married. As the Brits say, we were like chalk and cheese. I felt like he was holding me back in my career plans, and he felt like I was dragging him behind the horse by his teeth. We were miserable." She couldn't imagine that happening to her and Jack now, they were both grown-ups and had established careers. If anything, they were both slowing down slightly, or said they were willing to, but she wasn't sure that was true either. They had both been on the fast track for a long time and were used to it. Modifying anything in their public lives wasn't going to be easy, and for now they didn't need to. They had no conflicts about each other's work.

"Maybe we just need to keep things the way they are for now," Jack said reasonably. "There's no pressure on us to get married. There's no statute of limitations on it. We can always do it later, if we want to, as long as you're not in any kind of hurry. I'm not. We don't want to have kids." He smiled at her. Everything about their current relationship worked for both of them, even the difference in their ages, which Valerie had almost stopped worrying about, and had never been a problem for him. The difference between fifty and sixty seemed negligible now to both of them, and everyone else. Who cared? They felt like equals in every way. "Don't fix what ain't broke," he said, smiling at her. And she liked the fact that he was open to marriage, but didn't need it, and neither did she. And their kids didn't seem to care either way. The press had spotted them together several times, but no one seemed upset or excited or even shocked about what might be happening between them. They were reasonable options for each other, they worked for the same network, they were both important in their field, and they had a fabulous time together. What more did they need? "What about living together?" Jack asked as long as they were on the subject of future arrangements. "Is that something you'd ever want to do?" For the past many months they had been together every night, going back and forth between each other's apartments, but neither of them really wanted to give their own place up, and they agreed that it was much too soon to make that decision. It was just nice to think about where they were going, and what they wanted to do, to discover what was off limits, and what might be a good plan for the future. He loved his apartment, and she loved hers. He wouldn't have minded her moving in with him, and would have liked it, but he didn't want to give up his place, and for now, neither did she. She didn't want to be that dependent on him, and maybe never would.

"I don't know," she said, looking thoughtful. "I'm not in love with my apartment, but it works for me. I suppose I could sell it one day." But in the meantime, she liked staying with him, and they stayed at hers several times a week when it was more convenient for her. They were both surprisingly willing to adapt to each other, and reasonable people. "Maybe if something comes up in your building, I could buy it and sell mine, and add it to yours. It might give us what we need." He liked that idea. There seemed to be solutions for everything. They hadn't faced any major challenges or roadblocks yet, and their trip had been absolutely perfect, and continued to be. Nothing was pressing them, neither of them was pushing, they had no arguments or disagreements. They had enough space to move around in. And for now anyway, they enhanced each other's lives and lost nothing in the bargain. It seemed ideal. She was meticulously neat around the house, and he was messy, but other than that, there were no problems, and she didn't mind picking up after him in order to keep things neat. It embarrassed him at times, but he said he was constitutionally unable to be neat, it just wasn't in his genes. So she picked up his clothes at night and hung them up, put his laundry where it belonged, and constantly tidied up his papers. It didn't bother her and he didn't care. It made him feel loved and taken care of.

They walked along the Seine in Paris, went to an art exhibit at the Grand Palais, had tea at the Plaza Athénée, and stuck their noses into every antique shop on the Left Bank. They had coffee at the Deux Magots in St. Germain des Prés, and walked all over Paris arm in arm, and stopped to kiss every chance they got. It was a city where you constantly saw people kissing. Public displays of affection in Paris were never frowned on, they were encouraged. It was the most romantic week Valerie had ever spent with any man, and they both hated to leave for London.

They spent five days there going to the theater, and an antique show. He took her shopping on New Bond Street and bought her a pair of silver lovebirds at Asprey. And once there, Valerie called Dawn and got started organizing April's wedding. Dawn was excited to help her do it. April insisted she only wanted the staff from the restaurant, Ellen and Larry, and Mike thought he should invite his editor, his friend Jim and his wife, and another writer April didn't know. And of course Pat and Maddie and Annie and Heather would come. At most, even including Ellen's three boys, it came to fewer than forty people. It would be easy for Valerie to do at her apartment, although Jack had generously offered his, but she didn't want him to have the inconvenience.

Valerie told Dawn she wanted the best caterer she could find, so April didn't complain about the food, and had Dawn call a judge she knew, and the florist she always used. Valerie wanted five round tables of eight set up in her living room, and chamber music and no dancing, since April said they wanted a lunchtime wedding, with guests arriving at noon. It was embarrassingly simple. They even managed to have invitations made, which would be hand-delivered two weeks before the wedding. By the time she and Jack left for Venice, the whole thing had been arranged. And Jack insisted he wanted to give a big party for them later, maybe after she'd reopened the restaurant, and had the baby, when it would seem more festive. Valerie and April were both touched by his offer. But for now the simple ceremony and lunch at her mother's apartment were all April wanted, and probably all Mike could handle. He was already nervous about it, although insistent that it was what he wanted to do too. And

April was ecstatic. She joked to Ellen during one of her acupuncture appointments that as it turned out, she would be married, have a baby, and a successful business at thirty, just as she had always believed she should. But this wasn't about "should," it was about being totally in love with the man she was marrying, and excited now to have his baby. Ellen was delighted for them.

The days Jack and Valerie shared in Venice were the best of the trip. The light was beautiful there in May, the weather was perfect, and the food was much too good. Valerie said she'd have to starve when she went home. They took gondola rides and went to churches, kissed under bridges, and wandered everywhere on foot. They went across the lagoon to the Hotel Cipriani for lunch one day, and went to see the glass factory in Murano the day after. They bought a chandelier together for his kitchen. Valerie insisted it would look great with the Ellsworth Kellys and convinced him.

They had their last lunch at Harry's Bar, took a final gondola ride under the Bridge of Sighs, and spent their last night at the Gritti Palace in bed making love, and then walked out on their balcony to look out over Venice in the moonlight.

"Could anything be more perfect?" he asked, as he put an arm around Valerie and held her close to him. It had been the perfect trip. "I think this was our honeymoon," he said, smiling at her, and she nodded. They didn't need to get married, they already had everything, and best of all, they both knew, they had each other.

Chapter 20

April was at the restaurant every day, meeting contractors, and watching the people Larry had hired clean up debris, and remove everything that been damaged by water or fire. The basement was dry now, and the little they had been able to salvage was being stored there. The reconstruction of the restaurant still seemed like a mammoth project. Larry had hired all the people he needed, and he came by himself several times every day to oversee it, between the other jobs he was doing. April was there from sunup to nightfall, doing whatever she could, and constantly making decisions. It worried Mike that she was working too hard and doing too much, but there was no way to stop her, as usual.

He showed up one day at noon with lunch for her, and was horrified to find her pulling boards away from the wall with a crowbar. She was still wearing the rubber boots she had bought, and a hard hat she had borrowed from one of the work crews. She was a sight with her huge belly hanging out of her jeans, dirt all over her face, and work gloves, as she wrestled with the boards she then dropped at her feet.

"What in hell are you doing?" he shouted at her as she put the crowbar away. She could hardly hear him through the workers jack-hammering the floor in the kitchen. "You're going to have the baby right here, if you don't stop it!"

"I'm sorry," she apologized, but she didn't look sorry at all. She couldn't wait for him to leave so she could go on working and do more.

"You know, this may come as a shock to you, but they can do this without you. Women in their ninth month of pregnancy are not usually considered part of the workforce on this kind of project. Maybe you should join the union." She took the hard hat off and wiped her face as she grinned at him. The truth was she was enjoying helping with the work, and he knew it. Nothing would have slowed her down or kept her away. April was only happy when she was working. She sat down on a stack of bricks as he sat down next to her, and handed her the sandwich he had brought her.

"Thanks, I was starving," she said, as a truck arrived and the driver walked toward her. They were expecting more electrical fixtures, and she hoped this delivery was them.

"I have baby furniture for April Wyatt," the driver said, pointing at the truck. "From Valerie Wyatt." April had forgotten all about it. Her mother had mentioned it before she left.

"I don't live here anymore," she said, indicating the shambles around her. "Could you deliver it somewhere else?"

"In the city?" The driver didn't look pleased.

"Yeah. Uptown." He nodded. He could see that there was no way she could accept it here.

"Someone should have called us," he grumbled, but wrote down Mike's address. "Is there anyone there to accept it?" And of course there wasn't. Mike was going back to work and she was busy here.

"How about four o'clock?" she asked him, and he grudgingly agreed, and walked back to his truck and drove away. April knew she could be back at Mike's by then, and she would be exhausted before that anyway, so ready to go home. She had been at the restaurant since eight o'clock that morning.

"How much is there?" Mike asked her as she finished her sandwich. He had a small living room and bedroom, a tiny office, and a kitchen the size of a closet. There was no room for a lot of additional furniture there, in fact none at all. But she didn't want to hurt her mother's feelings. And the baby needed a place to sleep. She knew her mother had bought a crib and "a few other things" before she left for Europe. April had borrowed almost everything she needed from friends, and her mother had bought the rest, even a fancy layette from Saks that was due to be delivered any minute too. She was all set now. And in her own empty, nearly unfurnished quarters above the restaurant, it wouldn't have been a problem to house the furniture her mother had bought. At Mike's, it could be.

"I'm not sure, but we'll move it back over here, as soon as we can move back in." He had decided to give up his apartment, since he'd never see her otherwise. She was always at the restaurant, and she wanted the baby there with her. There didn't seem to be much point to his keeping his old place. As soon as the apartment upstairs was cleaned up, and the remodel was down to a dull roar, they were planning to move in. "Don't worry about it. I'll make room for it," she promised him. "How much room can stuff for a baby take?"

But she was in no way prepared for the full set of nursery furniture her mother had ordered. When the driver showed up at Mike's at four o'clock, he brought up a crib, a chest of drawers, some kind of table with a place to change diapers on top, a toy chest, a rocking chair for her, and half a dozen framed watercolors of Winnie the Pooh to decorate the walls. Valerie had thought of everything, and knew April wouldn't buy it. She was afraid she'd get it at Goodwill.

"Holy shit," April whispered, as he brought the last of it in, and the crib had to be assembled. She asked the driver if he could do it for her, and he wouldn't. He was sweating profusely from dragging it all up the stairs, and it took up every inch of Mike's apartment. He had had to put the rocking chair and the toy box in the kitchen. Mike was going to kill her. She had no idea what to do with it, or how to make it fit, and she hadn't wanted to hurt her mother's feelings by sending it back. In her own apartment, it would be fine. In his, it was a disaster.

She managed to wrestle the parts of the crib into the bedroom after the driver left, and then dragged the rocking chair in. If she squeezed the crib in next to the bed, there was a possibility it might fit. The rest was a problem.

She shoved the white chest of drawers with scalloped edges into a corner of the living room, and the changing table next to it. He didn't have a coffee table, so she put the toy box in front of the couch, and she stashed the Winnie the Pooh drawings behind it, for lack of anywhere else to put them. She didn't think Mike was ready to have her put Winnie the Pooh on the walls instead of his collection of photographs by Ansel Adams. She looked around the room after that, and had to admit that the living room looked terrible. The white baby furniture was cute, or would have been in a nursery, but it stuck out like a sore thumb, and they'd have to climb across the rocking chair to get into the bed. It was an obstacle course of babydom, but there was nothing else she could do.

Mike wasn't prepared for it when he got home that night, and he looked like he was going to have a stroke when he walked in. He had imagined a little basket in a corner somewhere, or maybe a miniature crib. Instead there were boxes all over his bedroom, waiting for him to assemble the crib, and baby furniture everywhere. He looked like he was going to hyperventilate and nearly did.

"How can a baby need so much stuff?" She didn't tell him that friends were going to drop off the rest of what they needed in the next few weeks, a sterilizer, pajamas, diapers, a stroller

Ellen was lending her, a high chair from one of the waitresses, a car seat one of the busboys didn't need, and things she didn't even know about yet and had no idea how to use. And Ellen had told her she'd need a plastic tub with a sponge insert to bathe the baby. April hadn't thought of that. Mike sat down on the couch staring at the toy box, and feeling sick.

"I'm sorry." April looked at him apologetically. "I know it's a mess. We'll be back at my place soon." In a single afternoon, the baby had moved in. For the first time, he felt the way he had after the sonogram, and he looked it, which worried April more than a little.

"We can't live like this. For chrissake, April, the baby will weigh five or six pounds. Why does it need all this furniture?" Her mother had bought what she would have for a magazine lay-out, and it was lovely stuff, but it had taken over Mike's postage-stamp-sized apartment, and was a warning to him that this seemingly tiny being was about to take over his life, in ways he hadn't understood till now, even in his panic.

"Why don't we put the crib together? And then the bedroom won't look so crowded," April suggested. As it was now, they couldn't even go to bed that night until they assembled the crib, because the bumpers and mattress and a white eyelet canopy were lying on their bed. "I'll help you."

"Do you realize that I have no mechanical skills?" he said miserably. "I don't know a screwdriver from a hammer and I can never read instructions. Whenever I get something that has to be assembled, I wind up throwing it out. I can never figure out what to do with the nuts and bolts. You need an engineering degree to put this shit together."

"We'll figure it out," she said soothingly. "We'll do it together."

"I need a drink," he announced, and went to the kitchen to pour himself a glass of wine. "What's that thing?" he asked, pointing at the changing table as he came back into the room. He looked extremely crabby and completely panicked.

"It's to change the baby on," she said, embarrassed.

"Why can't you change the baby on your lap, or on the floor or something? Do you realize the Olympic equestrian team doesn't use this much equipment?" April herself was living out of one small bag, and had three dresses in his closet. All she wore now were jeans, T-shirts, and rubber boots.

April went into the bedroom then to get started on the crib. She tore the cardboard away, looked at the instructions, and realized that Mike was right. Putting it together was more complicated than it appeared, and Mike came in a few minutes later and set down his glass of wine. He didn't mention the rocking chair or the mess in the room. He just walked over to her and put his arms around her as she wrestled with the boxes.

"I'm sorry. I wasn't prepared for this. And neither were you. You've got enough on your mind with the restaurant. You don't need me making it worse." He knew she had met with insurance adjusters the day before, and they had been a pain in the neck.

"Give me the instructions," he said, looking at them, and then went to get his tools.

It took them two hours of hit and miss, and several false starts, but they finally got it together. The mattress was in, the bumpers were attached, with little lambs on them, and the canopy was even on the crib. They both looked as though they'd run a marathon as they collapsed next to each other on the bed.

"Childbirth must be a snap compared to this," he remarked, and then was sorry the minute he said it. He looked at her mournfully, missing the restaurant for exactly the reason he had written about in his review. "I need comfort food," he said unhappily. April smiled at him and got off the bed.

"That's the easy part," she said, as she kissed him and left. Mike lay in bed watching TV, and fifteen minutes later she appeared in the doorway. "We may not have the restaurant. But you have me. *Monsieur est servi*," she said, bowing as low as she could given the beachball at her middle.

He followed her into the living room where she had set the small round table they ate on, and a stack of her delicious pancakes were on a plate with warm maple syrup beside it. She had even made a plate of them for herself—the menu sounded good to her too.

"Ohmigod," he said, like a man dying of thirst in the desert. "That's just what I needed." He sat down without another word and devoured them, and then sat back in his chair with a profoundly satisfied look. "Thank you," he said, looking peaceful finally. "Maybe everything will be okay." And then he shook his head as he looked around. "I had no idea babies needed all this stuff."

"Neither did I," she said honestly. Neither of them had thought about it, they were too busy dealing with everything else.

"I guess it doesn't matter," Mike said sensibly. "We're moving out anyway, and thank God your place is bigger than this." She was relieved by that fact too. Living as tightly as this long-term would have been miserable for them. She hoped to be back in her apartment by July, after the worst of the reconstruction was done and they wouldn't be breathing plaster dust day and night, which wouldn't be good for the baby either. Too much furniture in a cramped apartment had never hurt a child, even if it unnerved Mike.

He helped her do the dishes after dinner, and they went back to their bedroom. They brushed their teeth and got into bed, and lay looking at the rocking chair at the foot of the bed, and the elaborate crib beside it. Valerie had bought them beautiful things, just too many of them.

"It'll be weird when there's someone sleeping in that crib," he said softly, and looked at her in the moonlight streaming into the room. They could no longer get to the window to pull down the shades, unless they stood in the crib to do it.

"Yes, it will," she agreed, nodding, but their baby was a very real presence to her now. It was bouncing all over the place at the moment, probably from the pancakes and the sugar from the syrup. She had noticed that whenever she ate sweets, the baby hopped around for hours.

And then without another word, he reached for her, still shocked that he could want her so much even though she was so extremely pregnant. There was something so tender about her now, and so womanly, he couldn't keep his hands off her. He wasn't sure if that was normal or not, and he worried that it was uncomfortable for her, but she was touched by it, and always responded to him. They made love in the moonlight and forgot about the baby for a little while, and clung to each other, swept away by their passion.

Chapter 21

WHen Valerie and Jack got back from Europe, they were busy with a mountain of things they had to do. She had decisions to make about some of her licensing agreements, shows to plan, and an offer from her publisher to do another book. And she had to attend to the last details of April's wedding, and still had to pick the wedding cake. And Jack was just as busy.

She spoke to April the night they arrived, who said that the reconstruction of the restaurant was off to a good start, although it looked a mess, but she sounded happy. She was excited about the wedding. Valerie told her that Dawn had done a great job handling the details before her return. She had talked her through them in dozens of calls from Europe.

Their schedules that week were relentless, but by Friday night, Valerie felt as though she had a grip on things and that all was under control. Her first days back from a trip were always a nightmare. She managed to order April's cake on Friday afternoon, since April had explained exactly what she wanted. She wanted a delicate almond-paste icing and a chocolate and mocha filling with a hint of orange. The baker wasn't happy about it but he agreed to do it to April's specifications. She would have made it herself if she had time, but she had no kitchen to do it, and Valerie assured her it would be fine.

When she left her office on Friday, Valerie went back to Jack's apartment. They were spending the weekend there. Their back-and-forth life between the two still seemed to be working, although their lives were hectic. There had been a photograph of them together in Paris, and *People* magazine had called her office that afternoon to find out what was going on. Dawn had cleverly acted like it was no big deal, and explained nothing. They would find out on their own anyway.

Valerie got to Jack's apartment before he did, and she thought he looked serious when he walked in. She was taking a bath, and he sat down on the edge of the tub with a somber expression. He didn't say anything at first, and then he kissed her. She thought he looked depressed, which was unlike him.

"Bad day?" she asked sympathetically, and touched his hand.

"Yeah. Kind of. Just the usual hassles after a trip. You have to pay the penalty for all that fun, I guess." He smiled at her, but it was wintry. She didn't press him about it, and figured he would tell her what was bothering him eventually.

It wasn't until Saturday afternoon, as they walked in Central

Park on a beautiful warm May day, that he did. He had been quiet for a long time as they walked along, and then they sat down on a bench and he looked at her and spat it out.

"The network wants to move me to Miami." He looked devastated, and they both knew what it meant for them. Her show was here, and she couldn't move with him. They could commute on weekends if they wanted to badly enough, but it wouldn't be the same.

"Why?"

"God knows. They think it makes more sense. It's a bigger job attached to the network there. I'd be commentating more stuff, not just football. I'm happy with what I'm doing, and I guess I should be flattered. It's more money, more prestige." He hesitated then. "But I don't want to leave you. I love what we have, and I love you. Long-distance relationships are hard and most of the time they don't work. I don't want to be commuting at my age. And I don't want to live in Miami." He looked desperately unhappy.

"Did you turn it down?" Valerie asked quietly, hoping that he had. She had no right to influence him, or interfere with his career, and she wouldn't, but she knew that it would not be good for them if he moved. And she couldn't move with him, she wasn't about to leave her show for him. Nor did she expect him to retire from broadcasting for her, or negatively impact his job. She couldn't do that to him. This was a big and very unhappy news flash for them, and she didn't see how he could refuse it, or why he would, even if he didn't love Miami.

"I told them I'd think about it," he answered. "And I will. I guess our 'what if' games in Paris about what would happen if one of us had a job opportunity that required giving up the other, or hurting them, weren't so imaginary after all. I guess this happens. They made it very clear that they expect me to do this. I can say no, but they won't thank me for it. Valerie," he said slowly, "how do you feel about it? What would you do?" He really wanted her input and guidance to help him make the decision.

"Those are two separate questions," she said quietly. "How do I feel about it? Sad. I don't want you to move away. I love our life together. Maybe it was too easy and we were too lucky for it to last. Maybe life just isn't that simple. What would I do? Honestly, I don't know. I wouldn't want to screw up my career, but I wouldn't want to leave you either. I'm glad I don't have to make that choice. And I don't love Miami either. It's fun for a weekend, but I wouldn't want to live there. But you have to go where the job takes you, and where the big bucks are for you, and the important promotions. You're too young to retire." And she felt that she was too. "Just know that whatever you do, I'll understand and we'll make the best of it. I could come to Miami on Friday nights, and take an early flight back on Monday. Others do it. Politicians do it all the time, commuting from Washington, D.C., to their home states in California or the West. CEOs do it to work in one city and join their families in another. It's not easy, but if we want to, we can do it." She meant it, and he looked profoundly touched as she said it. "Just do what's right for you. We'll figure it out for us later." But she was worried that living in

Miami, he'd go back to the bimbos and young girls. He would be alone a lot of the time, and maybe eventually the old temptations would reclaim him. She felt very insecure, but she didn't share that with him. She thought it would be unfair to do so. He had enough pressure on him already from the network. He had made that clear. They weren't threatening to hurt his career if he didn't go, but it wouldn't help it either. No matter who you were, they expected you to go where you were sent. Even a big star like him. He felt it like a physical blow. Everything had been going so smoothly for them, and now this.

They walked slowly back to his apartment, and didn't speak. They both had a lot on their minds. He kept to himself for most of the weekend, and she offered to go home, but he said he didn't want her to. He wanted her with him, but she felt as though she'd already lost him. This time the "what if" game was real.

They didn't make love that night, which was rare for them. They just lay in bed and held each other. He looked lonely and scared. He talked to his agent about it on Sunday, and his attorney. His agent said it was up to him, and didn't think they'd penalize him if he didn't do it, and his attorney advised him to move to Miami. In the end, the choice was his.

Valerie went to meet April on Sunday afternoon, at the restaurant. She was working there alone, cleaning things up, and still throwing things away. She stopped for a few minutes to talk to her mother, mostly about the wedding. It was a week away, and she was excited, although she said that Mike seemed very stressed about the baby again. It was becoming very real, particularly with all the baby furniture in the apartment, and Ellen had dropped off the bathtub and the stroller.

"He'd better show up at the wedding," Valerie warned, and April nodded.

"He will. He's just scared. I guess I am too. It's a big change." So was getting married. It all was. Life, the fire, relationships, babies, marriage. They were all big bites to swallow. And Valerie had her own. She didn't say anything to April about Jack's potential move to Miami. She didn't want to upset her. She had enough on her mind with Mike, the fire, and the baby. Her due date was two weeks away. They were down to the wire.

On Sunday night she and Jack went to a movie. They both agreed that it was better for them to get out and be distracted. They had pizza for dinner at a restaurant called John's, but both of them were feeling down and had trouble coming up with conversation. She returned to her apartment that night without him. It was the first night they had spent apart in months. Valerie thought he needed space, and she said that to him. And if he was moving away, they'd better get used to nights alone again, although she didn't say it. The relationship had taken a step backward with the offer from the network, and it was painful. Both of them were afraid of what it would mean for them. And neither of them liked it. Valerie was doing everything not to pressure him in any way. But she was sad, and he could see it. So was he. It was just life. Things happened, even if you found a great woman or guy. Something like this could come along and toss everything right out the window. She hoped that wouldn't happen to them, but they both knew it could, and they were mourning it already.

They saw very little of each other the following week, although she slept at his apartment. She didn't want him to think that she was withdrawing from him. She wasn't, she was just busy, and she got back to his place so late every night that he was half asleep when she got there. She'd get into bed with him, and he'd wrap his arms around her and pass out. They kept meaning to make love, and didn't. They were always rushed, or running to a meeting. And Valerie had no idea what he was doing about the decision, and didn't ask him. She was fairly certain he would go. She thought she probably would in his shoes, although she wasn't totally sure, but she thought so. You couldn't build a career and an image for all those years and then toss it in the trash because you didn't want to move to another city. There were sacrifices you had to make. And sometimes, at the worst of times, those sacrifices were people. Maybe this was one of those. She knew she had put her marriage on the line for her career years before, although she'd been younger and on the way up. Would she make the same choice again today? She didn't know. She was glad she wasn't the one having to make the decision. She didn't envy Jack. And it was a wild guess as to whether going would improve his career or not going would hurt it. No one knew. And it wasn't only about money. The network held the cards here. Other networks would have wanted him, but he was well established with this one, and had been for twelve years. Valerie was giving Jack all the space he needed to make the decision, and all her sympathy and support because it was such a tough one. She knew they loved each other, but what that translated to in real life, when the chips were down, remained to be seen. She was trying to be adult about it, it was the only advantage to age: the ability to be disappointed and survive it, because you had done it before.

The week of the wedding, April was at the construction site of the restaurant every day. Mike was busy at the paper. Everything was ready for the baby at the apartment, and they were exploding at the seams, and so was April. She looked as though she was literally about to pop, and she felt it. She could hardly sleep at night now, so she padded around the apartment, folding things for the baby, tiny shirts and nightgowns and pajamas, and little caps and blankets and booties and sweaters. She had gone on a washing frenzy a few days before, washing everything. And she had to walk up and down three flights of stairs to do it, and didn't mind. Mike told Jim at the office that she was going a little nuts, and Jim assured him it was to be expected. He said all women did at the end of the pregnancy. It was their way of preparing for the baby, frantically building their nests. Some days, Mike tried to pretend it wasn't happening, just so he could relax. And it was reassuring for him to check things out with Jim, who was an old hand at this. He had been through it three times before and his wife had just gotten pregnant again, so they had that in common too, although Mike could barely imagine one child, let alone four.

He had made a reservation for them at the Carlyle, for their honeymoon. They were only staying one night. It was all he could afford, but he wanted it to be perfect for her. He had gone to see the room himself. And he never mentioned that the bride was nine months pregnant. He just hoped they wouldn't be spending the night at the hospital instead. It could happen. The doctor said she was ready, and she was having a lot of contractions. He kept begging her to go easy on the construction work, but as usual, she wouldn't listen. She carried lumber, used the crowbar, took things to the Dumpster. She even moved some bricks around. April was a workhorse who had no idea how not to be. Mike accepted that about her now.

She talked to her mother the day before the wedding and realized that Valerie was sad.

"Are you okay, Mom?" she asked her, sounding concerned.

"I'm fine, sweetheart, just busy." She sounded depressed much more than busy. April mentioned it later that night to Mike.

"I wonder if everything's okay with her and Jack."

"Why wouldn't it be?" The last time he had seen them, they had looked like newlyweds themselves.

"You never know," April said wisely.

Miraculously, April had found a dress that fit her for the wedding. She and Ellen had gone shopping and had found it at Barney's. It was a wide white silk swing dress with a halter top that showed off her shoulders. It was the only part of her now that didn't look ready to explode. The dress was short, and she was going to wear high-heeled sandals with it, and carry lily of the valley that her mother had had flown in from Paris. It was hardly a traditional wedding dress, but it was perfect for what she needed. And Pat was giving her away. Ellen was her matron of honor, her sisters were her bridesmaids, and Maddie had found matching sky-blue linen dresses for them, to save April the trouble, and she was grateful for her stepmother's help. Her mother was doing all white flowers in the apartment, orchids, roses, and more lily of the valley.

By Friday night, everything was set up in Valerie's apartment, and she was staying at Jack's, as she had all week. There was too much activity in her own, and Dawn was staying there to help set up the wedding. All the guests had accepted, except two of the waiters who had to attend family events of their own. Everyone else was coming, including Mike's editor, Jim and his wife and kids, and Mike's other friend from the paper. He had asked Jack to be best man, which touched him, since Mike had no real family of his own whom he still saw.

The night before the wedding, Valerie noticed that Jack looked peaceful, and she had an eerie feeling, as though he had decided to let go of her, and continue on his own. There was a bittersweet quality to the way he looked at her, and she felt waves of panic engulf her, but she said nothing to him. She owed him that because she loved him. She was going to be brave about it, she promised herself, if he left her. Maybe he had decided not to try a long-distance relationship after all, and just end it between them when he moved away. She said nothing to him, but cried in the bathroom alone that night, and then put a good face on when she joined him in bed and they made love. Every time now she worried that it would be the last time. It was going to be hard to lose someone she loved so much, but she kept reminding herself that she'd live through it. She had no other choice.

And in their bed next to the crib that night, Mike and April were talking about their wedding. She knew that traditionally, they weren't supposed to see each other the morning of the wedding, but they had nowhere else to go. Her mother was at Jack's, her apartment was all set up for the wedding, there was no room for her at her father's, and Mike wanted to be with her, and didn't want to go to a hotel alone. So they were at his place, in bed, whispering in the moonlight on their wedding eve.

"Are you scared?" she whispered. They were like two little kids giggling in the dark.

"Kind of," he acknowledged. It was easier to say in the darkness, although he was willing to admit it to her.

"Me too. I'm more scared of having the baby than about what happens after that. What if it hurts too much and I can't stand it?" She was frightened of that now. What if she went nuts from the pain or totally lost it in front of Mike? It would be embarrassing to have him see that.

"We'll get you lots of drugs," he promised. "Other women

seem to get through it." He hoped it wouldn't be bad for her. He had been terrified when she'd been in the hospital after the fire, and he was dreading the pain she'd have to face now. They both were.

"My mom's really been working hard on the wedding," April said, snuggling up to him, with his arm around her shoulders. It didn't surprise him. Wyatt women seemed to work hard at everything and shirked nothing. He admired that about them. April was no less conscientious than her mother. She was doing the job of ten men at the restaurant, even nine months pregnant, but it didn't seem to do her any harm.

"I'm sure it'll be beautiful," he said gently.

He was used to the canopied crib beside their bed now, and it no longer surprised him. He wondered what it would be like when someone was in it. Or when she sat in the rocking chair nursing their child. He had a feeling it would be sweet to behold.

When he finally turned over and turned his back to her, and she cuddled up behind him, he could feel the baby kicking. It was relentless, and he fell asleep to the soft rhythm of the kicks, wondering how she could sleep at all.

Chapter 22

The morning of the wedding, both April and Mike were extremely nervous. The tension of the day, and all its implications, had gotten to them both. He was getting ready at his apartment, and April was going to dress at her mother's. Ellen came by in a cab and picked her up, and they went uptown together. April knew her mother had a hairdresser and manicurist waiting for her, and her dress was already there.

"See you later," she said, and kissed Mike goodbye before she left. He had just cut himself shaving and had little bits of toilet paper stuck all over his face, glued there by blood. "Try not to kill yourself before the wedding," she teased him as he glared at her and then burst out laughing.

"Okay, so I'm nervous. Get out of here, before I change my mind." They were a classic shotgun wedding, with her nine months pregnant after a one-night stand. She couldn't help laughing about it, and again with Ellen on the way uptown.

"He's a good guy," Ellen confirmed on the way to Valerie's apartment. And Dawn was waiting for them. They had all gotten used to her looks by then and her extremely punky outfits, pierces, and tattoos. She had done the streak in her hair light blue for the wedding. Working for Valerie had not made her more conservative. Valerie didn't care since Dawn was impressively efficient and had been a whirlwind helping with the wedding.

Ellen was carrying her dress, which was the same pale blue as April's sisters'. But hers was short, like April's, and her sisters' gowns were long. Valerie had decided to wear mauve, in vaguely related tones. She had found a lavender organdy cocktail dress that she thought was suitable for the mother of the bride.

As April arrived at her mother's apartment, Valerie was leaving Jack's. He was still sound asleep and she left him a note, telling him that she loved him and she'd see him at the wedding. She wasn't sure why, probably because of the pending decision about Miami, but she felt now as though every day they shared was their last. It was a depressing feeling, but she tried not to appear worried as she hurried the three blocks to her own apartment. She found April and Ellen getting their nails done in the kitchen. If you didn't look at April's stomach, she didn't even look pregnant—the weight was all right there. And she had gained less than she was allowed.

"So, ladies, how are we doing?" Valerie asked them as her

assistant handed her a cup of coffee. She was wearing jeans and a T-shirt with sandals and she looked almost as young as her daughter. She had called Alan Starr the day before for his reading on the wedding, and he said everything would be fine. She hadn't asked him about Jack's decision about Miami. She didn't want to know and hear the bad news. She could guess all by herself without being psychic. He really had no choice but to go, and she was sure Jack knew it too.

April was having clear nail polish put on, and she was going to have her hair done in a loose braid with lily of the valley woven into it. Valerie looked in her refrigerators, and all the flowers for the wedding party were there. The rest had been delivered by the florist early that morning, and her living room was filled with white orchids and roses. The crystal and silver on the five tables gleamed. And there was a path through the living room for April and her father to walk when she went to stand before the judge with Mike. It was a very traditional little wedding, despite the unusual circumstances and the fact that she'd had only two weeks to organize it. But Valerie was good at that, and Dawn was a quick learner. The cake arrived half an hour later, followed by Heather and Annie carrying their dresses. Valerie put them in the guest room, and they bounded out five minutes later, looking for their sister. She was having a bath in her mother's pink marble bathroom, and emerged like a very pregnant Venus as her sisters stared at her belly.

"My God, you're huge!" Heather said with a look of amazement.

"Thanks, I know." April laughed. "I just hope I make it

through the wedding." She'd had contractions all morning, but she was sure that it was just nerves. The baby knew something big was happening. Its parents were getting married. April said as much to her mother, and Valerie smiled.

"Just try not to have the baby before we cut the cake," Valerie advised her, and they both laughed.

By eleven o'clock, all the women were in their respective rooms getting ready, and emerged right on time. Ellen and April's half-sisters looked lovely in their dresses, and their hair was done simply. Valerie was bustling around in her lavender organdy dress, putting her pearls on, and Maddie arrived to see what she could do to help them, wearing sober navy blue. Dawn was standing in the background wearing a short electric blue dress and high-heeled platform shoes.

And then they all went into Valerie's bedroom to see April. She looked absolutely beautiful in the white silk trapeze dress. The flowers were braided into her hair just as Valerie had suggested. And at ten to twelve, Dawn handed them all their bouquets.

The judge was there by then, waiting in the living room with a glass of champagne. He was an old friend of Valerie's, and happy to do it for her. Five minutes later, all the men arrived. Jack, Pat, and Mike, and Jim and Ed from the paper. Dawn pinned a tiny white rose to each of their lapels, except Mike who got lily of the valley, just like those in his bride's bouquet and hair. He looked scared stiff.

"Hang in, man, it'll be over before you know it," Pat teased him, and they all accepted a round of champagne as they chatted with the judge. Mike looked as though he needed it, and then Pat went to the back of the apartment to see his daughter.

The guests began arriving promptly at noon, and by twelve-thirty everyone was there. April and her father were chatting quietly in her mother's bedroom then.

"You look beautiful," he said to his daughter. She really did look like a bride, even in her condition, and she looked radiant. Everything had turned out well.

Valerie didn't even have time to see Jack or talk to him once the guests started arriving. She smiled at him across the room, and for a minute wished the wedding were theirs. Then at least she could be sure she wouldn't lose him. But even wedding vows didn't guarantee that, as they all knew well.

At twelve thirty-five, the small chamber group began playing Handel's "Water Music," and April came out on her father's arm, with her sisters in front of her. And Mike gasped when he saw her. April looked beautiful, and as she turned to him, she beamed.

Valerie, Pat, and Maddie were all standing together in the front row, with Jack just behind her. She turned to look at him several times, and he gently touched her shoulder and squeezed it. He leaned forward once and whispered, "Everything is going to be okay." She didn't know if he meant for April, or for them, but seated in the front row, and during the ceremony, she couldn't ask. She nodded, and whispered something to Pat about how beautiful their daughter looked. And then after a few words, the judge pronounced them husband and wife, and they kissed. They greeted all their friends with smiles and hugs, and

April and Mike were both wiping tears from their eyes. It had been a perfect little wedding.

"You did a beautiful job," Jack complimented her when she turned around to face him after the ceremony.

"Thank you," she said, looking up at him with the weight of the past week in her eyes. He could see it and it touched him. "I'm not going to Miami," he said simply, not wanting to keep her in suspense a moment longer. He had decided the day before, but wanted to sleep on it. He had called his agent and attorney that morning before the wedding.

"You're not?" She smiled broadly at him. "Are you serious? But what about your career?" She was worried about him, and didn't dare ask him what had made the decision for him. Not wanting to live in Miami, or them? It didn't matter. He wasn't going. She wanted to cry in relief as she put her arms around him and kissed him.

"My career will survive it. I'm not going to turn my life upside down at this point. I think it boils down to what we've both agreed on. There comes a time when you have to make sacrifices. I've *always* given up my personal life for my career. I just didn't want to do that this time. It's time to do something different." She stared at him in amazement. He was telling her that he had done it for her, that he had given up a promotion and more money for her. And the worst part was that she didn't know if she would have had the guts to make the same choice in his shoes. But Jack had done it. And maybe next time, if the choice was hers to make, she would too. Just as he had said, there came

327

a time when there was more to life than just a career and blind ambition. And Jack knew, as he looked at her, that whatever happened between them in the future, he had made the right choice for him. And for her too.

"I was so sure you were going," she said to him in a whisper. "I felt like I'd already lost you."

He shook his head firmly as he looked at her. "You didn't. And I'm not sure you could. We survived last December together, at the network. I didn't go through all that to find you, and then throw it all away." And as he looked at her, she wasn't sure she would either. They had both grown up, and something in them had ever so subtly changed. Their ages no longer mattered, but their goals and values did. Jack was thrilled not to be going to Miami, and to stay in New York with her, and the network would live with it. They couldn't have compensated him enough for losing her.

"Thank you," she said as she stood close to him. "Thank you." And with that, the others joined them, and they spent the afternoon talking to April and Mike's friends and her employees from the restaurant.

The last of the guests left at four o'clock after an excellent lunch, and several very touching speeches, notably one by April's father, where he said how proud of her he was and that this was the best shotgun wedding he'd ever been to. Everybody laughed loudly. There was no point pretending it wasn't.

April tossed the bouquet just before she left. And with a firm hand and practiced eye, she threw it straight at her mother, who caught it with a startled look.

"Now what am I going to do with *that*?" she said to Jack, who was standing next to her as she held it, and he laughed at her discomfited expression. She looked like she was going to throw it right back at her daughter. She wasn't ready for that yet.

"Save it," he said easily. "You never know when we might need it. The next time they ask me to move to Miami, I might force you to marry me and go with me." He didn't ask her "what if," and she didn't say she wouldn't. She was enormously touched and impressed by what he had done for her in refusing the network's offer. He had done it for himself too.

And then April and Mike departed to their room at the Carlyle. When the last of the guests left, Valerie took off her shoes and smiled up at Jack. It had been a beautiful wedding, and a magical day, not just for the bride and groom, but for them too. He put his arms around her then and kissed her, and she sank against him with immeasurable relief. She had been terrified of losing him, and brave about it. She felt as though they had won the Super Bowl on this one, and she felt very, very lucky and blessed.

In their honeymoon room at the Carlyle that night, April and Mike had ordered room service and were watching a movie. April was happy but exhausted, and they chatted about the details of the wedding, and what a wonderful day it had been. They both agreed that her mother had given them a perfect wedding, and April looked over at her husband with a grin.

"And I even managed not to have the baby!" she said proudly, as though she'd had something to do with it. And for once it was hardly moving, as though it was worn out too. It had been a memorable but very long day for all of them.

"Try and not have it tonight either. As long as we have the room, we might as well enjoy it."

"I'll do my best, but I can't promise anything." Her dress was tossed over a chair, and she still had the lily of the valley in her braid. She was still a bride, and not yet ready to be a mother. At least not tonight. She wanted to enjoy their honeymoon.

"Are you having contractions?" he asked, looking worried.

"No more than usual. I think we're okay for tonight."

He relaxed when she said it, and he would have loved to make love to her on their wedding night, but he didn't dare. She was so close to delivering that he was afraid to start something if he made love to her, and neither of them was up to dealing with her having the baby that night. They were exhausted. Instead they were happy to eat omelettes from room service and watch movies. She called her mother to thank her again before they went to sleep, and Valerie sounded happy.

"I think she's okay again," April said to Mike as he started to fall asleep. April knew that something had been bothering her mother, but whatever it was, it seemed to be over now. April was glad, she wanted her mother to be happy. "I wonder if they'll ever get married," she mused, but Mike didn't answer. He was already sound asleep and snoring softly.

Chapter 23

April went back to work at the restaurant on the Tuesday after the Memorial Day weekend as though nothing had happened. She was just as busy and energetic, although she seemed to be slowing down a little, not that most people would have noticed. But Mike did—he knew her better. She seemed a little bit more tired, and it was harder for her to get up in the morning, but she kept on going. By Friday, he teased her that she was obviously never going to have this baby, and it was clearly all a trick to get him to marry her. They had been married for six days, and were very happy.

He came to visit her on Friday afternoon when he finished work, and she was working with the plumber and the electrician in the kitchen. She had just purchased a brand-new stove for the refurbished kitchen, and she was excited about it as they pored over the brochures. Mike came up behind her and put his arms around her.

"How are we doing?" he asked her cheerfully. He was looking forward to spending the weekend with her, and who knew, maybe they'd have the baby. Her due date was the next day, although babies never came on time. She could have another two weeks to wait, according to her doctor, but April didn't mind. She had lots to do.

He noticed that she was holding her back as she talked to the electrician. Mike asked her about it as they left the restaurant, and she said she had pulled something that morning, but it was nothing. They went for a walk as they left the restaurant and she was rubbing her stomach, and struggled more than usual to keep step beside him. And then she stopped and held tightly to his arm as he watched her. Something was happening. She looked different, although she insisted she was fine.

"Then what was that?" he asked her suspiciously when she stopped again.

"Just a cramp. I carried some boards out to the Dumpster." He rolled his eyes and shook his head, but at this point, if she had the baby, it was fine. "I've been having them all day," she added, and he looked at her and laughed.

"I think maybe you have denial. Has it occurred to you that you might be in labor? I'm no expert, but you have all the signs." He'd been reading about it lately, just to prepare himself. She had back pain, "cramps" that were probably contractions, and she was having trouble walking when she had them. He sug-

gested they take a cab home, and when he hailed one, she doubled over. This time it *was* a contraction, there was no question
about that. And she couldn't walk or talk.

"Have you been timing these things?" he asked, as she got
into the cab with him.

"I don't have my watch on. I forgot it on the sink this
morning."

"April," he said, trying to feign a calm he didn't feel. Suddenly he was panicked. What if she had it in the taxi, or alone at
home with him? What would he do? He took a breath and tried
to talk to her calmly. "I think you're having the baby. Let's go to
the hospital and have them take a look."

"That's silly," she said at the look on his face, and then she
had another pain, and she stopped talking to him again, and his
suggestion didn't seem so silly. When she thought about it, she
had been having cramps all day, and her back was really hurting
now. She could feel pressure bearing down on her, and she
looked at him with wide eyes. "Maybe you're right," she said
softly, holding tightly to his arm, as he changed the address he
had given the cabdriver and told him to go to the hospital instead. And this time he timed the contractions. They were regular and three minutes apart. She looked terrified when he told
her. "I don't think I'm ready," she said in a nervous voice.

"Yes, you are," he said soothingly as she looked at him with
wide eyes, suddenly worried about him too.

"What about you? Are you okay? If this is it, are you in, or do
you want me to call Ellen?"

He didn't even hesitate. She was his wife, and this was their baby. "Don't worry about it. I'm in. I'm fine. And so are you." He held tightly to her hand and continued to time the contractions. They had gotten longer and harder since they'd gotten into the cab. "It's a good thing I showed up, or you might have had the baby on the floor of the restaurant. Didn't you think about what was happening?" She shook her head.

"I was too busy. I just figured I pulled a muscle this morning."

"Some muscle," he said, looking distracted as they got caught in Friday afternoon traffic and he told the driver to hurry. "I think my wife is having a baby."

"Please, not in my cab, sir." The driver looked imploringly at him in the mirror, and Mike told him to go faster. April had stopped talking completely by then and was grimacing in pain as she clutched him.

"Do you want me to call your mother?" he asked, and she nodded. There was no question in either of their minds now, she was having the baby. The contractions were coming fast and furious, and she had probably been in labor since that morning. He called Valerie, and she said she'd call Pat, and they'd come to the hospital to wait for the good news. Mike just hoped the good news didn't happen in the taxi.

The driver slid into the emergency room driveway and came to a stop as April's eyes widened with terror. "I think I'm going to throw up," she said, looking scared and sick, and Mike shook his head. He knew what that meant. He had done his homework. She was very close to having the baby. "Get a nurse!" he shouted at the driver, "or a doctor!" The cabdriver ran into the hospital, and a nurse came out a minute later pushing a wheelchair. She was wearing scrubs, and she was a big African-American woman with a head full of tiny braids and an enormous smile as she greeted April.

"Come on," she said firmly, "let's get you out of this cab. Dad, give us a hand here," she said, looking at Mike, and he nodded.

"I think I'm having it," April said, with a look of total panic.

"No, you're not," the nurse said firmly. "Let's get you into the hospital first. You don't want to have that baby in a taxi. It's a mess!" she said, and April laughed at her although she was having a pain, and the nurse and Mike lifted her into the wheelchair. Mike handed the driver twice what the fare had been, thanked him, and ran after the nurse, who was pushing April. She started to cry as they lifted her onto an exam room table. The nurse asked April what her OB's name was, and then told another ER nurse standing by to get the OB on call, and then call April's own doctor. The nurse told April she was going to check her, and she and Mike helped April take off her jeans and T-shirt and put her in a gown, and laid her back on the table.

"Don't push now!" the nurse warned her, still smiling. There was an aura of competence and warmth about her that reassured Mike. Things were going very fast.

"I'm not," April said through clenched teeth, "but I want to. It's pushing very hard. Can I have drugs now? This really hurts." She looked imploringly at Mike, and he looked at the nurse. She was checking April, and then smiled at them both.

"We're going to have a baby here in about two minutes, before the anesthesiologist can even get here. You're at ten, and something tells me you have been for a while. First baby?" April nodded.

"What were you doing that you missed the signs?" She had pulled off the end of the table, and set up stirrups and leg supports and eased April's legs onto them gently as April looked at her in terror.

"I was carrying some old boards out to a Dumpster. I can't have a baby now. I'm not *ready!*" she shouted, suddenly angry and frightened. She was losing control, but Mike was steady as a rock beside her.

"Oh, yes, you are," the nurse said calmly. "We don't get a lot of moms in here who miss the signs of labor because they've been carrying lumber. Are you a construction worker?" she asked with a broad grin. She was rapidly taking out instruments and keeping an eye on April.

"No, I own a restaurant," she said, grimacing with another pain, but she wasn't screaming. Mike was stunned by the process, and how quickly it had all happened.

The nurse turned to Mike then, and the doctor hadn't come yet, but they seemed to be doing fine without one. "Dad, would you like to see your baby's head?"

"Can you see it?" April asked, smiling, and then she had another pain that was the worst one she'd had yet, as Mike held her shoulders and then peeked and saw their baby's head crowning.

It had short dark curly hair, and then it retreated slightly when the pain ended.

"Okay, Dad, you hold one leg, I'll hold the other, and Mom, when the next pain starts, you're going to push as hard as you can, holding your breath, and we're going to have that baby in your arms in about two minutes. Come on now," she said. The pain had already started, and April was pushing, and as she did, the baby moved steadily forward and shot right into the nurse's hands as April let out a long low scream Mike hadn't expected. He looked at April in terror, but she was smiling and crying and the nurse was holding their baby and handed him to Mike as soon as she wiped him off and wrapped him in a blanket.

"You have a son," the nurse said as the doctor came through the door. Her own doctor hadn't made it, and the one on call at the hospital had showed up in time to cut the cord. Mike was horrified to realize that they had left the restaurant twenty minutes before. April had had the baby seven minutes after they arrived. The cabdriver didn't know how lucky he was.

Mike leaned over April, still holding the baby, and put him on her chest. She touched him and looked up at Mike, and both of them were crying and smiling at the same time.

"Sam," April said, whispering his name.

"I knew it was a boy," Mike said, looking at him proudly through tears of joy. They hadn't weighed him yet, but he was a big baby. The nurse was guessing nine pounds, and he had almost delivered himself. April was saying it hadn't been bad at all, as Mike rolled his eyes. It hadn't looked easy to him, but it hadn't been as awful as he had feared, and the miracle of one human being coming out of another had totally amazed him as he watched their son being born.

The nurse had left the room for a minute, as the doctor delivered the placenta and cut the cord, and she looked at April when she got back. "There's a mess of people out there asking for April Wyatt. Is that you?" She smiled her big wide motherly smile that had reassured them both.

"It was," April said happily, holding her baby, as Mike looked proudly at them both. "I'm April Steinman now. I got married last Saturday," she told the nurse, who laughed warmly.

"Well, that's a good thing. After we clean you up a little, do you want them to come in?"

She looked at Mike to be sure it was all right with him, and he nodded, knowing that this was the happiest day of his life, even if he had been terrified of it before, and he had never loved April more. He was fine about having her family come in. They were his family now too. And so was Sam. Forever.

"Okay," April said. She had started shaking, and they covered her with a warm blanket. They had taken her feet out of the stirrups, and the nurse told them the shaking was normal and would stop soon.

And a minute later her whole family came in. Her father and Maddie, Annie and Heather, and her mother and Jack. The room was full of people, exclaiming about the baby, talking to April and Mike, and wanting to see Sam. April looked blissful as she held the baby, and Mike was standing close to her, telling her how much he loved her, as everyone congratulated them. Valerie was looking at the baby with tears in her eyes and holding Jack's hand. And suddenly Mike realized that everything was all right. This was a whole other life from anything he had known as a child, among people who loved each other, the baby, and even him. And little Sam was the most welcome baby in the world.

The others left after a few minutes, and he and April kissed, and then she leaned down and kissed their baby and whispered, "Happy birthday, Sam."

There had been no way of knowing all those months before, but the worst birthday for some of them had turned out to be the best birthday after all.